I0676438

AIRSHIP 27 PRODUCTIONS

AN AIRSHIP 27 PRODUCTION

Domino Lady-Volume One
"Love is a Battlefield" © 2015 Greg Hatcher
"The Domino Lady Rolls the Dice" © 2015 Gene Moyers
"The Case of the Model, Madness & Murder" © 2015 Tim Holter Bruckner
"Domino Lady Finds a Few Good Men" © 2015 Kevin Findley

Published by Airship 27 Productions
www.airship27.com
www.airship27hangar.com

Cover Illustration © 2015 Fred Hammond
Interior illustrations © 2015 James Lyle

Editor: Ron Fortier
Associate Editor: Ray Riethmeier
Marketing and Promotions Manager: Michael Vance
Production and design by Rob Davis.

ISBN-13: 978-0692426142 (Airship 27)
ISBN-10: 0692426140

Printed in the United States of America

10 9 8 7 6 5 4 3 2 1

DOMINO *Lady*

Volume One
Table of Contents

LOVE IS A BATTLEFIELD

By Greg Hatcher

"The professor will see you shortly, Mr. Rosen."

Paul Rosen nodded at the hulking butler and the giant left him alone in the professor's study. The room was dark, but for the dim yellow light from a single standing lamp. There was only one window behind the desk, with red velvet drapes drawn over it. Mahogany bookshelves filled with academic texts lined the walls.

Money, Rosen thought. *Psychology must be quite a racket to furnish a place like this.* But he'd already known there was money involved; the envelope full of cash in his jacket pocket attested to that. Despite the rich décor—the chairs facing the desk were upholstered in maroon leather, and the Persian rug was large and thick—there was still something off about the room, something that made Rosen hold himself tense and ready.

"Mister Rosen."

The voice came from behind him. Rosen turned to see a bespectacled man smiling at him. He was tall, dressed in a gray suit with a black bow tie. He looked to be in his mid-sixties, with sunken cheeks and a high forehead, graying hair swept back from it in a widow's peak. "Professor Murdwell?"

"I am he." Murdwell inclined his head slightly toward the chairs. "Please have a seat." Without waiting for Rosen, he stepped around him and sat behind the desk, laying his hands flat on the blotter and facing straight forward.

Rosen sat. There was silence for a moment.

Professor Murdwell continued to smile.

Rosen shifted uncomfortably in his chair and finally said, "Well? Your nickel, Doc."

"What do you know about psychology, Mr. Rosen?"

The question took Rosen off-guard. "I guess it pays well," he said. "You seem pretty well fixed."

"I have created a unique niche for myself." Murdwell's smile looked a little smug. "Psychology, broadly speaking, is the science of the mind, the study of human impulses and instincts. Most people bumble through their lives with very little thought given to the reasoning behind their actions.

5

Were one to question the average man in the street about why he is doing what he does, doubtless the answer would be in some way related to money or shelter or sex or some other basic need. Man is a simple animal."

"It's the Depression, doc. People are just scraping by."

"Yes. But even when a society's populace is well off, they still are living largely unexamined lives. This gives an enormous advantage to those of us who have made a study of human impulses and the thought processes that are used to facilitate them, or in some cases mask them. You, for example."

"What about me?" Rosen was starting to get angry. "You got me here with a note implying I did something bad in Colorado, and then enclosed a hundred bucks telling me to be here at three today to get some help for that 'problem.' Well, I'm here. Skip to the end. What's it about?"

Murdwell was unmoved by Rosen's rising temper. "I knew you would come. My invitation was at once threat and bribe. You might have resisted either one individually, but both together would bring you here at the appointed hour as surely as the sun rising in the east. Once here, I knew you would be nervous and defensive; this room is designed to provoke that response in one of your sort. It is filled with symbols of power and authority, the lighting places me in silhouette, your back is to the door. Were I meeting a different man I would have arranged a different setting designed to maximize my advantage. As it is, you are nervous, restless, feeling threatened, and this is making you angry. You are about to threaten violence."

Rosen snapped his mouth shut. It was true.

Murdwell spread his hands. "You see? I am an expert. For the last few years I have been putting my expertise to use as a consultant, and as you remarked yourself, it has been lucrative. But now I have a challenge that requires certain special assistance. Your assistance, Mr. Rosen."

"Me? Why me?"

"Your history with women."

Rosen sat up straight, stung. "Look here! That girl killed herself, I didn't...."

Murdwell raised a hand. "Not just the incident in Colorado, though the consequences of that and your subsequent relocation here to Los Angeles did provide myself and my employers with convenient advantages. No, I mean the entire history. You've never had a job, is that correct?"

Rosen bristled. "Hell, yes, I had jobs. I taught golf and tennis."

"Part-time. Certainly not enough to cover your living expenses. Those were always provided for by your lady friends, until the incident in Denver.

Since your arrival here, you have been unable to find any employment… or any new female companions to subsidize your lifestyle. Yes?"

"Lots of people are out of work." Rosen stuck out his chin. "And yeah, I had some women back in Colorado. So what? You act like I'm a criminal. I haven't committed any crimes, and as for the 'incident,' the cops cleared me the same day they found Jessie's body. Her suicide note made it obvious what happened. She was just a starry-eyed kid who thought I was…. Well, never mind. The point is I'm not… whatever it is you think I am. I've had some bad luck. That's all."

Murdwell raised an eyebrow. "I was not clear. I am speaking of your history as a 'kept man' because it's relevant to your qualifications, not because I intend blackmail or some other malice toward you. That's not it at all. No, Mr. Rosen, I want to offer you a job."

"What kind of a job?"

"Ah." Murdwell leaned forward, his eyes sparkling with academic enthusiasm. "Here we come to the heart of the matter. What do you know about the Domino Lady?"

"Huh?" Rosen blinked. It was hard to keep up with the professor; the guy was all over the place. "Just what I see in the paper. She's some kind of a thief, isn't she? Girl in a mask?"

"She sees herself as more of a crusader." A sour expression flickered across Murdwell's face for a moment but then the smile was back. "She has taken it upon herself to damage several powerful businessmen here in Los Angeles. Often she steals from them, but it is just as common for her to expose their corrupt practices and hand them over to the police. She is not beloved by the local law enforcement at all, but nevertheless her actions mark her as someone who believes in a sort of rough justice." He thrust a finger at Rosen. "And, you see, this is where I come in. I have been engaged to put a stop to this woman's activities. My clients…well, let us call them a consortium. A group of prominent businessmen are…."

"Feeling the heat. I get it."

Murdwell's smile was thin and knowing now. "Survival, Mr. Rosen. The human animal takes desperate action when it is threatened. At any rate, these men came to me. My expertise in the science of the mind has resulted in my ability to construct… a sort of personality profile, a theoretical model of any given person based on various evidentiary findings. This is a new science, but it has already begun to yield results. There was a case in New York, a town called Lackawanna, where a psychologist divined the identity of a killer based on what he revealed about himself through several taunting postcards he sent to the police. There have been others. A decade from now I would not be surprised if police departments put a forensic psychiatrist on staff simply to construct such profiles of notorious criminals."

Rosen nodded. He didn't really understand all of it, but he didn't want to look stupid.

Murdwell waved it away. "Forgive me. I find this history fascinating but you probably do not. The point is, there are very few of us doing this work and of those... I am the best." He leaned back and spread his hands wide. "I am also the only one to realize the retail value of this service to the world of business. Think what it would mean in a commercial negotiation to know the entire personality of your opponent, to be able to predict his moves and counter them before even he himself knows what they are! Or of the value to a criminal enterprise to know every reflex and mental quirk of an official in charge of an investigation. The applications are nearly infinite."

Jesus, he's doing this consulting thing of his for the mob. Rosen had suspected the doc was crooked. But he was interested now, despite himself. "And you can do this with the Domino Lady?"

Murdwell snorted. "My dear Mr. Rosen, I have already done so. There is a mountain of evidence out there; the profile itself was hardly a challenge at all. It was gathering and collating the data that was the difficulty. Fortunately, my employers are men of some influence, and they were able to find police reports for me... as well as reach out to some rather more unsavory persons who have had actual contact with the Domino Lady. After two months of work I have managed to construct what I consider to be a definitive portrait." He ticked off the points on his fingers. "There are no photographs but the description remains consistent. She is young, early to mid-twenties, and though she wears a mask that obscures her upper face, everyone describes her as beautiful. Her usual apparel is a long dress and some kind of cloak, and she rarely goes armed, though she does carry a syringe full of knockout drops that she has used many times to good effect. Her interactions with both police and criminals, despite occasional violence, largely have been roguish and theatrical; she leaves calling cards, even."

"I read about those," Rosen put in. "'Compliments of the Domino Lady.'"

"Yes, exactly." Murdwell nodded. "But the outré drama of these trappings, the cape, the mask, the cards, have obscured the real picture. Everything we know about how she speaks and carries herself... this is no greedy gutter wench trying to score some quick cash. This is a young woman who was raised in high society, a lady of privilege… and something happened to her, that privilege was taken away somehow. The Domino Lady does what she does out of emotion, not economic need. She created a character to act out her anger. I think she has found something else there as well, a sense of adventure and a newfound purpose. She has romanticized herself, constructed a separate persona that she can step into and become someone completely different… a disassociation to a degree that one rarely sees outside of an asylum."

Rosen found most of this academic jargon pretty rough going, though the word *asylum* made him sit up a little. "She's a nut?"

"Hardly. Not in the sense you mean. If anything, she is intensely calculated in her actions. But underneath that… she is still a wounded little girl. She mourns her loss. More than anything else, she rages against the unfairness of the world. As I said, she is a *romantic,* Mr. Rosen, in the classic sense of the word. Reality dealt her a blow and she seeks to deal it one in return. She wants to believe that goodness and justice and decency can exist. And that is how we'll trap her." Murdwell's smile grew predatory. "We'll give her something to believe in. We'll give her you, Mr. Rosen."

"What? Me? But I'm…."

Murdwell steepled his fingers. "Mr. Rosen. Let me be blunt. I sought you out because you are an accomplished seducer of women. Your skills in that area are such that until the incident in Denver, you were making a fine living at it, and even the unfortunate death of Jessica Vine can be attributed to… let us say, to your inability to moderate your appeal to the opposite sex. Whatever ostracism or humiliation you may have had to endure because of the Vine incident in the last few months, all it says to me is that you possess exactly the quality I need. My principals are prepared to pay you one hundred thousand dollars to seduce the Domino Lady and bring her to me… at which point we will put her out of business." The smile became predatory again. "Permanently."

One hundred thousand! Rosen swallowed. That was more money than… he couldn't even wrap his head around it. The room in that flophouse on Cahuenga Boulevard was costing him fourteen dollars a week and he could barely afford that. "I couldn't… I don't want any part of any killing."

Murdwell raised an eyebrow. "Neither do I. I'm a consultant and you are my employee. What our clients do with the information we provide is hardly our problem."

Rosen swallowed again. He knew this was wrong. He'd lived off women, used them, sure, but this… this crossed a line. Damn that cold, calculating son of a bitch and his damn smile. He was so certain Rosen would agree.

He'd even bragged about how predictable Rosen was. He probably knew Rosen hated him for it.

Doubtless he also knew Rosen had no choice. He was broke. Without the professor he wouldn't even be able to make rent on the flophouse; he was on track to end up just another loser on the bread line.

The human animal takes desperate action when it is threatened. "All right," Rosen said, heavily. "I'm in. But how do you expect me to find this woman? She's masked, no one knows who she is."

Murdwell glared at him. "I know *exactly* who she is. I just don't know her name yet. We'll find her, Mr. Rosen. After that, it's up to you." He handed him a large manila envelope. "Your instructions are in here, along with another five hundred dollars in expense money. Rent a car, something flashy, a young man's play toy. And get yourself some decent clothes. You must look the part. The plan as outlined begins with your introduction into high society at the annual Children's Hospital fundraiser ball, it's this weekend. The Birchwood Country Club."

"Country Club?" Rosen blinked.

"My researches have turned up three potential candidates who match my profile of the Domino Lady," Murdwell explained. "They are young and move freely in high society, they fit the physical description, and they have the right psychological profile. All three are expected to attend the ball. Your job will be to identify which of those three is the most likely to be the Domino Lady."

"How?"

"It's all outlined in the plan." Murdwell nodded at the envelope. "Study that carefully, then destroy it. Take care of the car and the clothes. Be ready. Saturday night, you will be going on the hunt once more. You remember the hunt, don't you, Mr. Rosen? Studying the women in a room, flirting with them, dancing with them... all the while calculating your chances and choosing the most likely? The only difference is, this time you will be employing those roguish charms of yours for a higher purpose."

"It's not as easy as you make it sound." Rosen shook his head. "Charm or no charm, there's no predicting what a woman will do."

"Ah, but that's where you're wrong, Mr. Rosen." Murdwell's eyes gleamed. "Predicting human behavior is my life's work. Events at the Country Club have been arranged like moves on a chessboard. Play your part as I have outlined and the Domino Lady will have no choice but to walk right into our trap."

The Birchwood was one of the few places in Los Angeles that managed to successfully cultivate an atmosphere of regal dignity despite being a favorite gathering place of the boisterous, new-money Hollywood glitterati that made up the society that had coalesced around the film industry over the last couple of decades. Producers, stars, studio moguls... all of them knew that membership in the Birchwood was a major signal to the industry that you had "Made It," and its legendary exclusivity was such that an invitation to any event there was something to be treasured. It was where the powerful and the ambitious went to see and be seen.

Once a year, all this naked ambition and ego was cast aside as the Birchwood opened its doors to the community for the sake of charity; the Children's Hospital Orphans Fund Ball was just as exclusive an event as any other held at the club, but this one permitted press coverage, and because of its size, required outside catering. Nearly a hundred extra support staff were hired from various restaurants and catering firms around the city just for the one night. There were dozens of photographers lining the gravel walkway from the parking lot to the main entrance to the club, and a privileged few were allowed inside the ballroom as well, provided they were able to manage their bulky flash rigs with discretion.

Ellen Patrick, being one of the better-known young socialites in Tinseltown, knew the annual ritual well. Her father Owen had always supported the Orphans Fund when he was D.A., and Ellen had made sure to continue that tradition after his murder a year and a half ago. She had presented a check for five thousand dollars to the fund earlier that afternoon. The hospital administrator had begged Ellen to let them make a big ceremony out of it at the ball this evening, but Ellen had demurred. "I would be too embarrassed," she had said, in the breathy, fluttery tone she had practiced, the tone that left most who heard it convinced that Ellen Patrick was indeed every bit as feather-headed as the gossip pages said.

But there was no question that Miss Ellen was going to be at the Ball. Her other self had business there. The Domino Lady had gotten word that Joaquin Vasquez was going to be there, as part of his ongoing efforts to distance himself from the Vasquez crime family, and she wanted to see this miracle for herself. Ellen had known Joaquin in her school days, and remembered him as an arrogant, entitled brat that stood out from the rest even in a school full of entitled brats. *Including me,* Ellen thought. *Be fair. I was pretty awful myself a lot of the time... Before.*

"Before" was all she ever allowed herself to reflect on her life before the death of Owen Patrick and the chain of circumstances that led to Ellen adopting the identity of the Domino Lady. She was shamed by a lot of it; mostly by her carefree assumptions about how the world worked, and her unquestioning acceptance of a life of privilege among the showbiz elites of Los Angeles. Her father's murder had shown her how rotten the underlying structure that maintained the elites really was, and she had determined then and there that she would devote the rest of her life to exposing it for what it was and bringing those corrupt men to justice.

And I'm doing all right so far. Ellen smiled. It had felt good to hand over that check today, especially knowing that the money came from the Vasquez syndicate. The Domino Lady had dealt them a pretty harsh blow by intercepting a payroll meant for opium dens in Chinatown; losing it would create havoc between the Vasquez mob and the Chinese Tongs that operated there. Hurting both organizations at the same time had pleased the Domino Lady, and in any case that cash would do a lot more good for the orphans. That was what she had been meant for all along, Ellen thought. She had begun her crusade in a whirl of grief and rage, but as she had built the legend of the Domino Lady little by little, she had realized that she had found a meaning in her life that had been utterly lacking before. So much so that more and more over the last year, "Ellen Patrick" had not really existed, except as a daytime mask for the Domino Lady. She felt foolish now, waving and smiling at photographers and blowing kisses to the other guests, but Ellen Patrick's socialite status was a valuable tool in the Domino Lady's arsenal. She had to put the time in to maintain it.

Don't be such a wet blanket, she scolded herself. *Have a little fun. You remember what fun was like, right? Have a drink. Flirt with the boys. The Domino Lady did good work. You deserve a victory celebration. And who knows? Maybe Joaquin's really different now. Lord knows I am.*

"Ellen! You look splendid, my dear." It was Barrett Steeves from Emperor Studios, looking very much the silver fox. He had on an immaculate white dinner jacket and his graying hair was elegantly shaped with just the right amount of pomade. The scent of his expensive cologne mingled with his cigarillo to create something that Ellen found at once nostalgic and a little nauseating. Tobacco and cologne always reminded her of her father. "I hear you are one of our secret benefactors."

"Oh, I kicked in a little. Dad always supported the hospital." Ellen smiled and waved it away. "How are you? Is Toni here?"

"She is." Steeves' expression turned a little bleak.

Ellen caught the flicker of concern and grew serious. "How's she holding up? That was such a terrible thing with Roger and the fire."

"You know, I had no idea she even knew that young man." Steeves harrumphed. "Certainly I would not have had any sort of problem with it, this is the twentieth century. I knew him a little, just seeing him around the back lot. It was Roger that did that spectacular fall for us in *Riders of the Range*. Extraordinary agility, that's why Buckner wanted him for *Chicago Fire Fighters*. Hard to believe that a stunt could go so wrong. Roger was a fine lad and a very careful stuntman. I'd have had no problem with him courting my daughter, hardworking fellow like that's much better than those damned prep school boys you girls used to run around with. But apparently Toni thought I would object... we never had a clue the two of them were engaged. Did you know?"

Ellen shook her head. "No, I've fallen out of touch with a lot of the old crowd. I knew she was seeing someone and it was getting serious, but until I saw those pictures in the paper...."

"Damned vultures, going right up to her seconds after she got the news and snapping away as she's weeping her eyes out. That was about the ugliest thing I've ever seen from people and I work in Hollywood for God's sake." Steeves glared around at the photographers circulating on the ballroom floor. Then he turned back to Ellen. "Truthfully, my dear, I have a favor to ask. I'm a little worried. I'd thought it would be good for her to get out, but I'm afraid I made a mistake. She took up station at the bar and hasn't moved since then." He sighed. "This is the first time we've really been out in public since then and I was hoping... well. Anyway, could you perhaps keep an eye on her? I'd hate for one of those damned bottom-feeding newspaper people to ambush her again tonight, especially after she's had a few drinks. Perhaps you could even persuade her to go home."

"Sure." Ellen flashed him a reassuring smile and turned toward the bar. She saw Toni Steeves sitting on a barstool, looking speculatively up at a tall man in a black tuxedo and a bow tie that was oh-so-casually just a little bit loosened for that rakish air. "Hi, Toni!" she said brightly. "Who's your friend?"

"Don't know," Toni Steeves said. She looked up at Ellen with watery eyes. "Ellen Patrick? I'll be dipped. How the hell are you? Tennis guy, meet Ellen. She played tennis, too, once upon a time. Good at games. That's our crowd. Very fit." She let out a hoarse, unclassifiable bark. Not quite a laugh and just short of a sob. Ellen realized that she was very, very drunk.

"Hey, Toni," Ellen said. "You feeling all right?"

Toni glared at her with bleary *hauteur*. "I've had four Manhattans. I feel marvelous. Why don't you just say, 'Toni, are you drunk?' Because I

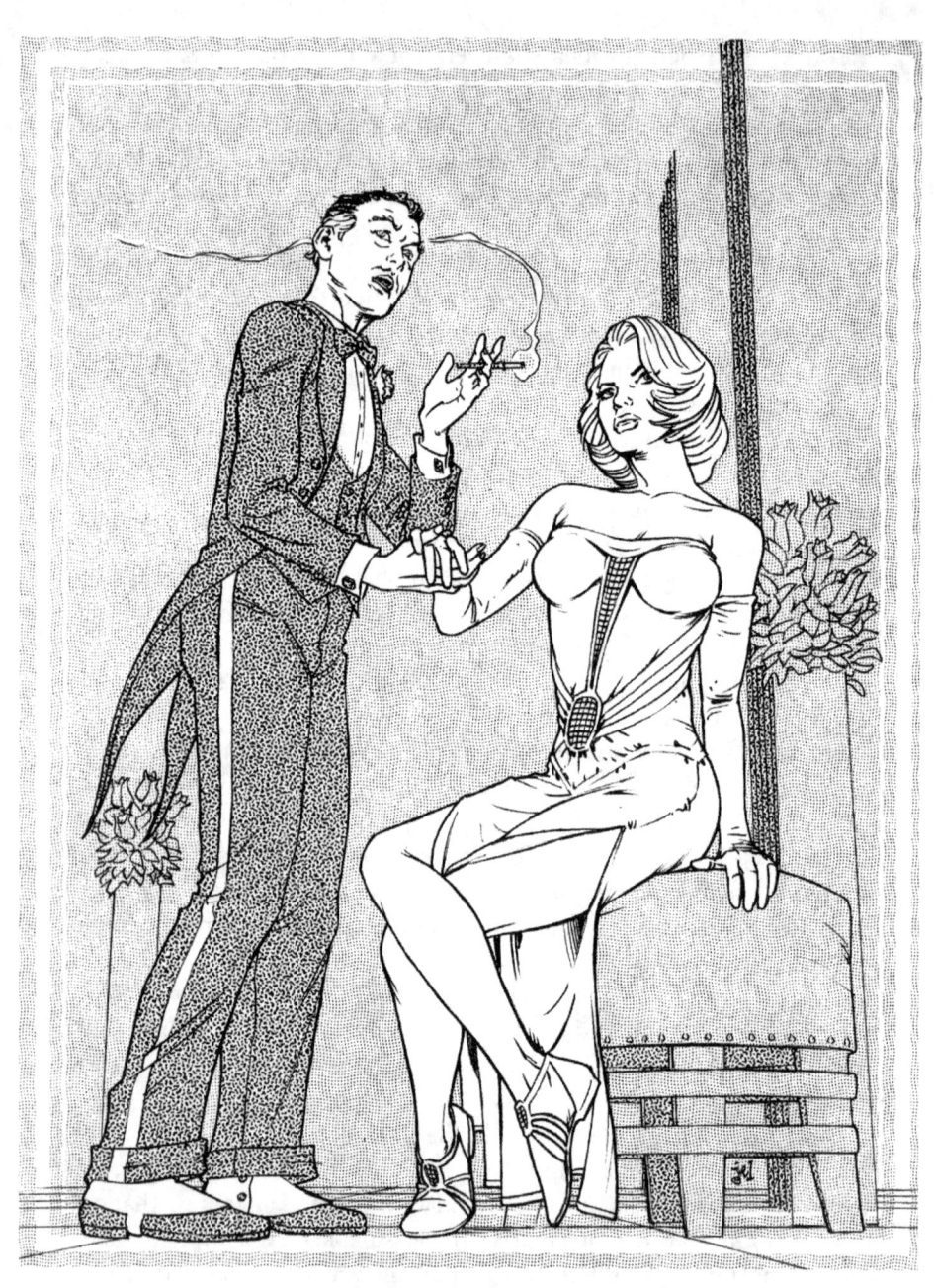

"I have a favor to ask."

certainly am. Buy me another one, tennis guy, and then we'll see how well this evening might turn out for you."

"I don't think so," the tall man said, with good humor. "I don't want you to think I'm easy. Maybe we should just take it slow for a while, eh?" He glanced over at Ellen, meaningfully. "Maybe there's some place upstairs where we could all relax? The lady looks like she might need to stretch out for a bit."

Ellen caught on at once. "Yes, Toni, come on now. Let's go up to the billiards room. You can lie down on the big velvet couch up there and we'll open a window for you. Get you some air. Come on."

The bartender had remained studiously neutral for all of this, but now he turned and drawled, "Billiards room's closed for the evening."

The tall man slipped him a folded bill. "Why don't you open it for us?"

The cash halted any further objection. Together they walked Toni over to the stairs, where the barman unobtrusively moved away the stand holding the velvet rope closing it off, and then replaced it once the three of them had passed. Once they had passed the landing and were out of sight of the main floor, the man slung Toni over his shoulder in a fireman's carry. She was completely unconscious by this point. By the time they had wrestled her onto the velvet couch, she was snoring; a ladylike, moderately high-pitched sniffle. Ellen worked off Toni's shoes and the man shucked off his tuxedo jacket and draped it over her as an improvised coverlet. They both stood at the same time, facing each other, and simultaneously burst out in chuckles.

"Thank you…" Ellen said, finally. "…uh… I can't call you Tennis Guy."

"Of course you could, pretty girls can say whatever the hell they want." He smiled artlessly, making the remark a joke and not a barb. "But I'm Paul Rosen." He held out a hand. "Tennis instructor, actually, not just a player."

Ellen shook his hand. "It wouldn't matter to me, I never get past the courtside drinks cart here. Nice to meet you. And thank you for your help."

Rosen shrugged. "Beautiful girl in distress. And anyway, you impressed me."

"Me? How?"

He grinned and raised an eyebrow. "I like that you're protective of your friend. From what I gather, that's not typical in Hollywood circles. You were swooping in to stop me taking advantage, weren't you?"

"Well…" Now Ellen was embarrassed. "Toni's good people. She's just a little dinged up. She lost her fiancé a few months ago."

"That's too bad. In any case, I'm glad you showed up. If I'd tried to get her up here alone I'm certain it would have been... er... misconstrued." Rosen smiled ruefully. "Shall we dare the ballroom again? Although I'm afraid I look a little disreputable."

"You look great," Ellen blurted, then blushed. She hadn't actually meant to say it out loud.

Now it was Rosen who looked embarrassed. He offered her his arm. "It would be poor form after this to offer to get you a drink, but perhaps you'd care to dance?"

Ellen smiled gently at him. "A dance sounds lovely. I'll just take a minute to let Toni's father know she's all right; he'll arrange to get her safely past the photographers and home."

An hour or so later, Ellen had decided she liked Paul Rosen quite a bit. They had danced and sampled the *hors d'oeurves* and chatted with several of Ellen's friends from her college days. They finally ended up back at the bar again, where Ellen decided to splurge for once. She ordered a Campari and soda and noticed that Rosen stuck to iced tea. "Are you in training?"

"Sort of." Rosen grinned, flushing a little. "Some of those Hancock Park ladies like to get in a couple of sets early in the morning. Trying that hung over... well, let's say that it took just the once to learn my lesson."

He looked so doleful that Ellen burst out laughing. "Poor you. We'll have to take it easy."

"Not too easy, I hope." Rosen's grin was just on the right side of suggestive.

Ellen felt her cheeks color a little. *He's cute and all,* she scolded herself, *but he's a distraction. Get your head in the game.* She straightened up and looked past Rosen to scan the ballroom floor. *Is Joaquin even here?*

He was, she saw. At the center of a small knot of photographers on the other side of the dance floor. He looked tired and sad, Ellen thought. *They've probably been asking about his family ever since he got here. Did he bring a date?* Didn't look like it.

There was a commotion by the main entrance, and then gunshots. That got everyone's attention.

Two men in black hoods entered, brandishing machine guns. "Joaquin Vasquez!" one of them roared. "Where is he? Where is the little turncoat?"

Joaquin Vasquez stepped forward. "I am here," he said. "What do you want?"

"What do you think, traitor?" The masked man fired another burst into the ceiling, causing more screams from the crowd. "We want to show you there is no escape from your heritage. We want to send a message to you and all your dog-brothers. You do not cheat the Red Dragon Tong!" He brandished the gun at the photographers. "Be sure to document this for your Western papers!"

Ellen stiffened. *This is...oh my God, I caused this! This is payback for the Vasquez opium money I took that night!*

She glanced around wildly, trying to think of some way to stop the gunmen. All her Domino Lady gear was hidden in her car including her gun and her knockout darts. *Never again without a weapon in the purse,* she vowed. *And no more carrying clutch purses, the hell with how unfashionable it makes me. Damn it anyway.* At least she was in flats if she had to run. She wondered if there was any way to get to a telephone. Of course there were none in the main ballroom, and they probably had disabled the one in the entrance by the coat-check. Upstairs? She looked over to the stairway entrance and sucked in her breath sharply at what she saw there.

Paul Rosen had surreptitiously unhooked the velvet rope from one of the brass stands, leaving him holding what amounted to a three-foot length of brass pipe with a square at one end. He hefted it experimentally, then clenched his teeth. "Hey! Think fast, creep!"

The gunman turned and Rosen hurled the brass stand at his head, square-end first, like throwing a hammer. It flew straight and true, hitting the hooded man's skull with a solid *thonk* and he went down like a sack of potatoes. Joaquin Vasquez threw himself at the other gunman before he had a chance to react and twisted the submachine gun away from him, and then the gunman found himself spun around by one shoulder. "Good night," Paul Rosen spat, and decked him with a right cross. The gunman staggered back and stopped, realizing that Joaquin Vasquez had him covered with the machine gun. He raised his hands. His companion sat up, dazed, and when he saw the gun aimed at both of them he did the same. Vasquez gestured with the gun and slowly both men removed their hoods, revealing them as Asian men in their twenties.

The crowd burst into applause. Ellen ran to Paul Rosen, who was cradling his right hand and wincing. "In the movies that never looks like it hurts," he said. "I think I broke my hand on that lunkhead."

"You're a lunkhead for taking such a crazy chance," Ellen snapped. "Let me see that hand." She took it in hers and turned it over. The knuckles were burst and bleeding. "Oh, Paul. We have to get you to a doctor."

"Can't you kiss it and make it better?"

Ellen looked at his ruefully smiling face and thought, *I shouldn't,* and then she thought she was tired of thinking. She took him in her arms and kissed him hard, not caring about the flashbulbs going off all around them.

"Very nice." Professor Murdwell smirked and tapped the newspaper photograph of Ellen Patrick and Paul Rosen embracing on the ballroom floor. The headline read, *A HERO'S REWARD!* "That was a clever improvisation with the rope stand. The script called for mere fisticuffs."

"The hell with you and your script." Paul Rosen was not going to be diverted. He was ready for Murdwell and his mentalist games this time. He pointed at the sidebar to the newspaper article. "Those two Chinamen? The guys with the guns? If you'd seen today's paper you'd know they hanged themselves last night in their prison cell!"

"Yes. Tragic, isn't it." Murdwell clucked his tongue. "Would you have preferred they be alive to testify? To swear under oath they had no connection with the Red Dragons? That they were, in fact, in my employ, the same as you?"

"I said I didn't want any part in any killing!"

"Oh?" Murdwell cocked an eyebrow. "And what part did you play in the deaths of those men, pray tell? If anyone took action, I assume it was undertaken by our sponsors. So? What do you care? Events have unfolded to our advantage. I recommend you leave it at that."

Rosen stared. The man wasn't human.

"You're thinking I'm a monster." Murdwell sniffed. "I don't mind. Most people would probably agree with you. I am…unconventional." He dismissed it with a wave of his hand. "Let us dispense with these other matters. I employed you for a specific task and it is that I wish to discuss." His gaze dropped to the Sunday edition newspaper photograph again. "Interesting that you landed Ellen Patrick. Observing the women I considered as possibles, I had almost made up my mind that it was Antonia Steeves that was our target; her anger burned so fierce and hot after the death of her fiancé… but apparently, from what you describe, that anger has turned inward. She is self-destructing." He shook his head. "Ellen Patrick, though. Despite the death of her father and the clear path to a revenge motive, all my researches led me to believe that she was too shallow an intellect for the Domino Lady. She was my third choice at best. But she was the one that took the bait. Her rescue of Miss Steeves, her reaction to the attempted kidnapping, her clear response to your perceived nobility. I had potential triggers sowed through that entire evening and of my three candidates, it was Ellen Patrick alone that answered to almost all of them."

"How are you so sure? You weren't there."

"My dear Mr. Rosen." Murdwell looked offended. "Of course I was there. Do you think me such a fool as to concoct this kind of an elaborate plan and then leave it all to chance? I was disguised as one of the photojournalists. I used my camera apparatus as cover to monitor the proceedings. I was watching Ellen Patrick from the moment she approached you. Her face was simplicity itself to read; the horror at seeing a crisis that her other self apparently had precipitated, the need to punish the wicked, the joy at finding someone else who shared her hunger for justice. She sees you as a kindred spirit now, someone who cannot let wrongdoing pass unavenged. Is this not so? Of all my candidates she is the only one that possesses those qualities and also has the social and financial mobility to sustain a second identity such as the Domino Lady. It must be her." He paused. "Well? What have you observed? You've had a week now."

"I'm... not sure." But in his heart, Rosen was sure. Hearing the professor lay it all out, it confirmed everything he had suspected.

For Rosen himself, it was a lot simpler: Ellen was a smart girl who pretended to be silly. He'd seen it. In her unguarded moments, she revealed an intelligence and depth that was far more than she showed to most people, and they'd had a few unguarded moments in the last seven days. Some really nice ones, if he was honest about it. He knew she didn't take him seriously, but she liked him and she trusted him. And he liked her, too, damn it. *So what if she was a little crazy? So what if it turned out she really did put on a mask and cape and...*

"Mr. Rosen." Murdwell's tone sharpened. "May I remind you that you were hired to do a job? You aren't actually developing some sort of infatuation...."

"Of course not." Rosen was gruff. "Don't be absurd. It's just... you may be over-thinking it. She's a pretty girl with more smarts than she lets on, that's all; playing the dumb blonde's a standard defense mechanism for girls in her set. And her daddy was a D.A., so of course she believes in law and order. But it's a long way from there to..."

"Yes, yes." Murdwell wasn't listening to him any longer. "You are right, we need a little more. We have a good candidate in Miss Patrick but it's not definite enough to move on. We'll need something further to draw her into the open. Someone to avenge. Someone to *rescue*." He snapped his fingers. "I have it! Young Mr. Vasquez was of use to us before; we can make use of him again. Return to your rental house and wait for further word from me. And, Mr. Rosen...." Suddenly Murdwell was staring directly at him and there was no smile on his face at all. "You were hired to play a part, and so far you have done exceptionally well. But do not for a moment think you are in a position to demonstrate any actual nobility. Should you attempt any foolish gallantry in defense of this woman, it might prove fatal. Do we understand each other?"

Rosen swallowed. After a moment, he nodded.

"Good."

Lucas Benford emerged from the rear entrance of the L.A. County Coroner's office into the alley. He let out a long, whooshing sigh and fished out a Chesterfield. He lit it and exhaled a cloud of smoke that dissipated slowly into the night sky. Addressing no one in particular, he said loudly, "I can letcha have ten minutes."

A figure emerged from the shadows: a woman, wrapped in a black cloak. She had long blonde hair that spilled down around her shoulders, and her upper face was obscured by a black velvet mask. The Domino Lady smiled gently at Benford. "Lucas, honey, I don't really need to look at those Chinese boys. I just want to know what you can tell me about them." A white-gloved hand emerged from the cloak with a twenty-dollar bill. "As a favor to me."

"Nance'll have my ass if he knows I'm talking to you." But the bill was pocketed quickly.

"I'll never tell. C'mon, Lucas, give." The Domino Lady leaned forward a little and flashed him a dazzling smile.

"All right." Benford took another drag on his cigarette. "First of all, they ain't Chinamen. One's Japanese and the other's Korean."

"What?" The Domino Lady's eyes squinted with puzzlement behind the mask. "That can't be right. They were Red Dragon...."

"Nuh-uh." The assistant coroner was emphatic. "Nope. Everything's wrong for Chinese. Bone structure, tattoos... all wrong. White folks don't think there's any difference, but anyone who's spent time in Asia knows there's individual facial characteristics to the different nationalities there, especially the cheekbones and the eyes. Not to mention one of 'em's got a tattoo in the wrong language. Those boys are not Chinese. Stake my pension on it. What's more, and if it gets out, heads are gonna roll—I better not see this in the papers—but them two didn't commit suicide. They were poisoned and then someone else strung 'em up. Ligature marks and lividity are all wrong."

"But that doesn't make any sense at all." The Domino Lady bit her lip. "Why...?"

"Don't ask me. I'm just the guy unloads the meat wagon on the night shift." Benford shrugged.

"You're more than that, Lucas." The Domino Lady smiled at the M.E. again. "You went to med school and you've got eyes. You proved that already. No one noticed this until now, though? Really?"

Benford shrugged again and stubbed out the Chesterfield on the brick wall. "Couple of Chinamen from the Red Dragons decide to off themselves, it's not a priority. I probably wouldn't have noticed anything if it hadn't been for the ligature marks being so light. Then I got interested. But I don't think I'm putting anything about this stuff in the report."

The Domino Lady let out a whistling sigh through clenched teeth. "Lucas, you know that...."

"Uh-uh." Benford shook his head emphatically. "I'm not any crusader. That's your department. I got a wife and two kids at home to think about. The D.A. got himself killed last year trying to strike a blow for justice and whatnot. We all learned our lesson then. Somebody got to those two guys in a holding cell at precinct headquarters and no one said boo. I know when I'm supposed to take a hard look and when I'm supposed to just rubber-stamp it."

The Domino Lady scowled at him.

Benford sighed. "Look. I'll tell you this. Somebody wants this to look like Tong war stuff and it's not. That's bad. That's why I'm talking to you. Everybody's tense about immigrants right now, whether they're coming up from Mexico or across the water. Nobody wants another riot. But I'm not putting Carol and the boys in anybody's crosshairs. If nobody picked up on this until now, it's because they aren't supposed to. Big people are making some kind of move. I can't tell you who. But it's not the Red Dragons."

The masked woman nodded after a moment, accepting it. "All right. Thanks for letting me know at least, Lucas. You're one of the good guys whether you think so or not."

"One more thing," Benford said as the Domino Lady turned to go. "Damnedest thing. You know the guns them two was carrying?"

"The machine guns?"

Benford nodded. "Yeah. Heard the guys talking about this when they brought in the bodies. Turns out them guns was loaded with blanks."

"Blanks?" The Domino Lady couldn't believe it. "But that's not..." She caught herself before she let slip that she had been an eyewitness. "Surely they couldn't have known they were shooting blanks."

"Heard it straight from the crime scene photog. Blanks. Like they were set up to get caught. Weird, isn't it?"

"Yes," the Domino Lady said slowly. "Yes, it is."

Ellen Patrick was still turning it over in her mind the next afternoon, when she and Paul Rosen ran into Joaquin Vasquez at the Birchwood tennis court. Ellen had quietly engineered the meeting; she remembered Joaquin liked his tennis game on Friday afternoon, and a couple of phone calls to the club that morning to inquire about Mr. Vasquez's reservation had confirmed that was still the case.

She'd brought Paul along both for company and for protective coloration, and because she knew having Paul there with her would give her the perfect excuse to insert herself back into Joaquin's social circle. "Joaquin Vasquez! It's been ages. I hope you aren't too traumatized from that nastiness at the Ball."

"Not too terribly," Joaquin admitted. "It was worse fending off the newspaper people after. It was such a mob I never even got to say thank you to the hero of the evening. Rosen, isn't it?" He held out a hand and Paul shook it. "Hell of a thing you did. I don't know many others who...."

Paul looked uncomfortable. "I was just mad," he said. "I don't like bullies."

"Have the police found out anything about what it was all about?" Ellen said brightly. "Why you? It's not more of those rumors about your family's business, surely."

"I'm afraid it's not just rumor, Ellen." Suddenly, again, Joaquin Vasquez looked tired and sad. "But they managed to target the one Vasquez that has nothing to do with any part of the import business. I have spent the last few years trying to make my own way in the world.... But my name can sometimes be a liability."

"I was just mad," Rosen said. "I don't like bullies."

"What are you doing now?" Paul asked him.

To Ellen's mild surprise, Joaquin actually flushed with embarrassment. "Actually, I'm a writer," he said. "On the Emperor lot. Right now I'm working on something called *Belles of Santa Maria*. Sort of a, uh, love story thing. Some song-and-dance numbers, salsa dancing actually. It's corny, but I'm proud of the work we're putting into it. The choreographer is amazing. We just got back from location shooting in Puerto Vallarta a couple of weeks ago."

"Why, that's wonderful!" Ellen put a little of her fluttery-featherhead voice into it. But she was genuinely pleased for him. "It sounds so romantic. Paul, you would never have believed Joaquin had a romantic bone in his body when we were at school, he was captain of the football team and got in all sorts of scrapes." She laughed and poked Joaquin playfully in the chest. "And look at you now. You big softy."

Joaquin grinned. It made him look absurdly boyish. "I'm not who I was back then," he said. "Your lady is too gracious to bring it up, Mr. Rosen, but I'm afraid I was a bit of a bastard back in our school days."

"Oh, I don't know about that," Ellen said, though privately she agreed with him.

"It's true." Now Joaquin's grin was rueful. "I... well, I guess I had a lot to prove back then. These days I am easier about my place in the world. Anyway, I must be off. I have my lesson with the club professional."

"Paul taught tennis, you know." Ellen nudged Paul. "Maybe you two could have a quick set some time."

"Well, it's been a while for me." Paul gave Ellen a sidewise look, "...but sure, that would be great."

"Couldn't you boys play today?" Ellen smiled at both of them. "I mean, it's such a lovely coincidence us running into you, Joaquin, and I think you two would have fun. The heroes of the Birchwood Ball should be friends. And to be honest, Paul, I think I'd rather sit and have a mimosa and watch you two play." She put a little extra into the smile.

As it had since she was in high school, Ellen Patrick's smiling face wilted the resolve of the men in her presence. Joaquin glanced up at Paul and, seeing his *why-fight-it?* expression, went to cancel the lesson. Then, matters decided, the three of them trooped off to the tennis court, where Ellen took up a seat at one of the umbrella-shaded tables courtside near the bar cart. Joaquin trotted out onto the court, but Paul Rosen hung back for a moment. He leaned in over Ellen and kissed her cheek, then whispered, "What are you up to?"

"Social engineering," Ellen whispered in reply. "I don't think he has many friends. Be nice."

Paul looked at her for a long moment, then nodded, satisfied. He turned and strode out on to the court. "Be gentle, now," he called cheerfully. "I can't afford to look too foolish in front of the lady."

Ellen regarded the two men with amusement and affection. She really was beginning to think she had been wrong about Joaquin. There genuinely was something new there that hadn't been there in the old days, and he couldn't help his name. As for Paul... well, he was proving to have real potential. He was smart and fun and easy to be with, and he didn't push her for more than she was prepared to give. He was almost *too* easy to be with, she reflected. She'd have to be careful not to give too much away. As it was he had seriously inconvenienced the Domino Lady last night; Ellen had run into some difficulty trying to find an excuse to end their evening early so her other self could get to the morgue for her appointment with Benford. Fortunately, Paul hadn't made an issue out of it, though she thought there might have been a flicker of suspicion in his eyes... *oh stop,* she scolded herself. *Cross that bridge when you come to it. You can't get seriously involved but you can enjoy his company. Have a drink and be relieved that you were wrong about Joaquin being involved in his family's smuggling ring.* She gestured at one of the club stewards. "Could I get a mimosa, please?"

The drink arrived in moments and she nursed it, taking only an occasional sip while she watched the two men playing tennis. They seemed pretty evenly matched. Joaquin was faster, and played with a little more flair, but Paul had better control of his game, often sending the ball with calculated precision to just exactly the wrong place for Joaquin to get to it in time to return it.

They were at one set each when another of the club stewards jogged up to courtside and waved at Joaquin. "A phone call for you, Mr. Vasquez. You can take it at the bar cart. There's a house phone there."

Joaquin nodded and strode over to the bar cart. The bartender handed him the receiver and Joaquin listened for a moment, then said something that looked to Ellen like *I understand. I'll be there.* Then he turned and came back to where Paul had joined Ellen at her table. "I'm sorry," he said tersely. "I'll have to cut our game short, Paul. Another time."

"That's too bad." Paul smiled. "Hope there's nothing wrong."

"No, no, just a problem at the studio. Some sort of emergency rewrite, and the director's losing the light or something." Joaquin's smile was so forced it was almost a rictus. "My apologies. I'll have a round of drinks sent." He gestured at the steward and then was in motion, heading out past the court to the parking lot before either Ellen or Paul could reply.

"Well, how about that?" Paul chuckled. "Never would have thought there was such a thing as a writer emergency. Only in Hollywood, I guess. Shall we see about ordering some dinner then?"

"No, no, that's fine," Ellen said quickly. "I think I'd like to call it a day as well. It'll be dark soon anyway, and I'm not feeling very good." She took a deep breath and added the one excuse guaranteed to end all further male inquiry. "I'm… pardon my saying it, but I'm a little crampy, I'm afraid. Could you take me home, Paul?"

"Of course." Paul instantly was all solicitousness. He insisted she wait while he brought his red convertible roadster around, and then drove her home in slightly awkward silence. Ellen smiled weakly at him but inside her mind was boiling. *If that was the studio calling then I'm Herbert Hoover. That was some kind of… threat, or something. He was terrified. I've got to ditch Paul and get over to Joaquin's place.* He was living in some sort of roommate arrangement in a house over by the new Farmer's Market, she thought he'd said, somewhere just short of Fairfax. Ellen was sure the phone call had been the newest foray from whoever was trying to implicate Joaquin in the Vasquez-Tong trouble, and she was determined that the Domino Lady would put a stop to it.

When they pulled up to her building, she got out of the car, then before going in she turned back and impulsively leaned in over the driver's side door and kissed Paul. "Sorry, darling. We'll do better next time."

"Next time," Paul smiled up at her. "Feel better, honey."

Ellen smiled back at him and then turned and ran up the steps.

Rosen watched her go, then put the convertible into gear. He drove around the block and found a parking place where he could observe the lot behind her building. He was certain that Ellen had ditched him to become the Domino Lady, and he had investigated the cars parked in the lot the day before. He had pegged a black Daimler sedan with blacked-out windows as being the most likely, and as he had suspected, he didn't have long to wait. Sure enough, he saw Ellen Patrick emerge from the back of the building, attired in a white dress and a black opera cloak. *No mask. She probably puts that on in the car.* She headed straight for the Daimler and got in. A few moments later, the engine roared to life and the Daimler spun out of the lot in a spray of gravel.

Rosen waited until the Daimler turned the corner, then put his own vehicle into gear again and followed.

The Domino Lady finished applying her mask and glanced at herself in the Daimler's rear-view mirror. *Looking good. All right, let's go.* She turned the key and the sedan's ignition responded with a reassuring rumble.

She had learned months ago on her first night out as the Domino Lady that string or even an elastic strap was no way to keep a mask on if you expected trouble, and ever since then she had used spirit gum to apply hers the way movie studio makeup artists applied a rubber appliance to an actor's face. This kept it tighter to the skin and didn't block her peripheral vision, either. She had made some changes to the domino mask itself in recent weeks; now the ribbing of the black velvet subtly altered the contours of her cheekbones, and she had also made the mask wider. This would be the first real test of it, though. Most of the time she tried to confine her exploits to places and people that had no intersection with Ellen Patrick, but tonight there was no way out of it; the Domino Lady had business with Joaquin Vasquez and that was all there was to it. She would just have to keep out of the light and remember to pitch her voice lower.

One hand on the wheel, she reached down and flipped open the glove box and fished out the new pistol Andrew had sent from New York. *All sorts of things getting a trial run tonight,* she thought. The syringe full of chloral hydrate that she usually favored as a weapon was really too unwieldy, and worse, the word was getting out about it. This pistol was a prototype, something her friend Andrew from Mayfair Labs had helped to engineer. It fired what he called 'mercy bullets,' non-lethal anesthetic capsules that shattered against an opponent when fired and caused unconsciousness within seconds of penetrating the skin. Ellen had wheedled one out of him with some story of wanting to show it to some friends of her father's in the Los Angeles Police Department. She was sure Andrew hadn't really bought it, but she knew he had a little crush on her and wouldn't give her away.

Dear Andrew. But of course now there was Paul. Damn it all anyway. The Domino Lady's lips curled in a grim smile. *For someone who swore off relationships, life's getting pretty complicated. Oh well.*

She pulled the Daimler up to the curb just outside of Joaquin's bungalow.

Movement flickered in her rear-view mirror and she glanced behind. A car with its lights off had slowed and stopped about thirty yards back. *Company. Well.* She wrapped the opera cloak around her and stepped out of the sedan. She strode up the path to the front door and saw that it was open.

Deal with my friend behind me first. She paused, waiting, listening. There was a brief rasp of gravel behind her and she whirled, gun out. It took everything she had not to let her jaw drop in shock.

"Don't shoot! Please." Paul Rosen raised his hands.

"Who are you?" The Domino Lady's voice was careful, controlled. "Why are you here?"

"I followed you…. I need your help. You know who I am." Rosen licked his lips and then went all-in. "…*Ellen.*"

Rosen watched her reaction. There was almost none. She had very tight control of her expression, but he could see the way her eyes narrowed behind the mask. *I almost can't believe it's her, the way she holds herself, everything is so different. Even her face…*

"My help with what? Never mind, it'll keep. Step ahead of me and keep your hands up." Rosen did so. She nudged him ahead of her with the snout of the pistol. "Go on in."

The living room of Joaquin's bungalow was a shambles. Chairs were overturned, there was a shattered vase on the floor near the fireplace mantel, and Rosen could smell cordite. Guns had been fired here. And… *oh, God. I knew the Prof planned something, but another killing, Jesus.*

There was a body on the floor in a pool of congealed blood. He knelt, fighting the urge to vomit, and turned it over. Dead, of course. One neat little bullet hole in the forehead just over the bridge of the nose. Not Joaquin. A young Latino man, maybe twenty.

"He shared the house with a friend." The Domino Lady's voice held an edge of suppressed anger. "They're framing Joaquin Vasquez for this. That means the police are probably on their way. Damn them. This was all staged. Again. Which means we need to move. Outside, now."

Obediently Rosen stood and she followed him back out to the street. "My car," she said. "You drive."

"Where?"

"Anywhere. Just away. Fast."

Once the car was moving, Rosen gave her a sidelong glance. The pistol was aimed straight at him, still. "Are you really going to shoot me?"

"I'm thinking about it. A lot." The Domino Lady sighed, finally, and lowered the gun. "All right, Paul. Let's have it. All of it. Start with that charade at the Orphan's Ball on Saturday. You were in on it, too, weren't you? The entire evening was faked. Everyone was playing a part but Joaquin, is that right?"

Rosen hesitated, then replied, "Yes. I was given a script. I imagine the gunmen were, too."

The Domino Lady nodded. "Okay. So who's writing your lines?"

So Rosen told her all of it: the professor, the envelope containing the list of possible candidates for the Domino Lady, and the instructions for getting close to all of them at the ball. He didn't pretty it up, not even when he had to explain about Jessica Vine in Colorado and how Professor Murdwell had been able to blackmail him. "But now... three people are dead. This is way over my head, Ellen. I don't know who else to turn to. I thought...maybe...."

"Don't call me Ellen when I'm dressed like this," she snapped. "You damn fool, this professor suckered you. You could have just walked away. He didn't have *anything* on you. The police back in Colorado cleared you, you said. But now you're an accomplice. You let some windy academic with a lot of highfalutin theory bully you into aiding and abetting a felony. You're an idiot. An idiot and a coward. And to think I thought you were... never mind. Let me think." She bit her lip.

Rosen didn't say anything. He knew she was right.

"But what's it all about?" The Domino Lady said after a moment. "Why go to so much trouble? Staging all this. It's not to benefit the Vasquez syndicate or the Red Dragons. Who's his target?"

Rosen looked surprised. "Why...you. The Domino Lady. I thought I explained all that."

She grimaced. "Yes, you did, and I don't buy a word of it. Of course he wanted me, too, and I'm ashamed of myself that I let myself be played like that... but he could have got me without all the theater. You said so. He had it narrowed down to just a few possibles. Sure, he planted you on me, but he also wanted the show at the Birchwood with Joaquin Vasquez, he used my raid on their payroll to kickstart his own campaign of terror. He's killed two people to make sure that played out the way he scripted it without any inconvenient questions from any follow-up investigation. And now Joaquin's friend. Why? What's the common denominator?"

"It beats me." Rosen shook his head. "You'd have to ask the Prof."

The Domino Lady nodded. "That's a great idea. Let's go do that. Right now."

"What? I thought…look, I'm out, I'm done," Rosen's voice rose an octave. "I don't want any more…."

"I don't give a damn what you want. You owe me, you lying son of a bitch. Anyway, I've still got the gun." She brought the pistol up again. No need to mention it was only loaded with mercy bullets. "Pull over as soon as you see a phone booth. I need to make a quick call. Then you'll take me to this professor."

Professor Murdwell's residence was a stately three-story home in Bixby Knolls. The house was huge, just barely short of being a mansion. The walls were white stucco, and the roof was red slate. There was a smaller roof over the entrance supported by white stone columns. There was a large lawn with several trees and a white brick wall surrounding the estate, and no driveway, just a walk-in gate at the front with a gravel path that led to the front steps. The Domino Lady instructed Rosen to park the Daimler at the end of the block, then the two of them walked slowly toward the house.

"You're just going up to the front door and knock?" Rosen was incredulous.

"Why not? I'm armed. You said he has just the one big butler. How big is he?"

"Pretty big." Rosen grimaced. "I'm sure he doesn't want to get shot, but I don't think he'll just roll over for us, either."

The Domino Lady shrugged. "We'll see." The butler probably also served as a bodyguard, and possibly the professor's personal torpedo. A mercy bullet would take him out of the picture and that left just the professor. She was confident that she could manage the professor and Rosen on her own.

It was full dark now, though not very late as yet. There were no lights on in the front of the house, but the moon was out and it gave plenty of light to see by. The trees on the lawn cast blue-black shadows on the white brick as they approached the entrance. The Domino Lady rang the bell and heard a distant *bong* from the depths of the house. A hall light came on and the door swung open. It was the large butler.

Before he could even open his mouth the Domino Lady fired twice in rapid succession: *Phut-phut.* The butler's eyes rolled skyward and he collapsed in a heap.

"Good God, you shot him," Rosen blurted.

"It's anesthetic." The Domino Lady glared. "Keep your voice down, the professor will be here any second. We need to drag this guy...."

"I think not, Miss Patrick." Another figure stepped out of the shadows on the lawn. It was the professor. In his right hand he held a .45 automatic. "As you can see, I am already here. I am armed as well, and this gun shoots real bullets. We were expecting you. Events went exactly as planned, thanks in no small part to your companion; Mr. Rosen is turning out to be quite an actor. I was only waiting out here on the lawn for half an hour or so before your arrival. Please drop your weapon."

The Domino Lady paused, calculating odds, then dropped the mercy pistol to the gravel.

Then, she whirled and slapped Paul Rosen with everything she had. It was like the crack of a whip. "You bastard."

Rosen just stood there. A red welt was forming on his cheek. "I'm... sorry, Ellen."

Professor Murdwell chuckled. "Now, now, Miss Patrick, we all have our parts to play. Mr. Rosen cannot help who he is, any more than you can."

"So I've heard." The Domino Lady faced him directly and put her hands on her hips. "Puppets on a string, according to you. And you're the puppet master. Is that it?"

"Very apt. I see what you are doing, Miss Patrick. Please just stop right there and get on your knees. Arms out. There will be no kicking or jumping or anything of that sort. I know that every iota of your being demands that you make some attempt, but it would be fruitless and I would prefer not to shoot you. Do not underestimate me." Murdwell gestured with the pistol.

The Domino Lady dropped to her knees and held her arms out. Murdwell nodded at Rosen. "Remove the cloak, there are concealed pockets. In fact, remove the dress as well; she has been known to carry a knife taped to her thigh. You see, Miss Patrick, this is the key to my success. Research. Your previous adversaries were very chatty about your methods, especially the ones I visited in prison. Most eager to help."

Rosen moved forward and did as he was told. He lifted off the black opera cloak and tossed it on the lawn, then hesitated. "The dress...I don't...."

"I don't want her getting up. Rip it." Murdwell's tone was exasperated. "Do it now. It's a bit late for gentlemanly scruples from you, Mr. Rosen."

The Domino Lady was expressionless behind her mask. Rosen reached a hand down the back of the white dress and pulled. The satin tore, leaving the Domino Lady in bra and panties. The satin pooled around her waist and thighs.

Murdwell looked her over carefully. There was nothing erotic about his examination, not the slightest hint of a leer. He might have been looking at a lab specimen on a slide. "All right," he said at last. "You may stand, Miss Patrick. Is the mask glued on, then?"

The Domino Lady didn't answer, but just glared at him as she slowly stood up. The satin fell to her ankles.

Murdwell tutted. "Spirit gum, I suppose. That means it would take some sort of acetone compound to remove it. It can wait. Rosen, gather those garments. We'll take the lady in to join our other guest in the cellar, and then we'll have to move Brunton to his quarters. How long will he be indisposed, Miss Patrick?"

"Sixteen hours at least. I gave him a double dose because he's such a big fellow." The Domino Lady's voice was level, though it held a slight edge. "May I at least have my cape back? Certainly you've proven I'm no danger to you now."

Murdwell considered it and smiled. "I think not, Miss Patrick. Even if the cape is free of concealed weapons, leaving you in your current state of near-nudity strikes me as good psychology. I don't wish you to forget I retain the advantage here. Inside, please."

The Domino Lady stepped out of the crumpled bit of white satin that once had been her dress and slowly walked toward the entrance, the professor behind her. Rosen scooped up the black cape and ruined dress from the lawn and followed.

The basement was dark and smelled of dust and furniture oil. And it was cold. The Domino Lady shivered and silently cursed the professor for leaving her in her underthings. The hell of it was, there hadn't been anything in the opera cloak. She had just wanted something to wear. The professor was right, she did feel at a disadvantage when trying to function in just brassiere and panties: not a terribly modest brassiere or panties, either. *Maybe the Domino Lady ought to consider longjohns.*

"…don't forget…I retain the advantage here."

At least she still had her shoes. They were sturdy black flats; no concealed weapons or anything, but she could run, and fight if necessary, without having to do it in high heels. And they were solid enough that she felt she could deliver the punishing kick in the balls Paul Rosen had coming, if she got the chance.

She had been falling for him. She could admit that to herself, though she would never have said it aloud. The professor had told Paul exactly what to say and do and it had worked like a charm. That was the humiliation that soured her stomach and left her cheeks burning. Was she really so predictable?

All right, enough with the self-pity, she decided. *You need a next move, Ellen. And a weapon.*

There was a rustle from behind her. "Who's there?"

The Domino Lady recognized the voice as Joaquin Vasquez. She remembered to pitch her voice lower, and she put a little bit of a rasp into it. "A friend. People call me the Domino Lady."

"Well, that's a plot twist." Joaquin let out a bitter chuckle. "Can you at least tell me what I've fallen into? Is this more of the Tong business?" He moved closer and she drew back. "Wait, are you *naked?*"

"Almost." The Domino Lady sighed. "Don't get any ideas."

To her surprise, Joaquin laughed. "Rest easy, miss. I'm... well, let's say my interests lie elsewhere."

"Oh?" Then she realized. "Oh. I see."

"I was disowned," Joaquin explained. "I am considered a blight on the family name."

There was an awkward silence.

"Families...can be cruel sometimes," the Domino Lady said finally. "Still, it's better in Hollywood for that... uh... lifestyle than in other parts of the country." It took everything she had not to exclaim, *Of course! How could I have not figured it out? Kicked out of the family business. Writing romance musicals in West Hollywood. Living with a male friend. And that overcompensating macho act in high school. The poor boy must have been miserable.* But Ellen Patrick was the one that knew Joaquin's background, not the Domino Lady. So all she said was, "Anyway, it's not the Tongs. It's all been staged. They're framing you. Can you tell me why anyone would want to start a war between your family and the Red Dragons?"

"I have no idea. Sincerely." Joaquin shook his head. "I received a call. They were threatening to expose me in the press... my living arrangements would be paraded through the newspapers, and also they threatened to name me as a conspirator in some sort of opium ring. They said I would be blacklisted. I was told to come here to discuss arrangements, and when I arrived a giant threw a bag over my head and manhandled me down here to the cellar. And that was all, until they threw you in here, too." He spread his hands helplessly. "It's a mystery to me why anyone would target me if they wanted to start a feud with my family's organization. I am the unwanted Vasquez. For the last five years or so I have been an outcast; my family considers me a disgusting embarrassment, and the rest of the world thinks I'm a criminal. Until I got my big break at the Emperor Studio I thought I was going to end up just another failed screenwriter. Thankfully they saw something in me. And then I met Ramon, and we became partners."

"Ramon?"

"A choreographer. My housemate." Joaquin paused. "My friend."

Oh, God. The Domino Lady sucked in her breath with a sharp hiss. "Mr. Vasquez, I'm so sorry. Ramon is dead."

Joaquin was silent for a moment. "You are sure?" he asked finally.

"I found the body." Impulsively, she laid a hand on his arm. She could feel him shaking silently. "Truly, I am sorry. None of this should have happened." *It's my fault,* she didn't add. *Because I was trying to put a stop to your family's operations in Chinatown, a mad scientist got a wild idea and now three people are dead.* She had to make this right.

"They will pay," Joaquin said, biting off the words.

"There's more to it, Mr. Vasquez. I think they're setting you up to take the rap. I don't know why. But we have to get out of here if we're going to put a stop to it."

"I agree." He shrugged. "But how? Are you planning to pull out a miracle?"

"I am, actually." The Domino Lady grinned. "Men really have no idea how much metal is concealed in a brassiere." She reached beneath her armpit and slid out two long thin strips of steel from where they had been hidden in a slim pocket along the underwire. "They missed my lockpicks."

This actually startled Joaquin into a laugh. "Astonishing. I'm going to remember this if I ever have occasion to write a movie about a female burglar. What else have you got in there?"

"Just feminine pulchritude, I'm afraid." The Domino Lady knelt by the cellar door and began to work at the lock, going by feel. "We're going to have to find weapons of some kind."

"The kitchen. There will be knives there." Joaquin's voice held a certain wolfish pleasure now. "Even the family black sheep is still a Vasquez. I have been throwing knives since I was a boy."

"Dangerous pastime." The door opened and the Domino Lady stood up. "Let's hope it pays off."

Paul Rosen stepped out on to the front lawn of Professor Murdwell's home and lit a cigarette. His thoughts were dark and his stomach was sour. Ever since they had found the body at the Vasquez bungalow he had been fighting an urge to vomit. He had spent the last twenty minutes dragging Brunton's unconscious body into the professor's front room where he had finally been able to manhandle the hulking figure up onto a sofa where he was now snoring peacefully. Then the professor had told him to wait there for further instructions, but Rosen had decided to wait outside instead. Being in there with Brunton was too reminiscent of being in a room with a dead body, in spite of Brunton's gentle snoring.

He thought again of the actual dead body he'd seen in the bungalow a couple of hours earlier, lying there in its sticky pool of blood, and this time he couldn't fight the nausea down. He threw the cigarette down on the gravel path and ran for one of the flowerbeds and threw up. He had eaten very little that day, so it was mostly dry heaves with a spray of acid and foam.

Finally the spasm passed and Rosen stood, panting, one hand on the white stucco wall of the house to support himself.

What have I done? was the forlorn thought that kept echoing in the back of his head. But the thing that was making him sick to his stomach was that he knew exactly what he had done. *Ellen was right. About all of it. But especially about me. I was just a coward, but now I'm accessory to a murderer. And he's going to murder Ellen and the Vasquez kid too.*

But what could he do? Rosen was no hero. In fact, Ellen was the hero; which pretty much made him the villain, didn't it? He hadn't known the roommate was going to be dead when he had followed Ellen to the bungalow, but he had still followed his instructions to the letter and confessed his complicity, then delivered her to Murdwell after "a brief show of reluctance." That was what had been in the script the professor had written out for him the day before. Rosen's horror at finding the Mexican kid's body had actually helped sell it. Probably why the professor hadn't told him in advance. But he'd gone ahead despite knowing it meant Ellen's death as well. Of course it did. Why kid himself about it?

The hell of it was, he could really fall for her. Maybe he already had, he admitted to himself. But he knew he had already lost whatever chance he had. Even if he went down to the cellar and sprung her, he knew that Ellen would never again look at him with anything other than disgust. He might as well just take his thirty pieces of silver and get out of L.A. as fast as he could. Start over. Somehow. Try and forget the frozen expression of the dead kid, and the hatred in Ellen's eyes for him that he'd seen under the mask.

Paul Rosen was so lost in his self-loathing reverie that he didn't see the three men approaching from the shadows until they were on him. One grabbed him and spun him around, and then one of the others slammed a sledgehammer fist into his stomach just as he was opening his mouth to raise the alarm, so that all that came out was a huffing grunt of expelled air.

They kept hitting him. His last conscious thought was a bitter, *I have this coming.*

No one interfered with Vasquez and the Domino Lady as they crept up the stairs and tiptoed into the kitchen. Apparently Brunton comprised the whole of the household staff. The Domino Lady had almost forgotten her near-nudity by this point; the important thing was that she was still masked and Joaquin hadn't made the connection with Ellen Patrick. That was enough.

Joaquin pointed at a wooden block that held a set of chef's knives.

The Domino Lady nodded at him. "You're the expert."

Joaquin considered it, then selected one with a long, flat blade about nine inches long. He ran his thumb gently along the edge of the blade and nodded, satisfied. "Fortunately, the professor is a gourmet. He does not skimp on his culinary accessories. This will do nicely." He glanced over to the Domino Lady. "You?"

She thought about it, but the truth was, she wasn't sure she had it in her to shove a knife into someone, even in self-defense. "I'll manage."

"In that case, I'll take two." He selected another, thinner one. "Very well. What now? Shall we try to find a telephone?"

"Let's just get out of here. My car is up the street." Then she remembered Paul still had the keys. "No, scratch that. Change of plan. We'll have to...."

They had been speaking in whispers. Suddenly they heard angry voices coming from the study and froze.

But no one was raising an alarm. It was an argument. "I paid you good money, Murdwell! I expect you to deliver!"

"I know that voice," Joaquin whispered.

The Domino Lady nodded. She did, too. It was Barrett Steeves.

Professor Murdwell sat behind his desk, his fingers steepled, one eyebrow raised in quizzical bemusement. "But I have delivered, Mr. Steeves. If you could just calm yourself, I will explain."

"I'm tired of your explanations!" Steeves was having none of it. "I hired you to do a job! You were supposed to take the Vasquez syndicate off my back! Do you have any idea what those people will do to me?"

"If they find out. I have assured that they will not." Murdwell was beginning to look a little annoyed. "My commission was to insure that you would emerge unscathed. I have done so. No one is going to connect you to the syndicate funds that you... appropriated. The Domino Lady will be revealed as the culprit, working in tandem with Joaquin Vasquez, and both will be found murdered with the finger of guilt pointing squarely at the Red Dragon Tong. It will be assumed that the two of them are responsible for the missing money, the sums owed to the Vasquez syndicate from the Tong for the smuggled opium from Mexico." He spread his hands. "Meanwhile, your finances are secure. How much have you skimmed from the Vasquez holdings? Five hundred thousand? A million? Surely this is a prize worth playing for."

"You think I get to keep all that money?" Steeves snorted. "Everyone thinks the movie business is Depression-proof. It's not. I never would have got into bed with the Vasquez mob if I hadn't been desperate to keep the doors open. I just needed some breathing room...."

"Yes, so you've said." Murdwell chuckled. "Of course you did. Otherwise you would have been poor. That's unthinkable for a man like you."

"I don't need your smirky sarcasm, either."

"Sarcasm? Hardly." Murdwell pursed his lips and clucked in sympathy. "I meant no offense. It's merely that I am fascinated with the lies you people tell yourselves. You've somehow persuaded yourself that operating a drug smuggling ring in partnership with a Mexican crime cartel is a charitable act. Really, you should feel smug. The idea of using location shooting in Mexico as a cover to get opium into the country was inspired, and certainly you had no problem underbidding the Chinese sources for the stuff the tongs had used previously. You have a gifted criminal mind, Mr. Steeves, as have I. The difference is that I've made my peace with it."

"Criminal mind? Well, maybe, but I never killed anybody." Steeves' voice had lost some of its bluster. "That's all on you. The two Chinks, the fairy dancer. And you're talking about killing two more...."

"Never killed anybody? Really? You mean the death of your daughter's fiancé was an accident?" The professor laughed. "What a remarkably fortunate coincidence that must have been, right after your production's return from making that Western in Baja. The one with the famous cliff fall."

"That wasn't me," Steeves said. His voice held a sullen pout. "That was Benito Vasquez. One of his boys had seen Roger poking around the wagon with the stuff hidden in it. I tried to tell them Roger was a good Joe but I guess they decided to make sure. I had no idea Toni was sweet on him. That all came out after, when those damn news vultures were swarming. Anyway, it's nothing near your body count; you can't just kill somebody whenever you need a handy...."

Murdwell shrugged. "You are in the business of make-believe, Mr. Steeves. You must understand the necessity of using props...*agh!*"

The exclamation was startled out of him by a knife that flew from the doorway into his upper chest, almost to the hilt. Joaquin Vasquez stepped into the room, the Domino Lady close behind.

Joaquin brandished his other blade at Steeves. "You're next. *Pendejo.* You think I am soft? You think I cannot kill? I will cut out your lying heart for what you did to Ramon."

Murdwell clutched at the knife hilt and bawled, "Rosen! *Rosen!* Get in here!"

The Domino Lady stepped over to him and grabbed the knife hilt and twisted. Murdwell screamed. A bubble of blood burst from his mouth. "Shut up and hold still," she told him. "He hit a lung but if you sit still it won't kill you. We've had enough out of you for one night." She looked up at Joaquin. "Where is that bastard Rosen, anyway?"

Steeves was still staring in horror at Joaquin. "I had nothing to do with any of it," he said. "I was just...."

"Yes. I heard what you were." Joaquin stepped forward and put the knife point to Steeves' throat. "You hired kidnapping, murder, who knows what-all... so you could keep your precious movie studio. You lied about everything. The only reason you took me on was my family name, wasn't it? You've been planning to frame me for over a year. Probably as soon as you started skimming. All my work, everything... it was meaningless. In the end I am still just a Vasquez, a criminal and murderer. Well then, pig, you will see what a murdering Vasquez can do...."

"Joaquin, no!" The Domino Lady's voice was desperate. "Please! He's not worth it, look at him, he doesn't even understand what he's done. He's just a cowardly old man who loves money. You can be better than this. I know you can."

Joaquin turned and looked at her. His expression was a terrible thing. Murderous fury and infinite sadness and a bitter fatalism, all at once. "And who gets justice for Ramon, then? Who do you think the police will believe? The Mexican faggot and the masked vigilante? Or the rich studio mogul? No, I must...."

There was a commotion from the entrance. Two large Chinese men entered, dragging a badly-beaten Paul Rosen. A third followed behind, cradling a machine gun in one arm.

The Domino Lady rattled off a string of Chinese. The man with the machine gun nodded. He stepped over to Steeves and gestured for him to stand.

"Who are these people? What...what did you tell them?" Steeves' voice shook with real terror now.

"I think you know who they are." The Domino Lady's grin was feral. "They're Red Dragon Tong. The real ones. I told them that you have hundreds of thousands of dollars of their money. They're going to have some questions for you." She turned to the Chinese again and spoke a few more words.

The man with the machine gun nodded. "*Tŏngyī.*" It was a grunt.

Steeves looked terrified. "What are you saying to him?"

"That you're the kind of filth who would sell out his own daughter's happiness for a few dollars, and they should be extra careful to make sure it hurts, and that it lasts a long time." The Domino Lady turned to Joaquin Vasquez. "Joaquin, they understand now that the Vasquez family has had no part in any of this. They'll leave you alone." She addressed the professor. "It was the butler, Brunton, that killed Ramon, wasn't it? On your order."

Murdwell looked up at her, eyes glittering with hate. "I underestimated you," he muttered.

"You aren't the only one who can arrange events. I made a phone call before we came here." The Domino Lady patted his cheek. "I don't particularly like the tongs. But I have friends in Chinatown. And as they say, the enemy of my enemy is my friend." With a savage smile, she added, "All this in bra and panties, too. Imagine how much I'd have been able to do to your operation with the psychological advantage of being fully dressed."

"You forget." Murdwell struggled to speak, his lips flecked with red foam. "I know who you are...I'll tell the world that the Domino Lady is really..."

Paul Rosen shouted, "No!" and lunged for the machine gun in the Red Dragon's hands. He grabbed it and fired a burst at Murdwell, stitching red across his torso. Then one of the other Chinese clubbed him to the floor. Before anyone could stop him, he pulled a pistol of his own and shot Rosen in the chest.

"Paul!" The Domino Lady rushed to kneel by him. A red hole gaped in his chest, welling dark blood, and she could see it was hopeless. Seconds left at best. "Why?"

"No telling what a woman will do... man either, I guess...." Those were Paul Rosen's last words. His eyes clouded and then he was gone, the body was empty; just meat, spilling red on the Persian rug.

The Domino Lady stood, slowly. She spoke a few more words of Chinese. The tong leader grunted agreement and turned to Barrett Steeves. Steeves began to squall in protest, and the man holding him clamped a hand on his throat and shook him the way a terrier would shake a rat. Steeves let out a gassy squeak and fell silent. The tong leader turned back to the Domino Lady, who nodded. They dragged Steeves out, leaving her alone with Joaquin.

And the bodies.

"What now?" Joaquin suddenly looked white and frail. Without his rage to fuel him, he seemed on the verge of collapse. "I still...there are so many questions."

"Lucky for you, they're questions no one will want to ask." The Domino Lady's voice was cold and distant. "Too many power players in town would get mud on them. All they're going to want is a fall guy to drop it on so they can hush it up. The important part is to make sure it's not you. Brunton's still out cold in the other room, he's the one that did the professor's hands-on killing anyway. Pin it on him. Just play dumb and keep your story simple. Give Brunton to the cops, tell them about Steeves and the smuggling, tell them the Tong intervened just as Steeves and the professor were putting the finishing touches on your frame. The studio has good lawyers. Get one on your side. And make sure the papers get wind of it. It's a great story. Conspiracy, studio corruption, murder, Chinatown intrigue… and it has the advantage of being true, even. Once they start digging it'll all come out and it'll clear you. Just leave me out of it."

"Leave you… but…" Joaquin looked at her as though he was seeing her for the first time. "I owe you my life."

"No. I owed you. Just…" The Domino Lady paused, not sure what she was trying to say. "Just get through this and… and live your life." She bent and fished the Daimler's keys out from Rosen's pocket, trying not to look at his dead face, and turned to go.

Joaquin said, "Wait."

She paused at the door and turned. "Yes?"

He inclined his head at Rosen's body. "I think we have both lost people tonight," he said slowly. "Whoever you are…. Whoever you pretend to be… please, you live your life, too. Be well."

The Domino Lady nodded, not daring to speak. She turned and strode quickly out toward the front door, pausing only to grab a trenchcoat off the coat rack in the vestibule and wrap it around herself before fleeing out into the street.

The Daimler was right where she'd left it. Of course, it had only been a couple of hours. It seemed like it should have been longer. She slid in behind the driver's seat and turned the key, and there was the reassuring rumble. She put the car into gear and sped away.

She didn't want to go home yet. She didn't want to be Ellen Patrick, to return to the shallow, insipid illusion she had carefully built over the last year. Not yet. She was sick of lies and illusions and all the different masks people wore, especially her own. She wanted something real.

She drove to a cliff out by Pacific Palisades, where she could see the ocean, and stopped. She folded her arms across the top of the steering wheel and let her head rest on them.

Then, finally, she let the tears come.

The End

AFTERWORD

*T*hey say that if art makes you uncomfortable, you're doing it right. I hope so, because God knows writing this often made me horribly uncomfortable.

There were several reasons. The biggest one was that I have never tried doing an adventure story with a female protagonist before... and Ellen Patrick, the Domino Lady, is a particularly challenging one to start with. If you know anything about the character's history, you probably know that Domino Lady stories generally include sex on some level. Her original 1930s adventures were done for one of the "Spicy" pulps, *Saucy Romantic Adventures,* and it was a given in the Spicys that at some point there would be a man and woman in a hot clinch, lots of innuendo, and ladies in various states of undress. (Even though, as Charles Beaumont famously said, a careful reading of the Spicy pulps actually did nothing to dissuade one from believing babies are brought by the stork.)

So the challenge is to write not just from a female point of view, but a sexy female's point of view. Traditionally, the most powerful weapon in the Domino Lady's arsenal is her smokin' hot body and her willingness to let horny hoods think they have a chance with her before she clobbers them. And there was an additional challenge as well: Ellen Patrick may be a freewheeling liberated lady, but I'm kind of a prude. The idea of writing something sexual and salacious is not in my wheelhouse. At all. Especially not the sniggering, adolescent version of sex we got in the Spicys. I'm something of a pulp traditionalist, but there are limits. The problem then became—how to do something that hit all the traditional marks of a Domino Lady story, yet was still something I was capable of writing?

What you just read is how I answered that question. Most modern writers, when they do a Domino Lady story, solve the problem of making her palatable to modern readers by making her a tough warrior woman who kicks ass and takes names. I didn't want to do that. It always seemed to me that the Domino Lady was a strategist, a trickster, and a thief. She outsmarts her foes, usually by getting them all hot and bothered and then, when they're panting with excitement, she jerks the rug out.

My idea, instead of trying to make her Batman in a dress, was to take the traditional Domino Lady tropes and up-end them; so in this tale, she is not the seducer, but the seduced. She does end up in a state of undress, but it's for purposes of the villain's strategy only, a gesture of his contempt... and the man she's nearly-naked with has no interest in her because he's gay. And so on. Using my usual technique of reverse-engineering a villain out of the hero, it occurred to me that the most challenging foe for the Domino Lady would be an ascetic, a man to whom sensuality would be foreign. An utterly ruthless creature of pure intellect, someone who views emotions as mere tools to manipulate people like pawns on a chessboard. Ergo, such a man couldn't be the seducer. He'd have to hire it out. That's where Professor Murdwell and Paul Rosen came from.

Somehow, while trying to do something that was a nod to the traditional Spicy pulps, I also wanted to do a story about love and romance and all the risks people take with each other when they embark on a relationship. I wanted the treatment of sex to be adult, but adult in a grown-up way, not an X-rated way. One of the things that makes a relationship truly adult is understanding risk and consequences. I believe that love makes us better than we would be otherwise, but I also believe that it can be pretty scary out there: people get hurt. Ellen Patrick and Toni Steeves and Joaquin Vasquez all are damaged goods in some fashion—and even the paid gigolo Paul Rosen is walking wounded, it's how Professor Murdwell gets to him.

So plotting this one was a bear because I was trying to straddle two traditions—a traditional 'spicy' approach, but one that wasn't quite so adolescent; something that brought a modern adult sensibility about love and romance to the proceedings. I think it turned out okay, but that's up to you readers to decide.

There are a couple of historical notes. I was determined not to do any kind of crossover because really I think that's just been done to death with the Domino Lady; she's met Sherlock Holmes and the Spider and the Black Bat and the Phantom and Dan Fowler G-Man. Even if Cap'n Ron hadn't asked us specifically not to do crossovers for this book, I would have eschewed it just in an effort to not return to such thoroughly trampled ground. But I couldn't resist throwing in a little nod to "Andrew at Mayfair Chemical"; I like to think that if Ellen ever did run into that particular hirsute pulp adventurer, they probably had a hot weekend in Manhattan at the very least. Certainly a wolf like Andrew would have been in there pitching with a girl as pretty as Ellen Patrick, anyway.

And there's always the research. Not that much of it actually made it into the story, but I had a lot of fun looking up things like how the coroner's office worked and how corrupt Los Angeles really was in the 1930s. (The answer is—*very* corrupt. If anything, this story downplays the situation.) The science of criminal profiling was indeed in its infancy back then, and the professor's anecdote about the psychologist who figured out the identity of the Lackawanna killer is true. Profiling as police departments use it today didn't really happen until the 1940s, so I figured a super-genius villain like Murdwell would be a decade or so ahead of the game. I was also fascinated to read about Frank A. Nance, Hollywood's "coroner to the stars," who probably witnessed more consequences of the ugliness beneath the glittery façade of Tinseltown than anyone else in the early days of the film industry. I didn't want to actually make him Ellen's law enforcement contact—I'm okay with name-checking real people in a story, but I'm hesitant to bring them 'on stage,' so to speak—but it occurred to me that with so many cops on the take, an assistant M.E. would probably be a much more useful inside man for the Domino Lady to have than someone actually on the police force. Hence, Lucas Benford.

That's the story behind the story. All that's left are the thanks to the usual crew—to my beta readers Anne Hawley, Sena Friesen, Tiffany Tomcal, Brekke Ferguson, Lorinda Adams, and Ed Bosnar, who provided not just helpful suggestions but also some badly-needed moral support when I was fumbling my way through trying to write from Ellen's point of view. Appreciation also goes to the mysterious "Lars Anderson," creator of the Domino Lady, an author who remains shrouded in mystery—no one knows if it was a pen name of one particular writer, a 'house' name shared by several different writers, or even a real guy who only stayed in the business long enough to write the original six Domino Lady adventures and then quit pulps forever. At any rate, whoever Lars was, he created a character that still captures the imagination of writers and readers to this day—Ellen Patrick is the perfect protagonist to try to bring a little justice to a place like 1930s Hollywood that runs on greed, illusion, and sex.

And as always, I appreciate my wife Julie's contribution: without her I would never have dared write a story about romance at all. She taught me that there really is such a thing as true love and it's worth fighting for, and that was a pretty heavy lift for her to get across to a crabby old guy like me.

GREG HATCHER - is a writer and teacher from Seattle, Washington. He has been writing for publication since 1987, but his work for Airship 27 is his first foray into pulp fiction and since that's a bucket-list item for him, he's still grinning about it. He was a contributing editor at *With Magazine* for over a decade where he won awards for both his fiction and non-fiction. Currently he does a weekly column for Comic Book Resources.com, as part of the *Comics Should Be Good* blog. In addition to all that, he teaches classes in writing and drawing as part of an after-school program created through the YMCA's Partners With Youth. He lives in an apartment just south of downtown with his wife Julie, their cat Maggie, and ten thousand books and comics.

THE DOMINO LADY ROLLS THE DICE

by Gene Moyers

"More champagne, miss?"

"Why yes, thank you."

Ellen Patrick took the glass of golden liquid from the butler and mused that prohibition was certainly not alive and well here at her friend's private party. It was a sunny summer day and the stunning young blonde threw her head back and shook her long luxurious hair. *It's a beautiful day to be alive*, she thought. Life had been slow lately, and Ellen Patrick had been more than happy to come to her friend Cindy Hansen's garden party. The tall, voluptuous woman was a striking figure in her blue sun dress, the exact shade of the sky on a cool spring day, as she moved gracefully amongst the well-dressed party goers. Nodding to a city councilman and his wife Ellen looked around for Cindy. She had been here moments before.

Handing her empty glass to a passing waiter, she started across the patio toward open French doors. Suddenly there came a shriek of fear, followed by cries for help. Ellen shot forward running like a deer despite the fact that she was wearing fashionable spike high heels. She streaked across the ballroom and turned down a wide hallway following the continued shouts for help. She recognized her friend Cindy's voice. Reaching an open door she dashed into a study. Bookshelves lined two walls and comfortable furniture was scattered about. A large window stood open letting in the pleasant sounds of the day. Behind a wide walnut desk a man lolled back in a leather chair. He was gray haired and wore an expensive suit. Even with his eyes closed Ellen recognized Raymond Hansen, Cindy's father. Cindy herself was draped across him and sobbing hysterically.

Dashing around the desk she grabbed for Raymond Hansen's hand. She could feel no pulse. Pushing Cindy back she placed two fingers to his neck and urgently asked her friend, "Cindy, what happened?" Cindy stepped back but just plunged her face into her hands crying. Ellen found a very weak and thready pulse in Hansen's neck. There was a commotion at the study door. A servant stood there hesitantly. Other servants and guests crowded in behind them. Pointing to the servant, she yelled, "Phone for an ambulance! Quick!" Ellen dragged Hansen out of his chair to the

47

floor. His limp body was a dead weight but Ellen was athletically built and her one hundred and twenty pound frame was stronger than it appeared. With Hansen stretched out on the floor she pulled off his jacket, loosened his tie and tore open his dress shirt. She could find no sign of injury or wound on him.

Frowning, Ellen stood up. The servant was speaking into a telephone. She brushed past him to Cindy. The young brunette was still sobbing into her hands. Ellen had no time for delicacies. She grabbed Cindy by the arms and shook her, "Cindy! Tell me what happened?" The girl stopped crying and looked into Ellen's eyes, but the blonde débutante could see her friend was in shock. Casting her eyes about she spied a half empty glass of what looked like water sitting on the desk. Grabbing it, she dashed it into Cindy's face. The young girl took a step back and spluttered.

"Cindy! What happened?"

Her friend stared wide-eyed at Ellen, "I came in. Dad was sleeping, I thought. Then I saw that," she pointed to a small bottle sitting on the desk. Ellen snatched it up and quickly realized that it was a strong sedative. The bottle was empty.

Ellen looked around; several people were standing silent in the room and more crowded the doorway. Taking charge, she commanded one of the servants, "Go to the kitchen and bring me back some salt, a lot of it." Then bending down she raised the unconscious Hansen to a sitting position and called for help, "You there, come here. We have to get him to a bathroom." Shocked out of their paralysis by the young girl's commanding tone, two men came forward and helped Hansen to his feet. At her orders they dragged him out into the hall to a nearby bathroom. Once there, Ellen had the guests hold Hansen up while she filled a glass full of tap water. At that moment the servant reappeared with a bowl of salt. Ellen poured a healthy amount in the water and swirled it about. "Hold his head back," she cautioned the men supporting Hansen. Then grabbing Hansen's nose she poured the salty water into his up-tilted mouth. The unconscious man swallowed, coughed, spit and swallowed again. Salty water sprayed everywhere but Ellen managed to get more of it down his throat. Out of water, she waited. Very quickly the unconscious Hansen was giving up the contents of his stomach.

Ellen let two of his guests support him at this point and stepped out into the hall. Pushing through the onlookers looking for Cindy, she was distracted by the sounds of a siren. Sidetracking to the front door, she threw it wide and waved the ambulance attendants up the front steps and through the wide doorway. She pointed the way to the bathroom and resumed her hunt for Cindy. She found the girl sitting on a sofa in the study. A servant was taking an empty water glass away. Judging that the stunned girl needed something stronger than water, Ellen located a bottle of brandy in a cabinet and brought a glass across the room.

Seating herself next to her friend, Ellen passed her friend the glass and urged her to drink. After she had taken a healthy gulp and coughed once, the color seemed to return to Cindy's face. Ellen waited. Finally Cindy turned to her, "Is he...?"

Placing her hand on her friend's knee she said softly, "No, he's still alive. The ambulance is here. There's hope. Is there anything else you can tell me?"

Cindy shook her head, "Just what I told you. I thought Dad had fallen asleep, but then I saw the empty bottle and the note." Ellen got up and walked to the desk. She found a sheet of writing paper with a note written on it. Addressed to Cindy, it was a regretful goodbye. Although not specific, Ellen knew a suicide note when she saw one. She picked it up and returned to Cindy's side, "Why would he do this?"

The young girl turned her tear swollen eyes to Ellen, "I'm not sure, but I can guess." She hesitated, "Dad took Mom's death hard. He drank a lot. Of course it wasn't always easy getting decent liquor, what with prohibition and all." She smiled, "He always said that life was too short to drink cheap booze. Eventually he started going to *La Fortuna* to drink with friends. Unfortunately he started gambling there as well. That's been going on for a while. I...I don't know for sure, but I think he must have been losing heavily lately. I know he's been worried and withdrawn. I asked him what's wrong, but he wouldn't tell me. He must think he's protecting me...." Her face crumpled and she started to cry again. Ellen looked around for a tissue, but her search was interrupted by the sounds of the ambulance attendants wheeling Raymond Hansen down the hallway on a wheeled stretcher.

Grabbing Cindy's arm Ellen stated firmly, "They're taking him to the hospital. You'll ride with me." Cindy could only nod. Pushing through the still startled guests, Ellen quickly located her purse. Dashing to her convertible, she shoved her stunned friend into the passenger seat and jumped behind the wheel. Gravel spat from under the rear tires as Ellen fed power to the powerful engine and they jumped forward. Reaching the street Ellen pushed the pedal to the floor and they quickly caught up to the speeding ambulance. They followed the white vehicle and its screaming siren the five minutes to the hospital.

Once there they found a place to park and rushed into the lobby. They were directed to the emergency room waiting area. It was too soon to learn anything, so Cindy left her name and they took seats in the waiting area. Ellen took a folded sheet of paper out of her pocket and passed it to Cindy, "This is the note your father left. No one has seen it but you and me. There are going to be awkward questions asked about your father's overdose. Destroy this and you can tell them what you choose."

Cindy nodded as she took the letter. She thought for a few moments before she tore it in half, folded the pieces and tore them again. She then passed the shreds back to Ellen, "Thanks Ellen. I don't know what would have happened if you hadn't been there." Ellen squeezed her hand and smiled.

Ellen questioned Cindy for more details of her father's recent actions. When she talked about gambling Ellen interrupted, "You mentioned *La Fortuna* before. Isn't that the floating casino anchored off the coast?"

"Yes. It's anchored just outside the three mile limit. That's why they can get away with gambling and running a speakeasy. The authorities can't touch them." Ellen nodded thoughtfully. She had heard of this floating casino but had never been there, though she knew a few friends who had been.

Her thoughts were interrupted by a white clad doctor who appeared in the waiting area gesturing to Cindy. She bustled over to him. He spoke quietly to her for a few seconds. Smiling, she rushed back to Ellen, "Dad's going to be all right. He should regain consciousness soon. He says I can go back and sit with him. Can you wait here for me?" Ellen smiled her agreement and Cindy left following the doctor.

Time passed as Ellen whiled the time away looking at outdated magazines. She wasn't really paying any attention to them. Instead she was going over ideas in her mind. She needed more information. Perhaps Cindy knew more, but there were also other sources. She had just made up her mind about who to call when Cindy appeared in the doorway.

Stubbing out her cigarette in an ashtray, Ellen stood up and went forward, hands outstretched, "How is he Cindy?"

"He's awake and doing fine. The doctor wants to keep him overnight, though. He says we were just in time. If you hadn't done what you did, he says Dad wouldn't have made it." She frowned, "I don't think he totally believed what I said about an accidental overdose, but there's really nothing he can do about it. I slipped the word to Dad to play along."

Ellen nodded, "I'm glad things worked out. Now, I'd better see about getting you home."

On the drive home Cindy related the conversation she had with her father at the hospital. Her father had been gambling a lot on the floating casino *La Fortuna*. His losses had grown large enough that he was faced with selling off their home and other assets. Charles Mertz, the casino owner, was pressuring him but not for money. Raymond Hansen was an elected county supervisor. He sat on several boards and advisory councils that decided everything from building permits to zoning. Mertz was threatening to sell Hansen's IOUs to a gangster. He was also demanding that Hansen give favorable votes to issues that Mertz would decide. Despondent over the situation, Hansen had decided on suicide. Since gambling debts were not legally collectible and his daughter of no political value, he thought that she might be able to escape the incident nearly undamaged.

By the completion of her friend's sad tale, Ellen was furious. This was just the sort of injustice that she sought to combat. Ever since the death of her father, Owen, at the hands of a corrupt political machine, she had sought to wreak destruction on society's leaches. Taking on the persona of the mysterious Domino Lady she took great pleasure in exposing corrupt politicians and robbing their crooked masters. Any funds she recovered on her forays against these criminals she contributed to charity or returned to their victims, although she always kept enough to finance her high flying lifestyle. Cindy's tale of woe brought out her fighting instincts. Sometimes she undertook her adventures to help out a friend or just for love of adventure. This time it seemed she might be able to combine adventure with a solid blow to some of the corruption that plagued her beloved Golden State.

By the time she dropped Cindy off at the Hansen home, she had the bare bones of a plan. Encouraging her friend to remain strong, Ellen pointed the nose of her car toward home. Once back at her fashionable apartment on Wilshire, she threw down her purse and moved to her liquor cabinet. A drink made, she leaned her shapely backside against the cabinet and glanced at her wrist watch. It was late afternoon, Saturday. Deciding that there was a good chance that he would be at home, she rummaged in her purse for her leather bound address book.

She set her drink down and thumbed quickly through it to the "M"s. A small smile crossed her face. Picking up the phone, she dialed 0. When the call was answered she asked for the long distance operator. There was a pause as a new voice came on the line, "Long distance."

"Operator, I'd like to place a person to person call to a Roger McKane in San Francisco."

"What is that number, please?"

Ellen quickly read off the number from her address book. There was a pause, "And your number?"

Ellen gave her home number and the voice replied, "One moment, please." Then the phone disconnected. Ellen hung up, leaned back on the sofa and sipped her drink. It had been a busy day, and the cold drink tasted wonderful. The phone soon rang.

"Hello."

"I have your party now." Then the same voice more distantly, "Your party is connected." There was a click and a familiar voice, "Hello."

"Hello, Roge. How's my favorite gumshoe? Still lurking around alleys in your trench coat?" Ellen laughed, a pure and honest sound.

"Ellen! Gosh, it's good to hear your voice! Where are you calling from?"

"Why, I'm at home of course. Where did you think I was?"

A pause, "Well it's been so long since I've seen you ,I was hoping maybe you'd come north for a visit."

Ellen paused teasingly, "Roge, I can't imagine you missing me that much what with all those lovely San Francisco girls just waiting for you to call."

"Now Ellen, you know that you're the only woman for me. But seriously, how have you been? And when am I going to get to see you?"

"I've been fine, and if you play your cards right you might be seeing me sooner than you think."

"Just say where and when. You know I'd go to the ends of the earth for you."

Ellen laughed again, "No need to go that far, darling, but I do need a favor if it's not too much bother."

"Say the word, Ellen. Anything for you."

"Well, I have a friend here in town who's run afoul of a shady gentleman. It seems she is being blackmailed for an indiscretion and is desperate. I've agreed to do what I can to help. What I need is all the information you can get me on a Charles Mertz. He's a professional gambler. I'll bet your firm has something in your files about him."

There was a thoughtful pause, "Mertz. I've heard of him. He runs that floating casino, off the coast doesn't he?"

Ellen was slightly surprised at this, "You've heard of him?"

"A little. Sometimes he sails that floating crap game up the coast to San Francisco. Whenever he does, the Coast Guard and Feds get all excited trying to keep an eye on him. Since he sells alcohol as well as runs gambling, there are a lot of lawmen who would like to get their hands on him. If your friend has gotten mixed up with him, that's bad news."

"It is. I've promised her I'd help. That's why I need anything you can tell me about him and his operation."

"Well, tomorrow is Sunday so the office is closed, but I could go in and take a look in the files. But I can't ask around the office until Monday."

"That would be great, Roge. Can you give me a call Monday night and let me know what you find?"

"I never need an excuse to hear your voice, dear, but yes, I'll call and let you know what I've found."

After goodbyes were said, Ellen made calls to several friends. It was fairly easy to find someone who had actually done some gambling aboard *La Fortuna*. Feigning boredom and the desire for new excitement, it was easy for Ellen to learn a good bit about the casino's operations. More importantly, she learned where boarding took place and the proper protocol for being admitted to the establishment.

Putting down the phone, Ellen stood up and stretched languidly. She glanced at her watch and decided that there was time for a leisurely bath before dinner. Unbuttoning her dress, she walked down the hall to the bathroom. It had dropped to her feet by the time she reached the bathroom door. Stepping out of it, she reached into the tub and adjusted the water temperature to her satisfaction. She added bubbling bath salts and then removed her silky black lingerie. Slipping into the tub, she leaned back, sighing deeply. Her eyes closed, but her mind raced ahead reviewing the day's events and planning her next moves.

By the time her bath water was growing cold she had firmed up her plan. A lot would depend on what Roge could find out, but she could do a few things. First she would call Cindy. Then it was high time she had a look at this fancy gambling ship, at least from a distance. Now for a dinner and good night's sleep.

Ellen woke up to bright sunlight streaming through the half open curtains into her bedroom. Stretching luxuriously in her oversized bed, she thought about the day to come. Eventually she got out of bed and slipped a long silk robe over her night gown and went into the living room. She made coffee and retrieved the thick Sunday paper outside her door and spent the rest of the morning killing time.

By noon she decided it was time to get moving and reached for the phone. It rang several times and when answered, Ellen asked for her friend Cindy. When she picked up the extension, Ellen spoke, "Cindy, I'm sorry to bother you, but I have something important to ask."

"Certainly, Ellen, what is it?"

"I need to know whether you have ever seen your father with a red and black circular ceramic casino chip?"

"Uh, yes, I think so. Or at least I've seen something like that."

"Good. Do you think you can find it for me?'

"I can try. Why is it important?"

"If you can find it, call me back and let me know. I'll tell you then. By the way, how is your father?"

"The hospital called and they say he can come home tomorrow."

"That's wonderful. Give me a call when you find that chip."

Ellen said goodbye and hung up. She was just stepping out of her bathtub a three quarters of an hour later when the phone rang. Wrapping a large plush towel around her, she dashed for the living room dripping water on the carpet. Grabbing up the receiver, she found Cindy on the other end of the line.

"Ellen, it's me. I found the chip. It was hidden in one of Dad's desk drawers. But why is it so important?"

"That is a very important chip. I found out from an acquaintance that it is given out to the regular high rollers who visit *La Fortuna*. I need you to loan it to me for a while."

"Certainly, I'd just as soon not have it around when Dad gets home. But what are you going to do with it?"

"That, my dear, is going to be my ticket onto *La Fortuna*. I need to check out that boat personally. I'll be by in a couple of hours to pick it up." She then quickly rang off and went to her bedroom to dress. She needed to make just the right impression tonight.

By four that afternoon Ellen was pulling up in front of the Hansen house. As she was about to knock at the front door, Cindy Hansen herself opened it. "Oh Ellen, what a lovely dress. Where are you off to?"

Ellen unconsciously smoothed down the front of the long royal blue gown. It was low backed and showed off a daring amount of her ample cleavage. It went beautifully with her long blonde tresses and creamy complexion. She had chosen it carefully to exude both sensuality and affluence. She was hopeful it would help her gain entrance to *La Fortuna*. She smiled, "Actually I'm going gambling tonight. Hopefully that chip will help me get a friendly reception."

Cindy handed over a red and black painted casino chip about an inch and a half in diameter, "Well, if this chip won't do it, I'm sure that dress will. You look wonderful."

Ellen laughed roguishly at this. After getting Cindy's assurance that she would not mention her plans to anyone and would conceal the chip's whereabouts if her father asked, she took her leave.

A leisurely drive took her south across town to Long Beach. With the directions she had gotten from her friends, she had no trouble locating the dock area closest to where *La Fortuna* was anchored off shore. She parked her car and walked a short distance along the pier to a boarding ramp surrounded by a small crowd of people. Night had now fallen and Ellen had added her black cloak around her shoulders. She carried a small clutch purse in her left hand.

The people were lined up under an awning that stood at the head of a sloping ramp leading down to a floating dock. Illuminated by hooded lights, a sign over the top of the awning proclaimed S.S. *La Fortuna*. Under the awning, a line of well-dressed people were queued up in front of a podium where a uniformed man was speaking to each person or couple before passing them down to the dock. Ellen joined the line and felt right at home. All the men were dressed in expensive suits or more likely evening wear. All the women wore fine gowns with quite a bit of expensive jewelry on display. The line moved quickly. The young ship's officer waved many people past with acknowledgement of their name and tip of his cap. Others he passed after a quick check of a clipboard he carried.

When she reached the front of the line, she summoned up her best smile and stepped up close to the young officer. He was thin and probably within a year or two of Ellen's age. His white uniform was sharply creased and he had two gold bars on his epaulets. To Ellen's eyes he looked bright and shiny and awfully impressionable. As he attempted to keep his eyes on hers and not her distracting cleavage, he asked politely, "Your name, miss?"

Smiling shyly, Ellen replied, "Ellen Page…"

The officer colored slightly as he consulted his clipboard. He raised his eyes and cleared his throat before replying politely, "I'm afraid I don't see your name on the list, miss."

Holding direct eye contact, Ellen slipped the fingers of her right hand into the front of her dress over her left breast and came up with the Fortuna chip. Holding it out to the officer, she tried to look slightly embarrassed, "I'm sorry, I didn't mean to hold you up."

His hand shaking slightly, the officer took the still warm chip from her. Licking his lips, he tore his eyes away from Ellen to examine the chip. It showed a ship silhouette on one side and an eagle on the other. Nodding, he passed it back to Ellen, desperately trying to keep his eyes on her face,

"*...if this chip won't...that dress will.*"

"Thank you, miss. I'll add your name to the list." He brought his hand to his temple in a salute and stepped aside for her.

Smiling, Ellen slipped the chip back into the front of her dress and proceeded down the ramp to the floating dock. Casino patrons were being helped aboard a forty foot launch there. It had been converted into a glassed-in water taxi with comfortable seats and good views. Settling into one of the seats, Ellen had only a few minutes to wait before the water taxi was filled and pushing away from the dock.

Although it was after dark, the warm summer night was clear and the water calm. This gave Ellen a fine view across the water and soon she could see their brightly lit destination. The ship was lit from bow to stern. She was showing the usual running lights and illuminated portholes but her masts and funnel were also lit up with colored lights, and there were what appeared to be long strings of lights strung over some kind of open upper deck at the stern. A bright searchlight shone down on the side of the ship where another almost identical water taxi was moored. As they got closer Ellen could make out more details. The ship was over two hundred feet in length. About a quarter of that was a low foredeck where the forward mast stood. The superstructure appeared to be two decks high and ran clear to the rounded stern. There was no aft deck.

As they approached to about a hundred yards from the ship, the moored water taxi blew a horn and stood away from the larger ship. Ellen's idling boat rocked in the wake of the leaving taxi and then slowly approached the now vacant landing stage that was hung over the ship's side. The helmsman expertly guided the launch alongside the stage and reversed his engine at just the right moment. Crewmen secured lines and the passengers started climbing onto the landing stage. A crewman helped each passenger out of the water taxi. Five metal steps ended at a metal landing where a metal hatch in the side of the ship had been latched open. There was a brief pause at this landing where Ellen watched in interest as the gentleman in front of her opened up his jacket and turned around. An officer nodded and he proceeded into the ship. As Ellen stepped into the ship, another officer in a white uniform saluted her. He was older than the young officer on the pier, and, Ellen noted, quite handsome. He quickly eyed her up and down and spoke, "Good evening miss, may I inspect your purse?"

Ellen gave him her best smile as she handed it over, "Of course, Captain."

Opening her small clutch purse, he glanced through it quickly. Ellen was very glad she had decided not to bring any of the varied and illegal tools of her trade with her. The officer handed her purse back and smiled in return, "I'm afraid the Captain is on the bridge, miss. I'm first officer Etheridge." Ellen gave him another hundred watt smile as she thanked him. He nodded and added, "Good luck, miss."

She proceeded up a stairwell, following the other customers, and found herself on the main deck. She had exited onto a long covered promenade deck that ran the length of the superstructure along the starboard side. The outer wall was pierced at regular intervals by large open window-like openings but it was quite sheltered. A burst of laughter and voices came from a nearby set of double swinging glass doors. Pushing through the doors, Ellen found herself in the casino. Well lit, it seemed to be about twenty-five feet wide. To her right was a wall pierced by large windows and a set of double doors. All around her the room was filled with blackjack and craps tables and roulette wheels. She judged that the crowd milling about numbered perhaps sixty or seventy. Ellen smiled and circulated. She passed by the forward windows and paused to look out at the illuminated foredeck. She could see the forward cargo hatch cover and beyond that the illuminated foremast. At the base of the foremast was a small windowed structure.

Ellen moved aft through the casino. It was about forty feet long and ended in a wall with wide corridors on each side. As she moved through one of these corridors past a featureless center structure, she decided this must house the ship's funnels that went down into the bowels of the ship. Past this center structure the room widened into another gambling space. This part of the casino was not nearly as busy but more customers were coming aboard by the minute and more tables were opening for play. Ellen slowed and pretended to watch the various games. She had been gambling before, what she was really doing was watching the layout, staff and any crew that passed through the casino.

There were double doors leading sternward into what appeared to be a bar, and she gradually drifted that way. As she passed a roulette wheel that was not in use she took a cigarette out of her purse and put it in her mouth. When she pulled out her lighter, she fumbled it and the lighter fell and bounced under the table. She bent down on one knee to pick it up, and while there she swept her hand lightly across the carpet under the table where the croupier stood. She quickly found a very slight raised spot under the concealing carpet. Ellen smiled to herself as she stood up again and lit her cigarette. Without doubt the spot was a concealed switch that activated magnets beneath the table. No doubt most of the games aboard were rigged in some way or another. It looked as though Mr. Mertz was cheating his customers as well as blackmailing some of them.

Ellen passed into the well-appointed bar. Deciding that she would look more casual with a drink in her hand, she ordered a glass of champagne before she continued her tour. Doors led aft from the bar. Here there was a large outdoor area with padded chairs scattered among potted bushes and flowering plants. This stern area was completely covered by the deck above but open to the sides and rounded stern. Open railings ran along the outside of this deck area. She could hear music coming from above. Leaning over the rail while she sipped and enjoyed the light sea breeze, Ellen decided this was almost pleasant. It was too bad that she was here on business.

An open stairway climbed to the next deck. Ellen took it and found herself on an open deck illuminated by strings of lights overhead. More large potted shrubs dotted the deck. A small spotlight illuminated a flag flapping slowly at the stern. The flag had two large alternating red and blue squares on a white field. The two white squares each had a star; one blue and one red. It looked familiar to her, but Ellen could not place it in her memory. It certainly wasn't the stars and stripes she knew. Forward large glass doors had been rolled back opening on a large dance floor. Several couples were dancing as she entered. Music was provided by a seven piece band. Her glass empty, Ellen stopped to listen for a few minutes before heading forward. Once on the other side of the funnel structure it was much quieter. It was an area of corridors and doors with cute names on them like "Mojave" and "Sequoia." Ellen stopped to listen at one for a few moments and could hear voices and the slap of cards. She decided that these were probably for private high stakes gambling. She eventually found herself at a gallery of windows overlooking the forward deck again. Stairs led upward and down.

Deciding she had seen enough here, Ellen headed down the forward stairway. Entering the forward casino, she mingled. She purchased chips and played roulette for a while, betting frugally to preserve her money. Eventually she moved on to the now busy rear casino and joined the noisy crowd around one of the craps tables. She was thinking of trying to find her way below decks when she spotted a familiar figure moving through the crowd. She quickly made her way to the bar and purchased another glass of champagne, then managed to reach the doors between the casino and the bar just as they opened to admit a white clad figure. Although she kept the door from hitting her, she squealed and spilled some champagne over her hand.

"I'm terribly sorry! How clumsy of me!"

"That's all right officer…uh it was Etheridge wasn't it?"

Handing her a handkerchief and taking her glass, the handsome officer nodded, "Yes, Keith Etheridge, and I must excuse my clumsiness, miss…"

"Ellen Page," she said as she wiped her hand.

"Well, Ellen, if I may call you that, will you at least let me buy you a drink to replace that one?"

"Why, thank you, Mr. Etheridge," she said, handing him back his handkerchief. He pointed back into the bar and Ellen casually took his arm as he led her in. First officer Etheridge bought her a new glass but declined anything for himself. Sipping, Ellen managed to steer him toward the shadowy stern deck.

"This is my first time aboard your ship, and I must say it is impressive."

Etheridge nodded, "I hope you're enjoying yourself."

"I am. Things are so organized. It must take a large crew to make all this run so efficiently." She waved her hand negligently.

Etheridge turned to her, "Not really. Most of the crew is just waiters and dealers. There are actually rather few of us actual sailors aboard. Just a skeleton crew to keep the engines running and in case the ship needs to be moved in an emergency."

Leaning back against the stern railing, Ellen feigned surprise, "Really, is that safe?"

Shrugging Etheridge moved closer to Ellen, "Certainly. We take extra seamen aboard if we're moving the ship any distance, but moored here for extended periods there just isn't the need."

Nodding, Ellen continued to probe gently for information, "And the Captain? Is he aboard?"

Etheridge laughed quietly, "Of course, he doesn't much care for the customers, so he spends a lot of time on the bridge. He'd stay there all the time if Mr. Mertz didn't insist that he mingle with them at least a bit every night. The customers like to see him in his uniform passing through. Probably makes them feel safe."

"Mr. Mertz? I've heard that name; doesn't he own this boat?"

"It's called a ship, actually. And yes, Mr. Mertz is the owner."

"Ooh, really? Is he aboard tonight?"

"Every night. He has a suite below. I'm surprised you haven't seen him yet. I just saw him forward."

Ellen touched his arm and smiled seductively up at him, "Do you have a suite also?"

Etheridge stiffened slightly and swallowed, "Uh, just a cabin actually, but it's nice. Perhaps I could show it to you sometime."

Finishing her drink, Ellen said, "I'd like that, but now I think I need another drink."

Offering his arm, Etheridge led Ellen back into the bar. He ordered her another glass of champagne and was just handing it to her when a tuxedoed figure entered the bar from the casino. "Speak of the devil," Etheridge muttered.

While the tuxedoed casino owner surveyed his little empire, Ellen looked him over. Mertz was middle aged, just going gray at the temples. He was tall and very thin. With his dark hair slicked back and thin hatchet face, he looked like a scarecrow with a good tailor to Ellen's eyes. His eyes were piercing and his pencil thin mustache could have just been a forgetful moment when shaving that day. Before Ellen could ask Etheridge for an introduction, Mertz's eyes landed on Ellen and he headed that way.

Etheridge straightened as he approached. Mertz spoke to Etheridge but his eyes never left Ellen. "It looks like a good crowd tonight, lieutenant. Are things going well?"

Etheridge stiffened to attention and spoke, "Yes, sir. Everything seems to be running smoothly. I was just on my way to the bridge to check in with the captain."

Mertz nodded, "Fine. But before you go, you must introduce me to this stunning young lady."

Ellen smiled at Mertz while Etheridge made the introductions. He then excused himself as Mertz was holding out his hand to Ellen, "It's a pleasure, Miss Page. I hope you're having a good time?"

"I am, Mr. Mertz. I was just heading back to the craps table."

"Well, don't let me delay you. Good luck, and I hope to see you here again."

"Oh, I'm sure you will. I find this place delightful."

Ellen continued back into the casino. She did not turn to look but she was sure that Mertz was studying her retreating form. As she squeezed in at the table, she smiled to herself. So that was Mertz. He certainly was a shifty eyed one. Ellen was willing to bet he didn't miss much. That was fine. She didn't mind him remembering her just so long as he remembered what she wanted him to.

Ellen spent nearly three more hours gambling and mingling with the crowd. She kept her bets small and didn't lose very much. By the time she was heading down to the waiting water taxi, she felt a lot more knowledgeable about *La Fortuna* and her gambling operations. Her next step would depend on what Roger could come up with. She was soon in her car and driving for her Hollywood apartment and her luxurious bed.

Monday Ellen slept late. After a pleasant lunch at one of the city's better restaurants, she was back in her apartment and awaiting Roger's call by 3 p.m. Not long before five the phone rang. When she was connected, Roger's pleasant voice came over the line, "Well, Ellen, did you miss me?"

"Oh, Roge, we just spoke on Saturday. I haven't had time to miss you much. Besides, I've been busy and I hope you have too. Do you have good news for me?"

"Well, it so happens I do have some interesting facts for you. You do realize that this fellow you're looking into is not a nice person, don't you?"

"I do. I'm hoping you can tell me just how bad he is."

There was a rustle of paper before Roger spoke, "It seems not much is known of Mertz until the early '20s. He got involved in running illegal liquor down out of Canada into Minnesota, Wisconsin and even into Chicago."

Ellen interrupted, "You mean he was a bootlegger with the mobs?"

"Not exactly. Apparently he wasn't mobbed up with Capone or Bugs Moran or even the Purple Gang. He was independently running hooch out of Canada and selling it to the highest bidder. As the war between Moran and Capone heated up, he apparently got squeezed by both sides. I guess that convinced him it was time to move on because he closed out his business and moved west to Vancouver and started running booze down into Washington State."

"So how did he get from there to here, and where did he get that ship?"

There was more rustling of paper. "Hmnn...apparently his ship started life as the *S.S. Caladan*. She was one of two passenger steamers built for the Dominion Steamship Company sailing the inside passage along the Canadian coast. In 1926 the *Caladan* ran aground on some rocks off Powell River. Unable to refloat her, the company gave her up to the insurance company. Apparently they were in financial difficulty and needed the money. Miraculously she didn't break apart and the insurance company managed to have her refloated and repaired in Vancouver. When they tried to sell her at a profit, Dominion Steamship sued to get her back. She was tied up in court for over a year. When the dust settled, the insurance company was glad to sell her cheap to one Charles Mertz. Mertz had her sailed down the coast to San Diego where she was refitted as a casino. She's been operating for nearly two years off the California coast, apparently making a lot of money for Mertz and his investors."

Ellen mulled over this information, "Do you have the name of the shipyard in San Diego that did the work?"

She heard Roger muttering as he shuffled papers. Then something hit her, "Wait a minute. Did you say *investors*?"

"No, and yes."

"What? I'm confused. What's no and what's yes?"

Roger laughed, "No, I don't have the name of the San Diego shipyard in our records. And yes I did say 'investors'."

"Well, tell me, silly. That sounds interesting."

"It is. Outside the three mile limit is international waters and Mertz can run his operation without worrying about the law, especially since his ship is registered out of Panama. But it wouldn't be hard to make running his business rough if the authorities really wanted to. They could harass his customers when they returned from his casino. They could search them for smuggled alcohol; deny him dock space for his boats, lots of ways to get at him."

"So why don't they?"

"Well, I made some calls and it seems that refitting his ship was pretty expensive. The word is that Mertz got funding from some influential Southern Californians. They invested in his business, and he cut them in on the profits. It seems he's also paying off a lot of local officials, as well. You know how it is, Ellen. As long as the money keeps flowing, people will look the other way."

Ellen grimly reflected that she did know how it was. This was an old story she had heard many times before. She could feel her temperature rising as her sense of right was assaulted. The crooks and corrupt officials never thought about the shattered lives they left in the wake of their greed. Her thoughts were interrupted by Roger speaking, "Hello. Ellen, are you still there?"

"Sorry, Roge. Just lost in thought. Tell me something, darling. Does your firm have any contacts in San Diego? I think I'm going to need a private detective to do some work for me there."

There was a slight pause, and when he spoke again Roger had a warning tone in his voice, "Yes, there's a guy there that we've worked with before. You're not getting in over your head here are you?"

Ellen tried to lighten her tone, "Now, Roge, I'm just trying to help a friend."

"Okay, here's his private number. His name is Mike Trent. He knows anybody and everybody down there."

Ellen quickly wrote down the number. "Thanks, Roge. You're a dear."

"Okay, when you do get in over your head, call me, all right?"

Touched by Roger's gallantry, Ellen answered gently, "I might just take you up on that." Promising to talk again soon, Ellen ended the call. Glancing at her watch, she realized it was just after five. There might still be a chance to catch this Mike Trent in his office. Quickly she placed the long distance call. When it was finally connected a calm voice said, "This is Trent."

"Mike Trent? My name is Ellen Page, and I was given your name by Roger McKane of San Francisco. He said you might be able to do some work for me."

Trent was agreeable when Ellen stated her needs. A price was quickly agreed upon, and Ellen promised to send a check immediately. After she hung up Ellen mused to herself that things were underway. It might take a few days to develop, but her plan seemed sound. But first: more research.

Over the next four days Ellen revisited *La Fortuna* twice more. Each time she took great pains to be seen as a steady gambler and drinker. She kept her bets small and kept moving among the tables to make it harder for anyone to see that her actual losses were relatively small.

She also took pains to cultivate the ship's officers and Charles Mertz himself. The young officer she had met on the dock was junior officer DuPree. Twenty-three and fresh out of the merchant marine academy, he was simultaneously entranced and intimidated by Ellen. She was already planning on special favors from him. First officer Etheridge was more experienced, but Ellen had convinced him she was a not-overly-bright thrill-seeking débutante. He certainly did not suspect her of anything as he attempted to become friendlier with her. Captain MacKenzie was a gray haired older man nearing retirement who didn't seem to relish his job captaining a ship that did nothing but float around at anchor. Ellen didn't waste her feminine charms on him; instead she treated him as she would her grandfather: some hero worship mixed with daughterly helplessness.

The few times she had managed a few words with Mertz, she had turned on the charm. It seemed to be working. He, too, seemed to think of her as a shallow rich girl. She had caught him watching her at the tables more than once.

"Thanks, Roge. You're a dear."

Saturday morning found Ellen nearing San Diego on the coast highway. Yesterday the detective Trent had come through with the information she had asked for, but also a bonus that she was going to look into first. She was somewhat familiar with San Diego and was able to locate the Pearson building fairly easily. It was shortly after eleven o'clock as she parked down the street from the eight story building. Many companies worked half days on Saturday and she expected the building to be open. It was, and she strolled into the lobby. As she studied the building registry, she noted the security guard sitting at the information desk.

Finding the firm of *Abernathy and Klein, Marine Architects* on the registry, Ellen strolled across the lobby to an open elevator. At her request the bored operator took her to the fifth floor. Once there Ellen quickly located the office and entered. A woman sat at a desk directly in front of the door. Behind her were two closed doors with names on them. To her right was a door marked *Records*. To her left, the wall was glass from the waist up and beyond the glass was a large, well-lighted room with several men working at drafting tables. Ellen hesitated and the woman asked, "Can I help you?"

Ellen smiled and, looking confused, asked for another firm on the same floor she had read off the registry. The receptionist smiled and quickly gave directions. Back in the hall, Ellen scouted the floor and located stairwells and restrooms. She then took the elevator down to the lobby. Exiting toward the front door she detoured to the information desk.

"Excuse me." The uniformed security guard put down his newspaper and looked at her politely. "I think there's a man who is in difficulty and needs help."

Alert now, the guard stood up, "Where was this, ma'am?"

"Up on the eighth floor. He was staggering along and even fell to his knees. I think he needs help."

Placing his cap on his head, the guard came around the desk, "I'll look into it, ma'am."

Ellen nodded and continued toward the front door. She headed for exit, and could hear the guard muttering something about "drunks" as he headed to the elevator. Once the elevator doors had closed, Ellen re-entered the building and made for the stairwell. She quietly climbed to the fourth floor. The layout was similar to the floor above, and she had no trouble finding the public restroom. Once inside she closed herself in one of the stalls and waited.

Time passed slowly. She heard footsteps in the hallway, and twice someone entered the restroom to use the facilities. By three o'clock she had not heard anything in a half hour. She cautiously left the restroom and looked around. It seemed that every office she tried was now locked. She decided to give it another hour before she made her move.

An hour later she pulled a black cloak from her oversized bag and swung it around her shoulders. She then positioned a black mask on her face and instantly became the Domino Lady. As she crept quietly up the stairs to the fifth floor, the masked woman thought about the casual white summer dress she had worn today. A white floor length formal had seemed a bit much for this casual office visit; this was the closest she could manage. Since she preferred to look her best if arrested, she decided she had better not be arrested today.

Once on the fifth floor she made her way quickly to the offices of *Abernathy & Klein*. The door was locked, of course, but it took only a minute or two of manipulation for the lock to click back and give the masked woman entrance to the office. Once inside, she did not hesitate. Ignoring the receptionist's desk and the partner's offices, she glided to the door marked *Records*. It was unlocked. Inside was a windowless dark space. A flick of a switch revealed a room half filled with shelves containing all manner of office supplies. The rest of the room contained several tall filing cabinets.

Smiling, she made straight for the file cabinets. Twenty minutes later she stood up and pushed the last file drawer closed with her foot. The only thing she had found that referred to Charles Mertz was one lonely file that contained only a contract for design work, some notes and several invoices and matching payment statements. Returning to the main office, the frustrated Domino Lady made for the closed door marked *James Abernathy*.

As she was reaching for the door knob, she glanced through the glass half window into the now darkened drafting room. In the gloom it looked as if there was something against the wall beyond the drafting tables. She moved silently to the drafting room door and found it unlocked. Entering the larger room, she moved to the far wall and was overjoyed to find several large plans cabinets. Each one was wide and deep with flat drawers no more than three inches in height. Using a pencil flash from her purse, she quickly located a drawer marked "F." Inside were stacks of large blueprints. Sorting through them, she quickly determined there was nothing marked *La Fortuna*. Frowning, the masked form closed the drawer and paused in thought. Then sidestepping, she opened a drawer marked "C." It took only a minute to find a stack of blue prints clearly marked *S.S. Caladan*. Another minute's perusal told her this was exactly what she had come for.

Rolling up the blueprints she tied them with a ribbon from her seemingly bottomless purse and closed the drawer.

The Domino Lady hesitated for a moment then withdrew a small card from her purse. She badly wanted to leave her trademark black and white calling card but didn't want to arouse suspicions that might get back to her target. Finally she opened the drawer and placed her card among the blueprints exactly where the missing ones would have been. It would be found, but not for a while, and all she needed was another week or so.

At the hall door the masked figure glanced out carefully before leaving the office and relocking the door. Quickly making her way down the stairwell, she bypassed the ground floor and went straight to the basement. Here the hallways were only dimly lighted, but it did not slow her movement to the rear of the building. The rear door was alarmed, but she made quick work of disconnecting the wires and opening the lock. Outside the alley door, several steps led upward to ground level. Removing her mask, Ellen looked carefully around. The alley was empty. She removed her silken cloak and stuffed it and her mask back into her purse. Then she casually strolled down the alley and out onto the sidewalk. The few passersby paid her—and the rolled bundle under her arm—no attention. Another minute and she was in her roadster, cruising silently down the street.

Ellen spent the next two days studying the blueprints of the *Caladan/La Fortuna* until she knew them like she knew her Hollywood neighborhood along Wilshire Boulevard. The shipyard had done extensive work to the *Caladan*. All the cabins, lounges and officer's cabins had been gutted. As she had seen, the main deck had been converted to one large casino bar with a covered, open area at the stern. The deck above had been converted to a lounge and dancing area, with private gambling rooms forward. Above this was the bridge, radio room and the open upper deck where the tall funnel and multiple life boats were.

Below decks there were fewer changes. Toward the stern were mainly crew's quarters and storage rooms. Amidships, the multi-story engine room and boiler rooms dominated. There were also assorted other areas such as the electrical generating room and pump room. Forward of the mechanical spaces, room had been made for officer's quarters including the captain's cabin and the two room suite for the ship's owner, Mertz. Forward of this was the ship's small hold. Apparently the shipyard had converted this extensively. There were now several walk in cold storage units there for food and drink. Also a personnel door had been cut in a wall for easy access. In the bows of the ship were storage and mechanical spaces.

Ellen was glad to see she could easily reconcile the ship's plans with the areas of the ship she had visited. Accurate plans meant that she was able to become familiar with those areas of the ship she might not be able to actually visit. She took special interest in "officer's country" and the mechanical area of the ship. She also took special note of the forward mast and superstructure on the bow.

By Monday Ellen was ready to move forward. She was sure she could get around quite well below decks on *La Fortuna*. She needed one more trip to the gambling ship to double-check a few things, but otherwise she was ready to put her plan into effect. The problem was she needed an extra set of hands. Ellen paced the living room as she smoked a cigarette. Cindy Hansen would be a natural choice, and it would be nice to give her a chance to strike back at Mertz, but Ellen hesitated in calling her. It would be dangerous, and she might need someone who could handle himself. Quickly making up her mind, she stubbed out her cigarette in an ashtray and reached for the phone, "Give me long distance, operator."

Once connected, she felt her pulse quicken as the familiar voice answered, "Hello."

"Roge, darling. I've missed you something awful."

"Ellen. Tell me you're here in San Francisco and on your way to see me."

Ellen laughed a clear honest sound, "There's nothing I'd like more, dear, but I'm afraid I'm still down south. However, I would like to see you soon and I have something important I need your help with."

"You know I'm yours to command, beautiful."

"Good. Now tell me you can take a day or two off and come visit me."

"Well...I do have some vacation time coming. What do you have in mind?"

Ellen told him. She gave him an abridged version of the truth about the Hansens and Charles Mertz. She told him that Cindy was being blackmailed and Ellen had agreed to help recover the incriminating evidence. By the end of the conversation, Roger had agreed to come to L.A. and escort her to *La Fortuna* on Saturday night. Nodding to herself, Ellen hung up and planned her last reconnaissance trip to *La Fortuna*.

By now Ellen was recognized by most of the crew and staff on the ship. She was passed aboard with a minimal glance in her clutch purse. Once in the casino, she kept on the move playing a few minutes at roulette before moving on to blackjack and then craps. She noted which officers were on duty, keeping a special watch for the captain. Before she moved to the lounge on the deck above, she spotted young officer DuPree passing among the tables. She timed her arrival at the stairs to meet him, "Why officer DuPree, it's a pleasure to see you this evening."

The young officer colored slightly as he touched his hat brim, "Good evening, Miss Page."

"Come now, Brian, I've told you before to call me Ellen."

Officer DuPree glanced around before replying in a low voice, "You know I have to keep up appearances, Ellen. Thankfully, the captain and first officer aren't around just now." His smile softened, "I've missed you, Ellen. Where have you been the last few days?"

"Oh, you know, parties, lunches, the usual," Ellen waved her hand airily as they walked aft. "But where is the captain? Surely it's not his night off?"

"No. He and the first are up on the bridge going over maintenance logs or something. Lots of paperwork to run a ship, you know."

Ellen reached out and took young DuPree's arm and said, "Then this is the perfect time for you to take me on that tour you've been promising." As she spoke, Ellen reached into her purse and brought out a cigarette.

Brian nearly broke his wrist getting his cigarette lighter out to light it. "Well, you have been wanting to see below decks." He glanced around and smiled conspiratorially at her, "I suppose it's as good a time as any. Let's go."

The young officer quickly led the way below. Passing through the casino, he smiled and greeted several gamblers by name. They soon found a stairway going down. At the bottom Brian waved his hand forward, "Officer's country is that way. Let's take a quick peek in the engine room." He then led the way aft. Making several turns and passing through a few open metal hatches, the pair soon came to a closed metal hatch labeled *Engine Room*. Unlatching it, Brian swung it open so Ellen could step across the coaming.

They were standing on an open walkway along the wall of the engine room. Below them were the two large reciprocating steam engines. The large fly wheel and huge moving piston arms were still, and the room was nearly silent. The only sound was the quiet hiss of steam somewhere below. The room was fairly well lit, and Ellen could see across the top of the engines to the other side of the ship. Turning to her companion, Ellen looked puzzled, "But the engines aren't running. And there's no one here?"

DuPree nodded, "It's not needed while we're at anchor. With proper steam pressure, they can be started quite quickly."

Ellen looked quizzical, "Proper steam pressure?"

"Yes. It takes over a half hour to start and bring all the boilers on line at full pressure. Right now we are only running on one boiler. That saves fuel and still gives us enough steam pressure to power the electrical generators."

Ellen had known this all along but continued to play the innocent débutante, "Oh, you generate your own electricity here?"

DuPree smiled indulgently, "Yes, it powers the lights as well as almost everything else."

"Ooh, can we see the generators?"

DuPree glanced at his wrist watch, "I suppose we have time." He led the way back along the walkway to the entrance, opened the hatch and passed through. Ellen followed and waited while he reclosed the hatch. They then located another stairway and descended to the level of the main engine room. They made several turns in the passageway to what Ellen knew was the port side of the ship and paused before a door marked *Generator Room*. Ellen could feel the vibration of the generator through the deck beneath her feet. Dupree turned to her, "It's a little loud in there, so we'll just take a quick look." He opened the hatch and stepped through. The whine from the large generator was loud but not deafening to Ellen's ears as she entered. The generator itself was a four foot high heavy metal shape with a spinning shaft turning it. A panel covered in gauges and dials was attached to its front. Massive insulated wires came from the generator, ran overhead to another wall and entered a long, ceiling high panel of what appeared to be massive circuit breakers. Next to the large breaker panel was a large diagram of the ship under glass. Next it was a telephone. Also posted near the telephone was some kind of list. Ellen glided over to the list and stared at it. It was a list of circuit breakers and corresponding compartments and machinery. As DuPree moved up beside her, she glanced across the panel of breakers, each manipulated by a large insulated handle. The young officer, smiling, spoke loudly, "Not much to see, I'm afraid."

Ellen shook her head, "This is really impressive. I'm glad I got to see it." They soon left the noisy generator room. Once in the corridor, Ellen leaned against the young officer and looked up into his eyes, "I'd love to see where your cabin is."

About to look at his watch, young DuPree instead beamed a huge smile down at Ellen and replied, "I think we have time for that." He quickly led them down a series of corridors. As they passed a door, Ellen glanced and saw that it was marked *Executive Officer*. She stopped and asked, "Is this Officer Etheridge's cabin?"

Nodding and pointing, DuPree said, "Yes. The captain's is just down there. Mine is forward of the hold, I'm afraid."

Ellen smiled, "Lead on." They made another turn before passing a door marked *Charles Mertz, Private*. She didn't stop or ask any questions but did look around, noting her location carefully. They went forward past the hold, Ellen taking careful note of their path. They then turned into a narrower corridor before coming up in front of officer DuPree's cabin. He smiled as he turned a key in the lock. He reached in and flipped a switch to light the room before standing back to allow Ellen to enter. The room was a small one with just enough room for the narrow bed, a clothes locker and a small desk.

Ellen was looking at her watch, "Oh my, I didn't realize how long we've been gone."

Surprised, DuPree answered, "Uh, we have been gone quite a while...."

"I don't want to get you into trouble." She smiled coyly, "Perhaps we can come back another time."

Obviously disappointed, he replied, "Sure. We can come back any time you want."

While DuPree was locking the door, Ellen looked down a forward corridor toward a stairway and asked, "What's down there?"

Pocketing his key, DuPree frowned, "Not much, the chain locker and storage mostly."

"Where does that stair go?"

"Uh, to the foredeck."

"Oh. Up by the mast and derrick."

"Yes, it comes up just in front of the derrick house."

"Would it be faster to go back that way?"

"Uh, yeah, I guess so."

"Good." Ellen set off toward the stairway. As she reached the foot of it, DuPree brushed past her with a smile. He climbed the stair halfway and reached up to undo and open the horizontal hatch. It swung open on a spring-loaded hinge, and Ellen felt a draft of cool air flow over her. She climbed the stair and took DuPree's outstretched hand as he helped her over the coaming to the foredeck. Ahead was the darkened bow. Turning, Ellen could see the brightly lit casino and superstructure. Above it was the dimly lit bridge. Between them and the superstructure was the tall mast and derrick lit up by colored lights. Just ahead of the mast was a small structure with semi open sides. Ellen pointed, "Is that where the derrick is operated from?"

Officer DuPree took her arm to guide her aft past the mast, "Yes, that's where we operate it when we're loading cargo into the hold. The anchor controls are there also." Ellen nodded.

As they reached the forward doors to the casino, DuPree held one open for Ellen and she preceded him into the room. As he did so, he caught sight of Officer Etheridge across the room, who smiled slightly to her and touched the brim of his cap. Also seeing Mertz, Ellen smiled and said, "Thanks for the tour Brian." She then turned and made her way to a craps table near the casino owner. She pulled some money from her purse and caught the eye of the croupier. He traded her money for chips, and she placed a bet on the table. She bet without thought and waited for an opening. Out of the corner of her eye she caught sight of Mertz, who had moved up to watch the action at the table.

Eventually the croupier called out, "New shooter."

Ellen stepped to the head of the table and waved her hand. The croupier obligingly pushed the dice across the table to her with his stick. Ellen placed a good sized bet and picked up the dice. She gave them a shake and flipped them down the table: they came up seven. The croupier pushed Ellen's winnings toward her and people placed their bets. Deciding to look carefree, Ellen let her money ride and flipped the dice forward again. The dice skipped down the table and ended up showing a six and a five. There was a murmur around the table and bets were shifted as the croupier pushed an even bigger stack of chips in front of Ellen.

Perspiration broke out on Ellen's forehead. She hadn't intended this. She knew that many people, including Mertz, were now watching her. There was also a considerable amount of money on the table in front of her. The smart thing would be to change her bet or pass the dice, but Ellen needed to appear frivolous. She let her bet ride and picked up the dice in her now sweaty hands. She shook them and gave them another flip down the table. They bounced against the far end of the table, rebounded and settled in place, one showing two and the other a one. The croupier sang out, "Three! The shooter craps out!"

Ellen backed thankfully away from the table. As she cleared the crowd, she was confronted by the thin figure of Charles Mertz. He smiled down at her, "That was unfortunate, Miss Page. I'm afraid the dice turned against you."

Ellen shrugged and smiled, "It's just money. It was exciting, though, wasn't it?"

"It certainly was. Can the House buy you a drink to make up for it?"

"Why certainly, Mr. Mertz. That would be very nice."

Once at the bar, Ellen ordered a glass of champagne. Glad for the chance to play the idle socialite, Ellen allowed Mertz to flirt with her. She wanted him to remember her as nothing but a brainless young girl. When he was finally called away by a steward, Ellen was relieved. Mertz's slimy charm gave her the shivers. Ellen spent another couple of hours gambling sparingly. She had seen what she came for and by midnight she was on her way home.

The next day a call to the harbormaster and a final call to Cindy Hansen completed Ellen's preparations. Roger was driving down on Friday. Everything was in place. Now there was nothing to do but wait.

Saturday evening, Roger rang her doorbell. Ellen thought him quite handsome in his black tuxedo. She was dressed in a long white satin dress that showed off her trim figure and bountiful cleavage. She carried a small clutch purse and wore her long black cloak to ward off the evening air. Roger was preoccupied on the drive from Hollywood. He worried that Ellen was needlessly endangering herself while relegating him to a supporting role. Smiling, she assured him that she was in no danger and that his actions would allow her to accomplish her mission without interruption. Little did he know that the foray Ellen planned was just the kind of situation at which the mysterious Domino Lady excelled.

She had planned their arrival at the dockside later than normal. When they sauntered up to the ship's landing point, arm in arm, it was just after ten o'clock. She greeted officer DuPree by name while he used a weak salute to cover his surprise at seeing her with a handsome escort. Ellen had perhaps the briefest moment of guilt when she saw the confusion on his young face. She was confident he was not involved in any of Mertz's schemes, and she regretted the necessity of toying with his emotions.

They were passed through and quickly embarked on the water taxi. The launch left for *La Fortuna* with only four guests aboard. At this time of night more people would likely be leaving than arriving on the ship—something Ellen was counting on. The night was warm and the seas calm

"Can the House buy you a drink?"

as they arrived at the gambling ship twenty minutes later. Roger was forced to open his tuxedo jacket for the mandatory weapons check but Ellen was known and the crewman gave her nothing but a smile as he waved her into the ship.

Once on the main deck, Ellen entered the casino on Roger's arm and glanced at her watch; they were right on schedule. They mingled, moving from table to table watching and gambling, sometimes together and sometimes apart. Ellen's main goal was to be seen and to locate the locations of the captain, first officer Etheridge, and especially Charles Mertz.

The captain put in an appearance not long after Ellen and Roger arrived. He spent a few minutes greeting customers and shaking a few hands and then retired to the bridge. Ellen felt confident that he would remain there for as much time as she needed. First officer Etheridge was there, circulating between the casino and second deck lounge. He greeted Ellen, who introduced Roger as a "friend." The first officer gave Roger the look any man gives to a possible rival, and Ellen was sure that both men attempted to get the better grip during their handshake. She pretended not to notice. She saw nothing of Mertz. Eventually she became concerned enough to question a passing waiter,, who told her that Mr. Mertz was playing in a private poker game upstairs. Relieved Ellen moved on.

By mutual agreement, Roger and Ellen met in the second floor bar at eleven thirty. While they sipped drinks, she spoke softly, "It's time. What does your watch say?"

Smiling, he glanced at his wrist and murmured, "Eleven twenty-nine."

She nodded back, "Exactly what I have. Good luck, and I'll see you on the other side." She leaned in quickly, gave him a quick kiss and glided smoothly away. Roger looked thoughtfully after her.

Ellen made her way down through the casino to the hat check located near the exit to the covered stern area. She picked up her cloak and moved out onto the covered deck. There were a few people there smoking or chatting while looking at the brightly lit coast. No one paid her any attention as she slipped quietly forward along the starboard outside promenade. She passed no one as she moved forward past the windows of the casino.

She quickly found a stairway and went down one deck. She made her way forward with her cloak over one arm and a happy smile on her face. She had a good story ready if she met any crewmen but made the quick journey without incident. In front of Mertz's office, Ellen swung the black cloak around her shoulders and fastened it at her throat. Reaching into a hidden pocket of it, she came up with her black domino mask and quickly fitted it to her face. The Domino Lady had finally made an appearance on the *S.S. La Fortuna.*

Opening her purse, the Domino Lady pulled open the lining in the bottom and removed two small metal objects. Glancing around, she knelt in front of the door and went to work. This was perhaps the most dangerous part of her plan. She was vulnerable, and anyone seeing her would quickly raise an alarm. Fortunately, the lock wasn't difficult, and in little more than a minute she had the door open. She passed quickly inside, located the light switch and flipped it. The office wasn't particularly large. Three walls were covered with wood paneling. The wall across from her was of metal and was pierced by two portholes. To her right was a good sized desk. To her left was a low side cabinet covered with liquor bottles and glasses. Near this was a door she knew opened to Mertz's bedroom. Directly across from her, under the two portholes, were two metal filing cabinets.

Locking the door behind her, the Domino Lady went directly to Mertz's desk. It was unlocked, and a quick examination of the drawers came up with nothing significant. She then moved to the filing cabinets. They were locked, but she made quick work of the simple locks. There she found what she had come for. The first held nothing but routine business paperwork, but the other was filled with files listed by name, some of which Ellen recognized as prominent Californians. She quickly located the file on Raymond Hansen. Pausing, Ellen glanced at her watch. It read eleven forty. Crossing to the liquor cabinet, she was just reaching for a bottle when she heard a step outside the corridor door.

Moving quickly, she flipped off the light switch as she heard a key inserted in the lock. In the darkness, the Domino Lady made for the connecting bedroom door. She made it through just as the corridor door opened. By the time the light flooded the office, she had the bedroom door closed with her ear pressed to it. She heard glass clinking and muttered curses. Silently turning the door knob, she eased the door open the tiniest amount. She saw nothing in the room for a moment, then realized that a figure was crouched down in front of the liquor cabinet. The figure wore a white dinner jacket and was looking into the cabinet. As she watched, she heard clicking then a metallic clack and Charles Mertz stood up with a bundle of cash in his hand. Counting through the large bills, Mertz did not hear or see the gentle movement of the connecting door closing silently.

In the darkness of the bedroom, the Domino Lady hiked up her long white dress. Attached to her thigh by a garter was a capped syringe. She removed the cap carefully by feel. With the hypodermic syringe ready in one hand, she reached for the door knob with the other. Taking a deep breath, the Domino Lady yanked open the door and lunged into the office. Mertz was reaching for the corridor door as he pocketed a large bundle of cash with his free hand. He sensed the quick movement behind him, but before he could turn, the Domino Lady had sunk the sharp needle into his neck with a deft motion. He grasped his neck, turned and managed to gasp out "Domino La…" before the quick acting drug overcame him and he sagged to the floor.

It took some effort, but the Domino Lady grasped him by the ankles and dragged him into the bedroom. Confident that the harmless drug would keep him unconscious for several hours, she left him on the floor. Removing the bundle of cash from his pocket, she returned to the office and relocked the corridor door. Time was now crucial. She grabbed a bottle of whiskey and upturned it over the open drawers of the file cabinet, dousing the incriminating files, then added another bottle for good measure. Lastly she opened both portholes. Grabbing a cigarette lighter from the desk, she moved back to the file cabinet and glanced critically at her work. The file cabinets were metal, as was the floor and bulkhead next to them. Any fire would be contained. The ship would not be in danger. The Domino Lady looked at her watch; eleven forty-three. It was time. She flicked the lighter to life and tossed it into the open file cabinet drawer.

Ashore, in an all-night diner, Cindy Hansen set down her coffee cup and glanced at her wrist watch. It read exactly eleven forty-one. According to Ellen that was exactly the time of slack water. She wasn't totally sure why that was so important, but she had promised Ellen she would follow her instructions exactly. Taking her purse, Cindy made for the telephone booth at the back of the diner. Once inside, she closed the folding door and lifted the receiver to an ear. She put a nickel in the machine and when a voice answered she spoke, "Operator? Give me the Coast Guard. I have an emergency to report."

In the lounge, Roger wandered around a bit watching the couples on the dance floor. When the wall clock read eleven thirty-five he made his way back to the bar. Getting the attention of the bartender he ordered a bottle of champagne in a bucket of ice. It was brought quickly, and the bartender asked, "Where do you want this served, sir?"

Roger replied, "I'll take it with me. I'm meeting a young lady." He smiled and winked as he passed across a bill, "Keep the change." The bartender gave him a knowing look as Roger left carrying the champagne in its bucket. It was easy to make his way through the lounge and casino. No one gave him a second look. Once he was going down the companionway below the main deck, he was on shakier ground. Any crewman who saw him was likely to stop and question him. He remained calm and went down a corridor and around a corner. With the ship's plans in mind, he was making for another stairway downward when a white-jacketed crewman came around a corner toward him.

Roger summoned up his best confused look as the crewman came to a stop in front of him. "Can I help you, sir?"

"Er, yes. I think I've lost my way," Roger slurred his words slightly as he smiled at the steward.

"What are you looking for, sir?"

"Well, I was going to the stern. There's a nice dark patio place there and I was meeting a young lady," he gave the steward a slight leer.

The steward nodded knowingly, "I'm afraid you're on the wrong deck, sir." He pointed, "Take those stairs upward and turn right toward the stern, keep going and you'll make it."

Roger waved his thanks and headed for the stairs. Ducking into the stairwell, he waited a moment and looked out. The steward was gone. Going down the stairs instead of up, Roger made it to the next deck. Sweating a little, he moved quickly around several turns and soon arrived at the door to the generator room. Once inside the vibration filled room, he drew a deep breath. He quickly scanned the layout. It was just as Ellen had described. Moving to a corner where there was a folding chair, Roger plopped into it gratefully. He wiped his sweating brow and looked at his watch. Pleased that it read eleven forty-two he muttered to himself, "How do you like that? Right on time." He set the champagne down on the deck between his feet and then hesitated. Shrugging, he pulled the open bottle out of the bucket. A few drops of water splashed on his tuxedo as he lifted the bottle to his lips.

Fueled by the alcohol, fire flared up in the open metal file drawers. The masked woman watched it for a moment before moving away. Unlocking the corridor door, she opened it slightly. As she stuffed the wad of bills into her small purse, she thought to herself that Mertz must have been losing at poker and come to his office for more funds. She shook her head. It looked as if it were going to be an unlucky night for him all the way around. Before she left the room, she took off her cloak and threw it toward the burning file cabinet. It caught on a corner and draped to the floor. Immediately the chemically impregnated cloth of the cloak went up in a ball of smoke.

The Domino Lady knew that within a minute it would be nothing but ash on the deck. Meanwhile, it was giving off prodigious amounts of smoke, as intended. Before she left the office, she reached into the front of her gown and pulled out a small black card. On it was inscribed *Compliments of the Domino Lady*. She smiled as she tossed it onto the floor of the office.

In the bedroom, she crossed the luxuriously furnished room to the corridor door and opened it wide. Again grasping his ankles, she dragged the unconscious Mertz out and some way up the corridor. Smoke was wafting into the corridor behind her. She reached up under her dress and came out with a cigar shaped metallic container. She gave it a sharp snapping motion with both hands and tossed it down the corridor past Mertz's office. The miniature smoke bomb immediately began puffing out gray smoke. Without a look back she turned and moved forward. Moving quickly down corridors and around corners, she met no one. Quickly she reached the foot of a steep stairway that ended at a closed hatch in the ceiling. She climbed them until she could reach the hatch handle. It turned easily. The hatch then lifted easily assisted by its spring mounted in the hinge. She climbed cautiously up and looked out. The shadowy forward deck was deserted.

Standing up, she boldly made her way the few yards to the small metal superstructure at the base of the main mast. She pulled open the door and entered the shadowy winch structure. There was a door opposite the one she'd entered. The rear of the structure was open from the waist up, looking out over the hold cover and derrick. Winch controls were just below this opening. Turning, she found more controls but could not make them out in the gloom. Searching the wall near the door, she found a switch and threw it. Lights came on illuminating the structure.

Standing exposed in the light, the Domino Lady knew she didn't have much time. She scanned the controls. There was an on-off switch marked 'Anchor' and a large lever that was connected to the floor. She pressed the 'on' switch and felt a hum through her feet. Then, taking a chance, she grabbed the lever in both hands and pulled it back with all her strength.

The champagne had tasted wonderful but Roger allowed himself only the one drink. He would need the rest of it. He waited watchfully, praying that the electrician or some wandering crewmen would not enter and find him. It might be hard to explain what he and his champagne were doing there. Time crawled as he worried about Ellen. His palms were sweaty, and he had just about convinced himself that something had gone wrong when alarm bells began to sound. That was the signal; Roger lifted the champagne bucket in his hands and walked to the large generator. Removing the champagne bottle, he upturned the bucket of ice water over the generator at the wiring connections. There was a flash of sparks that forced him to step back. More sparks flew and water that had splashed onto the spinning axle flew about. Immediately the generator began to slow. The noise and vibration diminished significantly. Smoke rose from the generator and the lights dimmed in the room. Roger then stepped over to the large breaker panel. He held the nearly full champagne bottle up high and upended it directly over the circuit breaker panel. Moving the bottle sideways to cover more area, he soaked the panel. Breakers began snapping open as more sparks flew. Roger didn't see the last of the champagne leave the bottle as the last breakers blew and the *La Fortuna* was plunged into darkness.

Knowing that she was visible to anyone looking into the winch structure, the masked woman bit her lower lip and repeated a quick silent prayer. The motor was turning, but she had no idea how quickly the anchor would lift. It didn't need to come all the way up; it only had to clear the sea floor enough for the ship to drift. She waited a moment more then moved back to the open forward hatch. She went down the ladder and looked at her watch. The winch had been turning for over a minute. It had to be enough. She turned to a red fire alarm box mounted chest high on the wall. Breaking the glass with the little hammer provided, she reached in and pulled the fire alarm handle. Immediately a loud bell began ringing. As she climbed again to the upper deck, the lights went out all over the ship. Reaching the upper deck, the Domino Lady found herself standing in near darkness. She reached up under her dress again and came out with the last of the cigar shaped smoke bombs. She armed it and dropped it down the hatch.

The ship was not in total darkness; a few dim battery-powered emergency lights gave some illumination. The alarm bells were silent, and the only sounds now were shouted commands and confused conversations. Shouted commands came from the upper superstructure, and she could see hand held lights moving about. The creak of ropes and pulleys came to her ears. As expected, they were lowering the boats. Walking to the ship's side, Ellen removed her mask and tossed it overboard into the darkness.

She then calmly moved aft toward the superstructure. As she passed through the crowd, she noted the conversations of those around her. There was a lot of confusion but no panic. She heard things like: "Why did the lights go off?" and "What was that bell?" Ellen attempted to calm people as she went, assuring them that it was just a power failure and there was no danger. She was pleased to see the first officer passing along the promenade supervising the boats as they were lowered to the main deck level. She moved closer to him and listened as a crewman ran up with a report, "Sir, the origin of the fire seems to be in Mr. Mertz's office. We found him unconscious in the corridor."

Not noticing Ellen, Etheridge replied, "What about the fire? Is it out?"

"They were extinguishing it as I left, sir. It didn't seem very big and was contained to the one compartment."

"Are you sure? There was an awful lot of smoke."

"Yes, sir. I don't know about that."

"And the lights? What happened to the lights?"

"Don't know yet. Someone has been sent to check, sir."

Smiling, Ellen turned and wormed her way through the crowd to the stairwell. She worked her way down and mixed with the throng around the lower open hatchway. One of the water taxis was just pulling away, crowded with patrons. Within two minutes another had pulled alongside and began taking off frustrated gamblers. Ellen glanced up and saw Roger sauntering down the corridor carrying of all things a champagne bottle in a bucket. He gave her a big smile as he came up, "What's all the commotion?"

Ellen spoke, "Don't know. The lights have failed." She raised an eyebrow and pointedly looked at the open bottle in his hand, "Did you stop off for a drink?"

Roger just smiled modestly, "I did have just a taste."

They'd worked their way out on the landing stage and another water taxi was approaching the ship when they heard the siren. Everyone stopped and watched with attention as the Coast Guard cutter approached quickly. She made a stirring sight cutting through the water, her siren blaring loudly. Her brilliant white hull was lit up from stem to stern, and search lights stabbed out, illuminating *La Fortuna*. A ragged cheer came from the patrons above. As Ellen and Roger stepped down into a launch, they could see the stars and stripes snapping in the wind from the cutter's bridge.

As the launch pulled away, it passed another civilian pleasure boat heading toward *La Fortuna*. Apparently word had gotten around, and people were pitching in to help out in what they thought was an emergency. Looking at the ship, she could see that it had visibly changed position, the bow now pointing toward shore. The cutter was alongside her now, and she could hear someone shouting through a megaphone. Flashlights moved about the decks. The lights were still out, so Ellen knew that they still did not have power to the winch. The question was, how far the ship would drift before they managed to drop anchor or get steam up.

She looked up at Roger, who had his arm around her, warding off the chill, "She's definitely drifting. I wonder if they'll get her under control?"

Roger held up the empty champagne bottle that he had inexplicably kept and shook his head, "Not any time soon, I'd think." He then pitched the bottle into the sea and laughed.

Ellen was curled up on her sofa in a set of satin lounging pajamas. It was only eleven so she was not in a hurry to get dressed. Right now she was absorbed in the Sunday newspaper. She scanned the front page between sips from her glass. The noise of someone rummaging around in her kitchen came to her ears. "It says here that the Coast Guard went aboard to help fight the fire, but it was already out. Apparently it was very small and did little damage but produced the smoke of a much larger fire."

A man's voice answered from the kitchen, "Was anyone hurt?"

"It says here that no one was hurt, just a few people shaken up."

"And the ship?"

"Hmnnn…It says by the time they realized the ship was in no danger, it had drifted into U.S. waters so the Coast Guard impounded it for alcohol and gambling violations."

"I'll bet that Mertz is just furious about that."

"Oh, yes, he's apparently already got his lawyers trying to argue that the Coast Guard boarded her illegally in international waters. Is there enough orange juice for another mimosa?"

"I think so. So, it looks like you've saved your friend from any blackmail."

"Definitely, it also looked like there was a lot of other blackmail going on there as well. Too bad they won't be able to add those to Mertz's charges."

Roger came from the kitchen with a full glass in his hand. He handed it over to Ellen and took her empty glass, "It looks like you not only saved your friend but put Mertz out of business permanently."

Ellen nodded, "I hope so. With his boat confiscated, he and his backers are going to be out a lot of money. I'm only sorry that we had to upset all those people last night." To herself Ellen thought about the information she would anonymously send to the newspapers about Mertz's backers and political cronies. That would really leave him out on a limb. She also thought about the cash, minus her gambling losses, that she would be donating anonymously to charity.

"Say, Roge, where did you get the idea to pour champagne on the circuit breakers?"

Roger plopped into a comfortable armchair and laughed, "You said you needed the lights and power off long enough for the ship to drift inside the limit. I thought that pulling a few breakers might not be enough, and without any heavy tools to smash things up I needed something to help out." He looked sad, "Waste of good champagne though."

Ellen threw her head back and laughed, "Don't worry, we have plenty."

The End

THE DOMINO LADY AFLOAT

*I*t turns out that stories are like wine. Sometimes they are ready to be written right away, and sometimes they aren't ready for years. That's how it was with the Domino Lady. I had wanted to write a Domino Lady story for a while now. I'm not sure why. I guess it might be because she got a lot of good publicity. Until recently I'd never read any of the original stories, but I'd seen some Domino Lady comic books and I had read some of the quite good new pulp stories being done and liked them. I was also intrigued by the way she was always portrayed: Long flowing white dress, black cloak and matching domino mask. She just looked so…elegant, and of course sexy. Maybe I was interested in the challenge of writing a female hero. I've never a written a story about one. Could I bring it off? Anyway the idea intrigued me.

I even went so far as to write up an outline for a Domino Lady adventure more than a year ago. It was a good solid idea but there was no immediate need for it, so I filed it away and promptly forgot about it. Meanwhile, there were other characters and stories to be written. Anyway, imagine my surprise when Ron Fortier put out a call for Domino Lady stories. I had the perfect story, all ready to go. I dusted off my outline, made some adjustments, added some details and off I went.

How did I come up with the idea? The original Domino Lady stories generally had very little mystery. The Domino Lady's target was usually identified very early. The stories were more about her using her feminine wiles to foil the corrupt activities she was targeting. So the only challenge was to pick a plausible target, have an interesting setting, and let the Lady have a go at it. Since the stories are set in California of the thirties I decided that a story set along the coast would be interesting. Prohibition and gambling go hand in hand with corruption, so that was also a natural pick. And the setting: In my childhood I used to watch a show called *Mr. Lucky*. It was one of those half hour adventure/drama stories that were all over television at that time. It was about a gentleman gambler who ran a floating casino on his yacht outside the three mile limit. He met all sorts of interesting people and had many adventures there. The setting fit my story outline perfectly, so I borrowed the idea of a floating casino and ran with it.

I ordered and read all six original stories for background flavor. One of them is set aboard a ship, which confirmed my judgment that a nautical setting could be interesting. This research also helped me keep my vision of the Domino Lady in the flavor of the original stories. So you will find no wild shootouts or our heroine using Kung Fu skills here. All we have is the Domino Lady doing what she does best: using her charm and brains to outwit and expose crooks and corrupt officials.

As for the writing, it was tougher to write than I thought it would be. As I said, I had no shootouts, car chases or fist fights to work with. Since this is my stock in trade, it was a bit of a challenge to find interesting scenes to fill the story. It definitely was a change of pace from my more action-oriented work. Still, it certainly gave me a chance to brush up on my conversation skills. It was a lot of fun, but challenging. Hopefully I have caught the flavor of the Domino Lady's escapades.

This story also had a personal feel for me. I spent a good part of my childhood in southern California, so the settings seemed very familiar and the time set during prohibition and the depression is classic pulp. All in all, I had a great time writing it. I think Airship 27's first Domino Lady book will be a big hit, and I'm glad I will be a part of it.

GENE MOYERS studied European and Medieval history at the University of Oregon. He is a former U.S. Army armor crewman. He worked in the High Tech industry for some time and ran a store front and internet hobby shop for several years.

An avid military gamer and role player, his favorite game was *Daredevils* set in the 1930s. His love affair with the 1930s and pulps in particular stem from his first time reading a *Shadow* novel as a boy. Although interested in writing since a teen, he did not turn to serious writing until 2000. He is the co-author of *GURPS Crusades*, published by Steve Jackson Games. He has a story published in *Ravenwood Volume II* by Airship 27. He has also written stories that will appear in the second volume of *Moon Man* and the first volume of *The Purple Scar*. When not working on Airship 27 projects, he is busy writing horror adventures for his swashbuckling character set in Colonial America.

Gene currently lives in Beaverton, Oregon with his wife and three lazy dogs.

THE CASE OF THE MODEL, MADNESS & MURDER

by Tim Holter Bruckner

The photographer, a fleshy man in a beret a size too small, cautiously circled his camera as if he expected it to snap at him. On the third pass, he stopped, turned his back to it and closed his eyes. He was silent for a long moment, his head titled back slightly as if in meditation. Then he turned, lifted the black cloth, leaned in to study the image on the viewfinder and lowered the cloth over his head. Another long moment of silence followed.

"Nita," he called, his voice just above a whisper.

His assistant, a pretty dark haired girl wearing an artist's smock a size too large, rushed to him and leaned in close as he gave her instructions through the black fabric hood. After a time, she nodded and went to the model posed on a black velvet chaise lounge.

Ellen Patrick wore a silver satin chemise that clung to her long elegant frame as if it had been poured over her from a pitcher of liquid starlight. With her pale ivory complexion and her long golden hair, lounging on the black velvet in front of a black, rhinestone studded curtain, she looked as if she were floating in the midst of a moonless midnight sky.

"Mr. Andre," the girl began softly, "would like to know if it would be possible to show a little more of your left breast."

"My left breast," Ellen repeated, smiling. Her décolletage was already so low, any further reveal and her portrait would be more in keeping with pictures found in *Nudie Cuties* and *Bare Beauties* than *Harper's Bazaar*.

"Yes, ma'am," Nita said.

Ellen adjusted her position and pulled at the fabric to expose more of her full bosom, the edge of the satin within a breath of pink.

"Let's just hope I don't sneeze," Ellen said, good humouredly.

The girl looked at Ellen a little confused and asked if she could bring her a box of tissues. Again, Ellen smiled, thanking the girl for her thoughtfulness.

Several shots later, Mr. Andre was satisfied with his work and had Nita thank Miss Patrick for her time. He would have a set of proofs sent to her apartment when they were ready.

Ellen was in the dressing room, having gotten out of the chemise and into a tailored emerald green outfit, touching up her makeup, when the door opened behind her. In the mirror, she saw the reflection of Nita, the photographer's assistant.

"There's a call for you, ma'am," the girl said. "It seems quite urgent. I can have it transferred here, if you like."

Ellen thanked the girl and went to the wall phone across the room. Nita turned to signal to someone and then turned back to Ellen to give her the okay.

Ellen picked up the receiver, "Hello," she said into the mouthpiece, "this is Ellen Patrick."

"Ellen, oh, thank God." The voice was so choked with emotion it was difficult to know who was on the other end.

"Connie?" Ellen said, "Is that you?"

"Yes, Ellen," Connie said. "It's me. Oh, God, Ellen, I'm in a heck of a jam. I don't know what to do."

"Where are you, honey?"

"The Hollywood Police station," Connie said. "Oh, Ellen, I've been arrested!"

Detective Danny O'Boylan was waiting outside the Hollywood Police station when Ellen's cab pulled up.

"Hey, gorgeous," Danny said as Ellen exited the back seat.

"Hello, detective," she said, leaning in to give him a kiss. As her lips pressed against his cheek, she felt his hand slide around her waist, pulling her into him. She almost raised her hand to his chest, to his shoulder, to around the back of his neck. But she didn't. There was too much history between them for that gesture to mean anything other than a renewed intimacy.

Ellen and Danny had dated. They might have continued had it not been for Danny's wife. A vengeful, hateful woman whose erratic mood swings made Danny's life, and in association, Ellen's, a waking nightmare. Danny and his wife, Delores, had been separated for some months. Delores moved in with her sister, Adel, who was renting a small stucco bungalow at the outskirts of Culver City. Danny didn't hear from his wife for weeks on end. Every now and then he'd get a letter asking for money. But there was never any correspondence that dealt with their relationship. Privately, Danny was hoping for a divorce. Delores had other plans in mind.

When Delores heard of Danny's relationship with Ellen, she went, as her sister later said, "bat shit crazy." She began following him. Showing up at the station, confronting him. Appearing out of nowhere to scream at him or beg his forgiveness. Dragging a screwdriver down the side of his car or breaking off his side-view mirror escalated to slashing his tires and, later, Ellen's tires. Showing up at Ellen's apartment in the middle of the night. More than once, the doorman at Ellen's apartment had to call the police to have the woman forcibly removed from the property. If it hadn't been for her husband, Delores would have spent many a long and lonely night in jail. Things seemed to calm down for a while. But it was just the calm before the storm.

One spring evening, Danny invited Ellen over to his house. He was going to cook her dinner and share a bottle of her favorite white wine. Afterward, they planned on driving up to the newly opened Griffith Park Observatory for a little convivial star gazing. They were on the patio listening to the radio, enjoying a warm spring evening when Ellen smelled smoke.

"Probably a spill in the oven." Danny said. "I'm toasting up some garlic bread."

He started to get up to check, but Ellen stayed him with a wave of her hand. "I'll check the oven and bring out the bottle of wine I brought. Opener in the drawer?"

He said it was.

"Danny!" she yelled from inside the house. "Fire!"

He bolted through the patio doors to see the living room bright with flame, waves of black smoke roiling across the ceiling. Within seconds the fire was feeding itself up the walls and across the hard wood floor.

"Ellen! Ellen!" Danny called.

She was in the kitchen. He ran to her just as a fist of heat knocked him back. The fire had flared up the wallpaper and around the molding, setting the kitchen door ablaze.

"Ellen! Ellen!"

"Danny!"

He ran out the patio doors, around the side of house to the kitchen window, used his elbow to break out the glass and started climbing in just as she was climbing out. He grabbed her under her arms and lifted her out of the window, making sure to hoist her over the shards of glass still embedded in the window frame. She collapsed into his arms. They'd almost reached the front yard when an explosion tore the side of the house away, knocking them both to the ground.

Delores O'Banyon was committed to the Horace Travers Memorial Mental Hospital. There would be no divorce so long as she was unable to fully grasp her current reality. For a woman convinced that she was about to be whisked away by her husband to begin their honeymoon, her current reality was as solid and steadfast as smoke.

Danny led Ellen to a bench beside the station entrance. When they had settled, he began.

"I know you have a million questions," he said. "Let me tell you where we are with Connie, and then you can ask whatever you like."

"Okay," Ellen said, trepidation sending a slight quiver in her voice.

He dug out a pack of cigarettes from his shirt pocket, bumped up two and offered her one. He lit both with the lighter she had given him for his birthday, two days before the fire. A wave of sadness fluttered through her at seeing his engraved initials on the case.

"We got a call at about one-twenty," Danny said. "Be at the Roosevelt Hotel at two. A guy is going to get murdered. Officer Dave Meadows got the call. You know Dave?"

She said she did.

"Dave was in the lobby at quarter to. There was a loud pop. Dave took off up the stairs. There was a scream. He identified it as coming from the second floor. He ran down the hall and found the door to room 256 open. He withdrew his weapon and entered the room with caution, indentifying himself. He found Connie standing over the body or her fiancé, Lance Holter. Holter was bleeding out, not yet dead, but a breath or two not far from it. Connie had a .38 in her hand. Smoke was still snaking from the muzzle. She was in shock, Dave said. Didn't know where she was. He was able to ease the pistol from her fist. He got her into a chair and called down to the front desk to send it to the station. Dave said it was like she was coming to the surface, like she'd been underwater. She saw Lance dead on the floor in a pool of blood, screamed and passed out. Cold. After we booked her, she had her one phone call. She used it to call you."

Ellen sat back, took a last drag of her cigarette before stubbing it out on the sidewalk. As she considered what Danny told her, she watched a mother wrestle her toddler out of the front seat of a car parked across the street.

"What did Connie have to say?" Ellen asked, turning back to Danny.

"Nothing," Danny said. "That's the thing. She doesn't remember anything about it. The last thing she remembers, she was on the phone to Lance making plans to meet for lunch. She has no memory of anything beyond that."

"It makes no sense," Ellen said. "You know she doesn't drive. So how did she get there? If she took a cab, there must be some way to trace that back."

"We're checking," Danny said. "But so far," he paused to look into her eyes, "Connie is going to be charged with murder."

Hearing him say it, say it out loud, made her feel ill. Connie and Ellen had been best friends since they both worked as carhops at Carpenter's Drive-in on the corner of Hollywood and Vine. Although Connie was some years older than Ellen, the differences in their ages seemed to make their friendship stronger and deeper rather than creating distance. They had even roomed together for a while. Connie was the sweetest, kindest, most compassionate woman Ellen had ever known. That she was in a jail cell accused of murdering her fiancé seemed impossible. Beyond impossible.

"I wanted to let you know what's going on before you see her," Danny said. "She's a mess, Ellen. Just wanted to let you know."

They stood and he led her to the entrance of the Hollywood Police Department. Ellen sat in the waiting area as Danny arranged to take her back to the jail.

"You'll have to leave that here," he said, indicating Ellen's purse. She handed it across the counter to the desk sergeant, who handed her a claim check to return her purse after her visit. She followed Danny down a long corridor, through a door, to another hallway lined with jail cells. A man was lying on the floor in the second cell they passed. The stink of urine and alcohol hit her like a slap in the face.

"He's a pastor," Danny said, nodding to the unconscious man. "Sad."

They passed a cell holding a couple of hard looking women. The redhead Ellen thought she recognized.

"The oldest profession with a new twist," Danny said. "They call her the Medium Madame. She can tell a man's future with amazing accuracy."

Despite the seriousness of the situation, Ellen couldn't help but smile. As they approached the last cell, they heard crying.

"I'll be just down the hall if you need me," Danny said, leaving her to walk the short distance on her own. She saw a chair had been placed near the cell and reminded herself to thank Danny for his thoughtfulness.

Connie was sitting on the edge of a steel framed cot, her face buried in her hands, crying softly.

"Connie?"

Connie looked up. Her eyes were red rimmed and puffy, her face swollen and blotchy with grief. There was a smear of something dark and wet on the cuff of her blouse.

"Oh, Ellen," Connie managed, before deep sobs constricted her voice.

"I'm here," Ellen said, pulling up the chair close to the bars that separated them. "Danny, I mean Detective O'Banyon, told me what happened."

"That I shot Lance?" she said excitedly. "I—I—I loved him, Ellen. I would never do anything to hurt him. Never!"

"I know," Ellen said, putting her hand between the bars. Connie's trembling hand in hers was cold and wet with tears. "Tell me what happened."

Connie's version of the events matched Danny's almost identically.

"And the last thing you remember before," she paused to consider how to phrase it, "before you found yourself at the Roosevelt was a conversation with Lance on the phone?"

Connie shut her eyes tight; trying to force away the image of her fiancé sprawled on the hotel room floor, his blood spreading out in a dark pool at her feet. After a long pause, she shook herself and looked at Ellen, holding tight to her friend's hand.

"We were going to try that new place on Highland," she said, in a wavering voice. "Then we were going to drive over to Tiffany's. The last thing… the last thing he said to me? He said, 'I love you, Mrs. Holter'."

With that she broke down, sobbing so violently that Danny made a move toward them. Ellen put up her hand to stop him.

"It'll be all right," Ellen said. "We'll find a way to make it right."

When Connie was able to settle herself, she looked up into her friend's kind and worried eyes. "Would you…could you…ask her if she would help me?" Connie asked.

"Domino Lady?" Ellen said.

"Yes," Connie said. "I think she's my only hope, Ellen. If anyone can help me, it's her."

Ellen gave Connie's hand a reassuring squeeze. "I can promise you, honey. The Lady is already on the case."

The cab ride from the police station to her apartment seemed to take forever. There was the snarl typical of late afternoon traffic, but in her heightened state of agitation, time itself seemed to mock her. She was a woman poised for action. She'd been advised—more than once—to be less rash and reactive and take more time to weigh and consider her actions. Good advice, she would have to admit. But sitting in this damned cab, wasting time she should be using to help her dear friend, as it crawled through bumper to bumper congestion made her antsy, anxious and heartsick. Connie was innocent. Of this Ellen had not doubt. How to prove it, that was the looming task. She had been caught, red handed, so to speak, with the smoking gun. And her only defense? "I don't know how I got here. I don't know what happened." It really was no defense at all. *Come on*, Ellen thought to herself, *move it!* If she thought getting out of the cab and hoofing it would get her home quicker, she'd have done it.

Every murder has a motive. Even those that seem random and driven by unchecked or uncontrolled emotion have some kind of motive behind them. But this murder? Where was the motive? She knew, without a doubt, Connie was innocent, consequently, she had been framed. Who hated Connie and Lance enough to destroy both of their lives? Was hatred the motive? Hatred over what? Of whom? And why...?

The cab pulled up in front of Ellen's apartment. She paid the cabby and headed to the entrance. Her favorite doorman, McNeil, was on duty.

"Afternoon, Miss Patrick," he called, moving to the door to open it for her.

"Good afternoon, Nick," she replied, using her nickname for him. "What's shakin'?"

"Lois and Burt had their baby," he reported. "Girl. Seven pounds, three ounces. And Mrs. Alsop accidently flushed her dentures down the toilet, again."

"She should buy them by the dozen," Ellen said, smiling. "Or keep her head out of the john."

She picked up her mail and headed upstairs. She made a quick call, changed clothes, and was in her car and on the road in less than half an hour. Traffic had eased and she was over the hill and into Studio City in forty minutes. A short jog down Ventura Boulevard, a left on Willis to Natick Avenue. She slowed as she neared a small, white clapboard bungalow, pulled into the long narrow driveway and into a garage, its doors open, ready for her arrival.

As she entered the back door that led into the kitchen she called, "Mrs. M.?"

"Ah, the Lady arriveth," a voice from the living room responded.

Domino Lady had a web of informants that stretched from one end of the state to the other with its most intricate weaving covering Los Angeles and its surrounding areas. But the person most responsible for maintaining the web and reading the twitch and tremble of each strand of webbing was Mrs. Eliza Morse. When Ellen first adopted her crime fighting alter ego, Mrs. Morse was there. Their history was a complicated one, to say the least. It was solving the murder of Mrs. Morse's only daughter—a solution which nearly cost Ellen, as Domino Lady, her own life—that sealed the women's relationship.

"I just made a shaker of martinis, if you want one. On the counter by the toaster."

Ellen paused, considered the offer, declined and headed into the living room. The entire north facing wall was a map of California; the west wall, a detailed map of L.A. and surrounding cities. Lengths of different colored thread crisscrossed both, secured by color coded pins. File cabinets lined the east wall, each stacked with color coded folders. Smack dab in the middle of the room, seated behind a mammoth mahogany desk, was the venerable Mrs. Morse. She was a generously proportioned woman, in her middle fifties with hair a shade of red not found in nature. She smiled as she watched Ellen settle into the only chair not doubling as storage unit. Although Mrs. Morse had lived in the states for thirty years, her English accent was as crisp and lilting as the day she got off the boat.

"Terrible that, about Connie," Mrs. Morse said.

"It makes no sense," Ellen said. She was going to tell Mrs. Morse about her visit at the jail when one of the half dozen phones arranged at the parameters of Mrs. Morse's desk rang.

"Hello."

She listened. Nodded. Looked over at Ellen. "Good," she said. "Thanks. Keep me posted," and hung up.

"What?" Ellen asked.

"I think the Domino Lady might want to pay Mr. Bradley Holter a visit," Mrs. Morse said.

"Lance's brother?" Ellen asked.

"The very same. He's been at the Five O'clock Club most of the afternoon. Seems he has a theory about his brother's murder. And he hasn't been shy about sharing it."

Ellen had not met Lance's brother but had heard plenty about him from Connie. None of it good.

"Might be better for the Lady to go in disguise," Ellen said. "He might be more inclined to share his view with a lonely, slightly tipsy escort."

"Lola?" Mrs. Morse offered.

"Lola," Ellen confirmed.

Ellen got up and made her way to a room at the far back of the house. It was simply furnished, with a bed and nightstand against one wall. Across from it was a long, narrow, multi-drawer desk. A lighted mirror on the wall occupied the center of the desk facing a swivel chair. Various bottles and jars were arranged neatly at either side. She went to the built in closet and opened its folding doors. To the right were hung a dozen Domino Lady outfits in her signature white, low cut, thigh-high slit gowns. To the left was a collection of costumes that would make any theater company bristle with envy. She selected a slinky red satin halter with a plunging neckline just this side of legal. From the overhead shelf she took down a hat box, set it on the bed and removed a long, auburn wig. Some minutes later she rejoined Mrs. Morse in the living room.

"Good evening, Lola," Mrs. Morse said.

"Good evening, Mrs. Morse, honey," Ellen said in the tuneful drawl of a southern belle. "He still there?"

"Jimmy said he's unlikely to be going anywhere under his own steam," reporting what the bartender at the Five O'clock, a reliable member of Domino Lady network, confirmed moments previously. "Your cab is wait-ing."

Ellen sauntered to the front door and blew Mrs. Morse a kiss.

"Why is it, every time I see you walk in that dress, I hear conga music?" Mrs. Morse said.

Ellen laughed," Don't wait up," she said, closing the door behind her.

Heads turned in lusty appreciation as the slinky redhead sauntered into the Five O'clock. A man sitting by the entrance was so taken with Lola, a.k.a., Ellen Patrick, if he would have been a little shorter you would have been able to hear his jaw drop with a thud onto the table at which he was seated. Jimmy, the bartender, caught Ellen's eye and nodded to the slope shouldered man sitting at the bar. She winked, and swayed ever so slightly, as if she'd had a couple earlier, on her way to the bar, each step a drum beat of erotic rhythm.

She took the bar stool one away from the man Jimmy had indicated.

"What'll you have, doll," Jimmy asked.

"Why," Ellen said, "I'll have what handsome here is having," nodding to Lance's brother, Brad, who at that moment, seemed to become aware of Ellen's presence. It took him a moment for him to focus: when he did, his grin spread from ear to booze flushed ear.

"Whiskey Collins," Brad said, "Two."

Jimmy nodded and moved a few feet down to make the drinks, being sure to substitute iced tea for the whiskey in Ellen's drink.

"I'm Lola Louise," Ellen said in a slow southern drawl, extending her hand.

Brad took her hand, held it firmly, lightly massaging his index finger against the underside of her wrist. The hungry look in his eye and the feel of his touch made her skin crawl, but she stayed fully in character.

She selected a slinky red satin halter...

"I'm Brad," he said. "It is my *pleasure* to meet you, Lola." He put a spin on the word *pleasure* that was so sophomorically loaded with double entendre, she almost laughed out loud. He looked like he could be Lance's twin but with all his features dulled and softened. And there was a thickness about him that spoke of years of an over fondness of alcohol.

"Likewise, honey," she said, as Jimmy placed their drinks in front of them.

For the next few minutes, she flirted with him, teased him, led him around their conversation as if she had a leash tied around his manhood. Then she let her expression go dark.

"Just terrible about what happened today," she began. "I was at the Roosevelt, visiting a special friend? When they said that someone went and got murdered. Right there in the hotel. Right in his own room." She shuddered at the memory.

His expression changed so dramatically, she thought he might be having a stroke.

"That was my brother!" he said. "That was my brother that got murdered by that bitch!" He turned to his drink, sucked down the last of it and motioned to Jimmy for another.

"Oh, honey, I'm so sorry. So very sorry. I didn't know," she said, reaching out to put a sympathetic hand on his knee. Even in his grief, the gesture was not lost on him. He covered her hand with his own and moved it higher on his leg a couple of inches.

"If you don't want to talk about it," she said, looking into his eyes.

That's all she needed to say for Brad to launch into his theory of the crime. According to Brad, Lance had been carrying on an affair with a woman named Iris London. The affair had been going on for some time and there was talk about them marrying if Iris could get a divorce. Iris' husband would grant her a divorce on one condition: she'd have to buy it from him. For ten thousand dollars she could be a free woman. Lance didn't have a hundred bucks, let alone ten grand, but he knew where he could get it. When Connie's father died, he left her a small fortune. The plan was for Lance to marry Connie, stay married long enough to make an annulment impossible, divorce her, take half of her inheritance in the settlement, give ten thousand to Iris' husband so she and Lance could finally be married. And it would have worked, if that bitch, Connie Lundgren, hadn't found out.

"She followed him to the hotel where she knew he was with Iris, waited until Iris left the room and then went in and shot him," Brad said.

"No!" Ellen said, in shocked disbelief.

"Yes!" Brad said. "And you know what?"

"I'm sure I don't, honey," Ellen said trying to slide her hand from beneath Brad's.

"When the cops found her? Found her holding the gun? Found her holding the gun standing over my brother's bleeding body? You know what she said?"

"No, honey, I'm sure I don't."

"She said she didn't know how she even got there. Didn't know anything about it. She said when the cop came in and set her down in a chair and took the smoking gun from her hand, that it was all news to her. Like she had some kind of episode. Some kind of amnesia! What a load! She thinks just because she'd got a bunch of dough, she's going to buy her way out of it? No way. No goddamn way. I'll see that bitch fry before I let that happen!"

"Oh, honey," Ellen said, full of compassion. She mustered up a tear, reached into her purse, withdrew a small, lace trimmed handkerchief and dabbed at the corner of her eyes. "Oh, honey, that's the saddest thing I ever heard."

She snuffled, dabbed, and excused herself to go to the ladies' room and collect herself. She'd be right back. She walked to the end of the bar, made a right down a hallway where the restrooms were located, and kept walking out the back door to a cab that Jimmy had called earlier at Ellen's signal.

As they drove to the Studio City house, she thought about what Brad had said. As crazy as it was—and knowing Connie as she did, it was plenty damn crazy—there was probably something to it. At least the part about Lance's affair. At least, it was a place to start looking. She'd have Mrs. Morse start digging into it first thing in the morning.

By mid morning of the following day, Mrs. Morse had compiled a substantial dossier on the Londons. Iris London was an artist's model having posed for cover art for magazines like *Master Detective*, *Thrilling Detective*, *Inside Detective* and *Spicy Detective*. Despite her marital status, she'd had several high profile affairs with men of power and influence in finance and show business. Now, in her mid thirties, both her career as an artist's muse and as a good-time companion were fading with her youth. Joseph London had been in and out of trouble with the law since his teens. There was almost no criminal activity that he had not been rumored to have been involved in or convicted of. Now, in his middle fifties, Joe had focused his nefarious endeavors to breaking and entering, shake-downs and blackmail.

Ellen's network had been shadowing Joe for most of the day. He visited his wife at her apartment just off of Franklin Avenue and stayed for an hour. From there he went to Jerkin's Tool and Die, a favorite spot for men of Joe's avocation for unloading stolen goods to be resold throughout Los Angeles in pawn shops and back-alley outlets. After two and a half hours in Jerkin's, he moved to Tully's Bar and Grill on the corner of Sunset and Western where he spent the remainder of the day. At seven-thirty, he went to his car, a little unsteady on his feet, opened the trunk, removed a large canvas bag, put it on the passenger's seat and drove off.

As he exited the highway, a burgundy Mercedes-Benz 500 K Roadster followed judiciously behind him. He parked on Olivia Avenue and walked through Grant Park, carrying a cloth bag that looked like a child-sized pillow case, to the alley behind Ellingsworth and Company, a small jewelry manufacturer specializing in simple wedding bands and earrings. It took him fifteen minutes to disable the alarm and break into the back door. He was inside the building for nearly half an hour. He exited with the bag nearly full and retraced his steps.

He had gotten about halfway through the park when he heard, "Hello, Joe. What do you know?"

He stopped dead in his tracks. From behind an old oak stepped a vision of spectral loveliness. She was tall, and dressed in a white satin gown that caressed each of her abundant curves as if it were a second skin. The bodice was cut daringly low, exposing the half-moons of full round breasts. A slit that ran up her hips nearly to her waist revealed long elegant legs. Her hair was long and shimmered golden in the pale moon, a playful curl cascading over her shoulders. She wore a black domino mask that framed her large blues eyes.

"Domino Lady," he said with a gasp.

"Joe London," she replied. "What you got there, Joey?"

She watched him weighing his options. She raised her hand, making sure he saw the chrome-plated .38 Special. Then she watched him reconsider his options. When it looked like had, he smiled, raised his hands in surrender and walked slowly toward her. Now, just a few feet from her, he reeled back and tried to slam the bag into her skull. Domino Lady ducked the assault with ease, came up fast, turned and hammered a judo chop to his Adam's apple. He made a thick choking sound, dropped the bag and collapsed to his knees, grabbing his throat in both hands. Domino Lady, scooching the bag toward her, adopted a casual stance and gave him a moment to recover.

"Let's talk about Lance Holter," she said.

"Who?" he wheezed.

"Please, Joe. Let's not play that game. You don't have the time. The cops will be here in twenty minutes. You can tell me what I want to know before they get her or after they get here. Up to you, Joey."

He tried to get up, but she dissuaded him with a wave of the .38.

"Lance Holter?" she said. "You know, the guy you were going to let marry your wife if he paid you ten grand?"

The look on his face told her she was on the right track.

"It wasn't like that," he said as if he had a throat full of sand.

"Tell me what it was like," she said. "Tick-tock. Tick-tock."

"Look," he said. "Iris and Holter palled around together for a while. Nothing serious. He had some dough and liked spending it on Iris and she liked having it spent. But then we find out it ain't his. He ain't got a pot to piss in. It's all coming from his fiancé. And he's got, you know, *secrets*. I been around awhile. Hard to shock me. I seen it all. But that guy? That guy took the cake for weird. I mean *weird*. So me and Iris, we figure he's going to want to keep things going with her 'cause she makes him think she's into his sick stuff, *and* he's going to want to keep his secrets secret, from his fiancée, until after they're married, at least. Then, when it's good and stuck, he divorces her and walks away with a boat of scratch. He gives Iris the ten and she dumps him. Simple, see?"

"Simple," Domino Lady repeated. "What do you know about his murder?"

"Nothing that ain't been bouncing around town," he said. "She found out, went to the hotel and shot him and then came up with this blank-out scheme. Now she's sitting in jail. But not for long. Her bail hearing is tomorrow. And with that kind of dough, she'll be out and living the good life in her Beverly Hills mansion like nothing ever happened. Poor folks get a kick in the ass. Rich folks get a pass. That's how it is. That's how it's always going to be."

Domino Lady dipped at her knees, picked up the bag, reached inside, grabbed a handful of rings and earrings and tossed them into the grass near Joe's knee.

"If I were you, Joe? I'd look into another line of work," she hoisted the bag over her shoulder and backed down the path until he was out of sight.

By the time she got to her car, she'd removed the mask and secured her hair into a ponytail. She put the bag in the trunk, took out a long, hooded dark overcoat, slipped into it and slid behind the wheel, starting the engine. As she turned off of Olivia Avenue, she was passed by a squad car with its lights off.

Connie's bail hearing was over in twenty minutes. There were no objections. Bail was set at fifty thousand dollars and she was asked to relinquish her passport. Not that anyone thought she was much of a flight risk. She looked wretched. In the two days she'd been in jail, she seemed to have lost ten pounds. There were dark circles under her red, swollen eyes. There was a noticeable tremor in her hands as she took up a glass of water for a drink. The murder of Lance Holter seemed more of an unfortunate event than a capital crime. Everyone in attendance acted as if the real victim in this case was Connie Lundgren. The poor girl lost her true love. Was charged with a crime she could not have possibly committed. And would have to live with the horrible, crippling guilt that she was not able to bear witness to the event which, in essence, would allow the real villain to go free.

"Just look at the poor thing," Ellen heard a spectator say. "It doesn't look as if she could hurt a fly, let alone kill the man she loved. Poor thing."

As Connie was being guided out of the courtroom by her attorney, she saw Ellen and smiled. Ellen returned the smile and put her hand over her heart and blew her friend a kiss. Tears welled in Connie's eyes as she passed out of the courtroom doors.

The courtroom steps were thick with reporters. The instant they saw Connie coming down the stairs, they seemed to swell like a dry sponge sprayed with water. Questions were thrown at her in rapid fire. Loud. Harsh. Brutal. Her lawyer held her tight to him, guiding her toward a waiting car. Flashbulbs exploded in her face. A particularly aggressive reporter pushed to the front of the group. Ellen recognized him. Skip Larson of the Los Angeles *Herald-Examiner*. He was a nasty little fellow who seemed to thrive on the misery he caused other people. More than once, he wrote scathing editorials about the reckless vigilante, Domino Lady, whom he called, "that maiden of immorality who fights crime dressed as a call-girl, thwarting the legitimate and noble work of the police to satisfy her own twisted need to satiate her thrill-lust."

When he learned that she, Ellen Patrick, was acquainted with the Domino Lady, he took after her with the same poisonous pen.

"There is no doubt that we are judged by the company we keep. Miss Patrick has chosen to associate herself with a woman of the lowest moral standards. Can it be long in coming that we shall begin to see Miss Patrick parading around town, like her comrade, in an outfit so scandalous, the Hays Commission would be forced to publicly censor her if she were to appear on film," he wrote.

"Connie! Connie," Skip yelled. "Isn't it true you murdered your fiancé when you discovered he was cheating on you? Can you comment on his wild weekends in Mexico?"

Connie glared at the reporter. Suddenly, her eyes rolled back in her head and she collapsed into her attorney's arms. He had to carry her to the car. A nearby policeman helped him ease her in the back seat. As soon as the door was closed, the car sped away. Ellen promised herself, Skip Larson and Domino Lady would meet soon and sort out a few things.

"So," Detective Danny O'Boylan said, sidling up to Ellen as she waited for a cab. "What did you make of all that?"

"Make of what?" she said a little more sharply than she intended. "Skip Larson is an asshole. That's what I make of it."

"No, not that," Danny said. "The hearing."

"What about it?" she asked.

"Ever seen a hearing that quick?" he said. "Over and done in less than half an hour. And Holter was barely mentioned."

"What are you getting at?" Ellen said, not caring if her annoyance showed.

"You have time for a cup of coffee?" he asked.

"Why?" she asked warily.

"There's a few things about this case that might be of interest to you," he said.

She felt like saying, "You mean about Iris and Joe London and the shake-down for ten grand?" But she mentally took a deep breath, waved the approaching cab off and turned to him, with what she hoped looked like concern.

"About Connie?" she said.

"About the whole damn mess," he said. "Murder and money. Never a good mix."

He offered her his arm and together they walked the half block to Ruby's Café. From the outside it looked like a dive. On the inside, it *was* a dive. What it lacked in décor and ambience, it more than made up for with the best fresh brewed coffee in the city and a sweet roll that could not be beat this side of the Rockies. They found a booth in the back, near the kitchen, ordered, waited until their order came a few minutes later, and then settled in.

"Okay, spill, detective," Ellen said playfully.

"I'm going to assume you already know about the shake-down," he said, taking a sip of coffee.

She tried to look surprised, but he knew her too well, and gave it up.

"And Iris and Joe London?" he pressed on.

Her smile told him everything he needed to know.

"You amaze me, Miss Patrick. You really do."

"So, tell me something I don't know," she said.

"You know why we can't track down how Connie got to the hotel that afternoon?"

As soon as he said it, she knew.

"Because she was in the hotel already? Spent the night?"

"Yep," he said. "With?"

She thought about it for half a second. "No clue," she said. "Her fiancé?"

"Nope."

She reached under the table and gave his inner thigh a pinch that made him wince.

"Iris London," he said, rubbing at the sore spot.

"You're kidding!" she blurted.

"I kid you not," he said, with good natured smugness.

She sat back in her chair with her cup of coffee and let it sink in.

"Well, I'll be," she said softly.

"Well, I'll be one with you," he said. "Who do you suppose the gun is registered to?"

"Iris London?"

"Lance Holter."

She made a show of letting her jaw drop.

"It gets better, or worse, depending on your perspective."

She raised her hand and made a pinching gesture difficult to misinterpret.

"Connie and Iris spent the night together," he said. "Lance stayed the night in the hotel, as well." Here he paused. "But not alone."

Again, she mimed a vicious pinch. "With?" she prodded.

"Anne Susan Lundgren," he said.

"Who?"

"Connie's sixteen year old daughter."

Danny and Ellen agreed to meet for dinner the following evening. Danny had to get back to the station, and Ellen had to get in touch with Mrs. Morse as soon as possible. Connie had a daughter? Ellen did the math. Connie Lundgren was eleven years older than Ellen. Connie often joked that she was a late bloomer. The difference in their ages never seemed to be an issue between them. In some ways, it balanced things out. Ellen was always mature beyond her years and Connie seemed stuck in her late teens. Connie had a sixteen year old daughter which meant that she was a mother at seventeen, long before Ellen met and befriended her.

Not once did Connie mention anything about having a kid. So far as Ellen knew, Connie was the only child of two devoted, loving and supportive parents. That she came from money was never part of who she was. She never put on airs. Often she said, "It's my parents' money, not mine." And that's how she lived. Making her own way on her own terms.

As their lives went in different directions, they drifted apart, as is only natural, but they still kept in touch with the occasional phone call or letter. And Connie never failed to ring up Ellen on her birthday, no matter where she was in the world.

On Ellen's twentieth birthday Connie called, "Happy birthday, kiddo!" she sang.

"Where are you?" Ellen asked, the static being so dense on the line it was difficult to hear what her friend was saying.

"India!" Connie said loudly. "I just now got off an elephant and I'm in love!"

"Really? Who's the lucky fellow?"

"His name is Raj. Five thousand pounds of handsome!" Connie said, laughingly.

So, Connie had a sixteen year old daughter. It was becoming clearer with each passing day that the Connie Ellen had known as a teenager was not the same person she knew now.

Back at the apartment she called Mrs. Morse and filled her in.

"Find out what you can," Ellen said, "Anything you can and get back to me."

She called Connie a dozen times that day and always got the same response. Connie was not taking calls under doctor's advice. She was sedated and trying to recover from her ordeal. Would…what was it? Miss Patrick? Would Miss Patrick like to leave a message?

Ellen decided it was time that she and Iris London have a chat. With some help from Mrs. Morse, she knew that Iris would be modeling at a

Life Drawing class at Los Angeles Junior College from 6:00 to 8:00. She planned to be there when Iris returned home.

It was seven o'clock. A light drizzle had begun. Ellen was on the road, top up, wipers swishing back and forth to a tune Ellen had stuck in her head. She decided to take Laurel Canyon Boulevard over into Hollywood to the Franklin Arms. At the crest of the hill, a pair of headlights swung into view behind her. Within seconds they were up on her and so close she could see the faces of the two men behind their windshield. She knew muscle when she saw it, and these two guys had muscle written all over them. Had the road not been so slick, she would have tried to out maneuver them. Ellen was an exceptional driver and knew this stretch of road like the back of her hand. But in these conditions, at night, it would be foolhardy to try anything.

Just around the bend was narrow road that went up into the hills, curved through several rustic vacation cabin spots, and down to a small bridge that would take her through to a rarely used exit back on the Laurel Canyon Boulevard. There were so many switchbacks and tight turns; it would be a miracle if her pursuers could keep up. And all she needed now was a little distance.

She made the turn, her tires screeching on the wet pavement. She watched the big, late model Buick fishtail as it made the turn. Within a couple of blocks she was already gaining ground. Two tight turns ahead and into a long narrow stretch that would take her down into the city.

She made the first turn and felt her back tires struggle for traction. Heading into the second turn, she saw with alarm that the road was blocked by a downed tree. She was trapped. No going back and no going forward. The headlights of the Buick caught her just as she exited the car, and she started running down the road toward the fallen tree.

The crack of gun fire sounded like a canon as it echoed off the surrounding forest. An explosion of shattered bark sent dust and debris into her eyes, making it hard for her to see. She felt the suck of air over her right shoulder with the second shot. She stopped, turned and put up her hands in surrender. Better to capitulate now and figure a way out than be dead in the middle of nowhere. Lucky for her, she thought, that she hadn't changed into her Domino Lady outfit yet. It, with her .38, was in a bag in the trunk.

They were after her, Ellen Patrick, not her alter ego, Domino Lady. What did that mean? One bruiser stood some feet away, the pistol trained on her. The other, a man the size of an industrial refrigerator, walked toward her, a smirk on his fist-hammered face. He said nothing but grabbed her arm and walked her to the Buick. He shoved her into the back seat and got in beside her as the other mug got behind the wheel. She smelled it before she saw it. She knew what it was, she'd used chloroform herself on several occasions. He brought the chloroform soaked cloth up and pressed it hard again her nose and mouth. She pretended to struggle, as he would expect her to do. But she made a point to hold her breath as long as she could and then feign unconsciousness. She was starting to get light-headed, that's when she went limp as a wet rag and slumped onto the seat.

"She's out," the guy with the chloroform said.

"If it hadn't been for that tree, she would have gotten away," the driver said. "And there would have been hell to pay."

"Amen to that," his partner said.

They pulled up into a cabin's rutted driveway, turned around and headed back to Laurel Canyon Boulevard. But instead of heading back into the valley, they continued down toward Hollywood. At Sunset, they turned right, drove another twenty minutes, pulling into a long, gravel driveway. Ellen felt the car turn onto a smooth turn-about where the car came to a stop. The guy with her in the back seat got out and lifted her from the car as if she were a child's toy. She stirred a little to let him know she was beginning to come out of it. He quickened his pace up to an entry way, through an open door, through a living room, down a dark hallway to a side room. He laid her on a bed that smelled musty of disuse.

"Nighty night," he said sarcastically and left, closing and locking the door behind him.

Sure she was alone; she sat up and tried to get her bearings. It was too dark for her to know anything about where she was. What she did know was that she was in a mess of trouble.

She could hear the faint sounds of people moving around in the living room down the hall. Every now and then a snippet of a conversation.

"You were lucky," she heard a man say. Then a response she couldn't make out. She eased off the bed to the window and cracked open the shade. The window looked out over a kind of patio. There were two chairs with a small table between them. She undid the window latch. The window was swollen shut from the rain, but it could be lifted when she put some muscle behind it. She heard footsteps coming down the hall, got back onto the bed and lay very still. The footsteps stopped just outside the door. She heard a key slide into the lock and, with a turn, the tumblers disengaged. The door opened slowly. Light from the hall fell in a distended rectangle

...she started running down the road...

across her, then a shadow within that rectangle told her she was being studied.

"Miss Patrick?"

The voice was soft and impossible to tell if it was male or female. Ellen stirred as if trying to lift herself to consciousness.

"What?" she said feebly. "What? Where am I?"

"You're safe, Miss Patrick," the voice said, coming into the room. The door closed, sending the room once again into darkness. She heard footsteps cross the room and the creak of a chair as her visitor settled into it.

"I apologize for any inconvenience," he said. Yes, it was a man. "But I needed to speak with you, and I wasn't sure you'd be willing to indulge me. Again, my sincerest apologies."

Ellen made of show of struggling to a sitting position.

"I don't understand," she said.

"Connie has been accused of some terrible things. Libelous things," he began. "When it gets out, as it will, as it always does, public opinion will be against her. In a court of law, public opinion can't matter. But it does. You're a friend of hers. You know her. But I'm guessing, by what you've been recently been told, you're not sure you know her at all."

"I'm confused," Ellen said.

"Of course you are," he said. "You know a good many influential people; one particularly influential person. I'm hoping, at the conclusion of our conversation, you will use your influence to help Connie in her struggle to clear her name and the charge of murder against her."

"And how do you plan to go about that?" Ellen asked.

"By telling you the truth."

Ellen settled herself, becoming more alert. "What happens after our *conversation*?" she asked.

"You will be returned to your car to do with the information I provide you as you please."

They were silent for a long moment. She heard the rolling song of chorus frogs nearby.

"Okay." She said.

"Okay," he said. "Did you know Connie has a twin sister?"

"What?" Ellen said with genuine surprise.

"I didn't think you did. I dare say not more than a handful of people do," he said. She heard him turn in his chair. There was a flare of a match, blocked by the back of his head. He'd lit a cigarette with his back to her to keep his identity in as deep a shadow as was the room. With the cigarette lit and the match extinguished, he turned to face her. As he took a long drag, the increased glow of its burning tip did nothing to illuminate her visitor.

"From an early age Cindy evidenced behavioral issues, which is a charitable way to put it. At seventeen, she ran away with a boy. Six months later she was back. At eighteen she gave birth to a daughter, Anne Susan Lundgren. Shortly after the baby was born, she again ran away. Cindy has been in and out of various institutions her entire life. She is now in upstate New York living in a facility where her condition can be treated humanely.

"Connie does not have a daughter," he said. The revelation of a child? The child is Cindy's, not Connie's. Uncovering the past is an imperfect activity, as you shall see," he took another deep pull on his cigarette, suppressed a cough and continued. "Lance Holter. I have to be quite honest and tell you I did not like Mr. Holter. But I was not engaged to be married to him, so what I think is of little consequence. Connie is a true innocent and easily manipulated by someone more worldly, shall we say? If his relationship with Iris London were as simple as a sexual affair, we'd be lucky. But, to be blunt, Miss Patrick, Mr. Holter was a junkie. And Iris London was his source, through her husband, Joseph. When Connie discovered the truth, she supplied Mr. Holter with the money to purchase his drugs. It seemed the lesser of several evils. The plan was, after they were married, he would undergo treatment to free him from his addiction. Are you with me so far?"

"Yes," Ellen said.

She watched the glowing end of the cigarette drop to the floor and heard a faint sizzle as it was extinguished in a wet spot on the floor.

"She was advised, most strongly, to break off the engagement, but you know Connie, there is no one more loyal to her friends and loved ones, despite the cost to her.

"We must go to the night before Mr. Holter's death to understand what happened." He took a deep breath, exhaling slowly, as if he anticipated the telling would exhaust him. "Connie received a call from Iris London to meet her at the Roosevelt Hotel. When she arrived, she was told that in addition to supplying Mr. Holter with his drugs, there would be an additional cost of ten thousand dollars to keep the whole thing under wraps. Blackmail, plain and simple. Connie knew what such a revelation would mean to her and her family, especially so close to the wedding, and decided to pay it.

"She also learned that her fiancé was staying at the hotel that same evening, in room 256. He was suffering from withdrawal. Sick and vomiting. He could be made right with a fix that Iris would be willing to provide, but she'd need half of the ten grand to comply. Connie had seen Mr. Holter in that condition only once. The thought of his going through it again made her heartsick. She agreed.

"Connie made a few calls from Iris' room, which led to her making a critically unfortunate choice. The money could not be delivered until the next afternoon, but it would be delivered. When Iris was certain she and Joseph would be paid, she went to Mr. Holter's room and advanced him enough of the drug to see him through to the next morning.

"Connie had kept in touch with her niece who had been living with a caring family for the past few years. Connie's parents had disowned the girl; transferring the sin of the mother to the child. Despite their objections, Connie maintained a loving and supportive relationship with the girl. Connie was rightfully apprehensive about the money being delivered to the hotel. And this is where she made her fatal mistake. Rather than ask someone like myself to arrange the delivery, she enlisted her niece, Anne Susan, to bring a package to the hotel. The girl knew nothing, only that her aunt asked a favor for which she was only too happy to comply."

Ellen was sitting Indian style on the bed, her elbows on her knees, chin on her fists, attentive to her visitor's every word.

"This is where cruel irony comes into play. If that is in fact the right term," he continued. "Anne Susan went to the front desk and asked for the room number of Connie Lundgren. Iris had booked her room under her own name but had booked Mr. Holter's room under Connie's name. The girl took the stairs up to the second floor to room 256. She knocked, heard someone in the room. There was no answer. She tried the door and found it unlocked. She eased into the room and saw a man sitting on the edge of the bed rocking back and forth, muttering to himself. He was disheveled; stains of vomit covered his shirt front. She turned to go. Mr. Holter—seeing the girl for the first time, and the package in her hand—thought she was delivering his fix. He lunged at her, blocking the door. She ran across the room. He caught her by the arm and began yelling at her. He had her pinned between the dresser and the wall. The girl was terrified, as you might imagine. He started shaking her, violently. Anne Susan saw a pistol atop the dresser next to his wallet and watch. She grabbed the pistol, begging him to move away. It looked like he was going to try and choke her. And that's when she shot him.

"Connie, being informed by the front desk there was a Miss Anne Lundgren on her way to her room, 256, panicked and ran down the stairs when she heard the sound of a gunshot and the girl's scream. Throwing the door open, she found Mr. Holter on the floor bleeding profusely. Her niece, in shock, standing with the smoking gun. She took the gun from the girl's hand and told her to go to room 316.

"'Go now!' Connie said urgently.

"The girl took off running just as the police officer arrived at the second floor landing. And the rest you know, I think."

"But who called the police? If it was an accident as you say, how could someone have called the cops in advance? A call came in at one-twenty and the murder happened at two."

"What I suspect," he said. "And this is only speculation on my part, because, at this point, I really can't say for certain. But I suspect that the call was a fabrication. Officer Dave Meadows may have been at the hotel for reasons of a non-official nature. It's not uncommon for the boys in blue to massage an event in support of a brother officer. But as I said, you know the rest, I think."

"He found Connie standing alone in the room with the murder weapon in her hand and her dead fiancé at her feet?" Ellen said.

"Exactly," he said. "That's the whole of it. Connie can't reveal the truth without involving her niece in a life altering scandal."

"And so, she took the blame," Ellen said.

"Yes, Miss Patrick. She did."

He walked toward her on the bed and handed her a black cloth hood. After she had it on, he led her out of the room, down the hall to the front door.

"I hope I can count on your help," he said. "She's going to need every bit she can get from all of us."

With that, someone held her arm and led her down the stairs to a waiting car. She was joined in the back seat by one of the two men who abducted her. A half an hour later, the car stopped and her hood was removed. Her car was bathed in the beam of the Buick's headlights, just where she'd left it. The two mugs drove off, leaving her alone in the brooding gloom of the forest. She got in behind the wheel, started the ignition, backed up into a driveway and headed for home.

Her mind was abuzz with what she'd just been told. As complicated a tale as it was, it was easier to believe than the alternative. The innuendo that Connie was somehow *involved* with Iris London? That Lance Holter had been having some kind of illicit affair with Connie's sixteen years old daughter? Or, that Lance was going to convince Connie to give him ten thousand dollars for which he would buy Iris' divorce and, after a suitable time, marry and divorce Connie, take half her fortune and then marry Iris? The version her abductor laid out, as convoluted as it sounded, actually made more sense and lined up more in keeping with the Connie she knew than the woman whose character had been perverted by rumor.

She walked into her living room at half past one in the morning and dialed Mrs. Morse.

"Hello," her voice was sharp and alert.

"Why aren't you asleep?" Ellen asked.

"Why aren't you?" Mrs. Morse returned.

And Ellen spent the next hour telling Mrs. Morse why.

Ellen managed a couple of hours sleep but it was a troubled, erratic sleep. The events of the past few days replayed in her mind like a broken record, over and over. It kept skipping back on itself until none of it made sense. A couple cups of strong coffee helped clear the fog a little, but with heightened clarity, more questions arose. At nine Mrs. Morse called.

"Officially," she said, "there is no Anne Susan Lundgren."

"What?"

"As far as I've been able to research, and granted, I'm still in the early stages," Mrs. Morse said, "but there is no birth certificate for a girl of Anne's name, age or general location of birth anywhere I've looked. Unless she was a home birth."

"Which seems highly unlikely, given who the Lundgrens are," Ellen said.

"I agree," Mrs. Morse said. "What are your plans for today?"

"I'm going to see if I can find the place I was taken to last night. Not to confront them, mind you, just to see if I can track down who owns the place and from there figure out who he is."

"The man who told you Connie's *true* story?" Mrs. Morse asked.

"I need to know what his connection to all this is," Ellen said. "Later, I'm going to pay Joe and Iris a visit. They're in every version and I think somehow much of this hinges on them."

"Be careful," Mrs. Morse encouraged. "This whole thing has got me a little jumpy."

"Me too," Ellen concurred.

They agreed to touch base later in the day and hung up.

She had a vague idea of where the place was and drove up and down Sunset toward Malibu with no luck. Unless she misremembered the twists and turns they took, which was more than possible considering she had been slightly affected by the chloroform, that little house at the end of the long gravel driveway had disappeared. For all she knew, they could have just driven around the block for half an hour and pulled into a place of Santa Monica.

It was getting late, and she needed to prepare for her evening's activities.

Joe London lived on the second floor in an apartment in the Toluca Lake district. To say the place had seen better days would have been an understatement. It had clearly been built before the development of Toluca Lake Park and would most likely not survive the expansion much longer. She drove around the block several times and saw no sign of Joe's car. She decided to let herself in and wait for him. According to her sources, he had been on a run in Burbank and would be home sometime in the next couple of hours. That would give her time to dig around a little in the man's apartment. Not that she expected to find anything directly related to the Connie Lundgren case, but it wouldn't hurt to look.

It took her less than a minute to pick his lock. It was dark inside the apartment. She hugged herself against the back of the door, stayed perfectly still and listened. Somewhere a faucet dripped and a clock ticked. But there were no other sounds. She made sure all the blinds were drawn, found a side table near an overstuffed chair on which stood a small shaded light and turned it on. The walls were covered in pictures of his wife. Nearly floor to ceiling, images of Iris London, in various states of undress, were pasted up like wallpaper. She had been a strikingly beautiful woman with a flawless figure. Iris as a scantily clad cowgirl. Iris posing as an Indian Princess. Several pictures of Iris, nude, sitting on the edge of a rock overlooking a reflective lake. There was even one of Iris as Joan of Arc, had Joan been inclined to forgo her armor.

Ellen slipped out of the hooded, ankle length coat she sometimes wore when working as Domino Lady. She'd learned that it was always best to reveal herself on her terms than to have a nosy neighbor report a strange woman skulking around in a slinky satin dress and have the cops show up unexpectedly. Domino Lady's relationship with the police was strained at best.

Off to the right of the living room was the kitchen. To the left, a bathroom and a bedroom. It didn't appear that Joe was overly concerned with tidiness or cleanliness. Plates of half-eaten food were stacked in the sink where the leaking faucet wore away a clean spot on a spaghetti encrusted plate. Newspapers were scattered everywhere, some weeks old. She ventured toward the bathroom, the .38 ready in her hand. There was a pile of dirty towels in a heap near the bathtub. The ring that ran around the tub looked as if it had been painted on. The sight of it almost made Ellen wretch. Taking the last few sheets of toilet paper, she closed the lid of the toilet trying not to look into the bowl. From the bathroom, down a short hall to the bedroom. She switched on the light. A blood stain the size of a hubcap spread out across the mattress with a trail of blood leading to the window out to the fire escape.

Domino Lady could not be seen coming out of an apartment where signs of foul play were in evidence. The way this whole thing was playing out, so far as she knew, the cops could already be on their way. She was closing the bedroom window curtain when there was a loud crack and thud as if someone pounded a hammer into the window frame. She dropped to the floor just as a second shot sent a shower of broken glass exploding into the room. She felt dozens of pinches of pain as small shards of glass cut into her exposed back.

She crawled across the floor to the light switch and turned off the light, then down the hall to the living room. Slipping into the coat, she turned off the living room light and eased the door open. Luckily for her, she'd parked the Mercedes away from the streetlight. Her .38 at the ready, she bolted from the apartment, down the stairs, across the walkway to her car. She sped down the street away from the building, checking her rearview mirror for any signs of a pursuer. She didn't let up until she got to the highway.

Her back stung and she had to drive leaning away from the seat. Before she realized where she was, she'd just turned onto Franklin Avenue. Joe was most likely dead or on his way to it. Domino Lady would need to see Iris, if for no other reason, than to warn her. She parked a short distance from the Franklin Arms entrance, walked quickly to the doors, through them and up the stairs to the second floor to Apartment 12B. She left her set of lock picks in the car and so knocked lightly. There was no response. She tried the knob. It turned easily. Cautiously, she opened the door and called Iris' name, her finger on the trigger of the .38. No response. She stood stalk still, listening. A radio played softly from another room. Again, she called the woman's name. And again, no response.

She closed the door and walked into the living room. The walls were painted such a shocking color of pink, she felt a little dizzy. Once she got her bearings and had a look around, it seemed both Joe and Iris shared the same appreciation of her, although Iris' collection of self images was a bit more restrained. Instead of the wallpaper approach from Joe's apartment,

Iris chose movie poster sized images framed in black, thick wood frames. There was no denying, Iris was a beauty, and she was a proud beauty at that.

Again, she called to no reply. She made her way slowly through the living room, sensitive to the slightest sound. Iris' apartment was laid out almost directly opposite that of Joe's. She leaned around into the kitchen. It was spotless. Another framed portrait of Iris as a farm girl with a basket of wheat resting on her hip was hung on the wall opposite the small dining table. Backing out of the kitchen, she headed to the hall that led to the bathroom and bedroom.

The bathroom was done up in shades of peacock blue. The only things that were not color keyed was the faucet, water taps and toilet paper. From the toilet seat to the bathtub plug, everything was blue. That *Blue Orchids* by Glenn Miller was playing on the radio as she exited the bathroom made her smile. The bedroom door was closed. She knocked. No answer. Every bit of her hoped Iris had gone out, suddenly. So suddenly, she'd left her front door open my mistake. Left the radio playing knowing she'd be back soon. Maybe a quick trip to the local market at the end of the block.

As Domino Lady eased open the door, her heart sank in despair. Iris London was propped up in her bed, nude, a bullet hole in the center of her forehead. Her eyes were open and there was an odd, unsettling expression on her face, as if she hadn't quite decided to die just yet. A ribbon of blood ran from the wound to the right at the bridge of her nose and followed the contour of her cheek to the narrow space between her ample breasts. *Strange Fruit* by Billie Holiday came on the radio as Domino Lady went to Iris, put her .38 on the bedside table and pulled the coverlet over her. She hadn't been dead long; there was still warmth to her body.

"Please don't move," a voice came from behind her. She knew that voice but there was something different in it now. There was a coldness, a detached amusement, that seemed to parody the woman she knew.

"Connie?"

"Ellen," Connie said. "Or should I call you Domino Lady? Turn slowly, and please don't make any sudden move to your gun. I really would hate to shoot you. Honestly. I'd just hate that."

Ellen turned slowly. Connie stood in the doorway, a chrome-plated .38 special, identical to one she used, clutched in Connie's unwavering hand.

"I bet you have a lot of questions," Connie said. "Let's go into the living room where we can be more comfortable."

She made her way slowly through the living room.

With the gun, she motioned Ellen out of the bedroom, stepping back to let her pass. Connie took a few steps back to retrieve Ellen's gun from the bedside table, then followed her into the living room, pointing to a chair near an end table, across from a black leather couch. She looked around the room, making a face.

"There's no accounting for taste," Connie said.

She settled back into the couch cushions, keeping the gun trained on Ellen the entire time. "So, did I kill Lance? Yes. Was Lance sleeping with my daughter? Was Lance a drug addict? Was she," Connie said, motioning with the gun to the body in the bedroom, "trying to blackmail me? It gets complicated after that. Would you like a drink? I know I would. It's been one hell of an evening, I can tell you."

Ellen was ready to decline but thought better of it and said that she would like one as well. Connie directed Ellen to a sideboard across the room where there were some bottles of liquor stored and a collection of glasses. Ellen poured them each generous shots of Old Taylor whiskey, placed Connie's on the arm of the couch and took hers back to the chair with her.

"Where to start?" Connie said, more to herself than to Ellen. "Can you take off that mask? It's a little disconcerting."

Ellen removed the mask, placing it on the end table. As Connie took a long drink from her glass, Ellen couldn't shake the feeling that there was something different about this Connie. The same but different. Was it in the way she moved? Spoke? The tone of her voice? The way she held her drink? What was it? What…was…it? Connie seemed captivated by the room. Her attention was focused on a large portrait of Iris as an Island Girl, in a grass skirt, posed mid-hula.

"I will miss her, you know," she said without taking her eyes off the image. She was twisting her ankle distractedly as she spoke. And that's when Ellen saw it, a purple birthmark about the size of a quarter just above the inside ankle of Connie's right foot. The Connie she knew did not have such a birth mark.

"When did Lance know you weren't his Connie?" Ellen asked casually.

Connie turned and looked at Ellen with venom in her eyes.

"She's dead, isn't she, Cindy?" Ellen asked.

Cindy picked up her drink, finished it in a single swallow and threw the glass across the room, shattering it against the far wall.

"The birthmark," Ellen explained, pointing to the spot on Cindy's ankle. "Even identical twins carry some mark of individuality."

Cindy bolted from the couch and backhanded Ellen across the face with the butt of the gun. Ellen tasted blood almost immediately and smiled as Cindy sat.

"Let's see if I can piece this together," Ellen began. "The part about you having the baby is true. Right? The part about you being in and out of institutions is also right. Here's where I think it gets complicated. Somehow or other, you got out of where they had you committed. Here's your sister, the good one, engaged to a nice guy, living a nice life, having everything you don't have or will never have as Cindy Lundgren. But as Connie Lundgren, it's all yours. You killed your sister and took her place. How? I have no idea. Things were going pretty well. You were getting away with it. But then Lance started noticing things. Did he see the birthmark? He was putting two and two together. You introduced Lance to heroin. Already an addictive personality, it wasn't hard to do. As he became more and more dependent on the drug, you lost interest. You became bored. And Iris was, if nothing else, not boring. How am I doing so far?"

Cindy looked amused. She sat back, drew were legs up underneath her and nodded.

"The whole blackmail thing was Joe's idea. You were treating Iris to the good life and Joe wasn't getting any of it. To keep him quiet, you were going to pay him. But as soon as he was out of the picture, and he would be with your help, the money would go to Iris. Were you two planning to run away together? But then the big wrinkle. Anne Susan shows up. She's not living with some caring, loving family. She's in a foster home. And hates it. And hates you. She tracks you down and, with a little digging, discovers what you've been up to. Whether she met up with Lance by accident or design, I have no clue. But they do meet and they begin an affair. You've abandoned Lance, and Anne Susan had no trouble taking your place."

Cindy reached across the couch, picked up Ellen's drink, raised it in a mock toast and finished it off.

"And?" Cindy said.

"And," Ellen continued, "you found out. And I'll bet this came as a big surprise to you, you became jealous. It was okay that you didn't want him but not okay for someone else to want him, especially your own daughter. You saw Anne Susan leaving his room that afternoon, barged in and confronted him. And when he admitted to it, you killed him. Joe and Iris were just loose ends you had to tie up."

"I have to say, Ellen, I'm impressed," Cindy said, getting up from the couch to the sideboard, pouring herself and Ellen a fresh drink while managing to keep the gun trained on Ellen. "Your reputation as Domino

Lady is well deserved," she said, coming back to the couch. "But you got one thing wrong."

"Yes?" Ellen said. "What would that be?"

"Connie's not dead," Cindy said with obvious delight. "She's in upstate New York. Drugged up to her eyeballs!"

Ellen tried to keep her expression emotionless, despite the surge of relief that spread through her.

"Even with the Lundgren family money, there's no getting out of this without a conviction," Cindy said smiling. "Connie will stand trial. Connie will be convicted. And then we'll switch places as we did before. And she'll know what's it like to be locked up against her will! For something she didn't do!"

Cindy took a long sip of her drink, staring at the portrait of Iris as the Island Girl.

"I really will miss her," Cindy said wistfully. "I really will."

"So, now what?" Ellen said.

"To be honest," Cindy said. "I'm not sure. I think we both know I can't let you live. The question is, do I kill Ellen Patrick or Domino Lady? Domino Lady has been part of this almost from the beginning. I bet it wouldn't be hard for the cops to pin Joe and Iris' murder on her."

"What happens to Anne Susan?"

"I could not care less," Cindy said, the consonants becoming a little soft from the alcohol. "Hopefully she'll have run away, or get lost. She's got to know there's no place for her here."

Ellen got up slowly, Cindy's gun following the arc of her rise. "Another?" Ellen asked. "I know I could use one."

Not waiting for a response, she took Cindy's glass back to the sideboard for a refill. With her back to Cindy, she filled Cindy's nearly to the brim, but poured half a shot of whiskey into her own glass, filling the rest with water from the ice bucket.

"You know," Ellen said, wincing a little as she settled back in the chair. "That whole goody-two-shoes thing could wear a little thin with Connie," slurring her speech just a little.

"I know!" Cindy said, adding a few more Os to the end of the word. "Do you know, by the time I had Anne, Connie hadn't even kissed a boy?" She adopted a high pitched sing-song voice, "Saint Connie. Saint Connie."

There followed a long silence between them. Ellen backed her drink, in two big swallows. Cindy did the same to hers and shuddered. Ellen got up, Cindy's gun following a little less precisely, went to the sideboard and fixed a couple more drinks as she had before.

"Could Iris really hula?" Ellen asked, handing Cindy her drink.

"Oh, she was a hell of a dancer," Cindy said. "A hell of a dancer. You know what she said to me just before I shot her?"

"No," Ellen said. She let her eyes half close and her head nod to the side before making the over-correction that drunk people sometimes do.

"She told me," Cindy slurred. "She told me she loved me."

"Ah," Ellen said, "That's sweet."

Ellen's head dropped back onto the cushion and within a few seconds, she began to snore.

Cindy laughed.

"She could tap dance," Cindy said, staring at the image of Iris as Island Girl. "Just like Ginger Rogers."

Ellen cracked an eye to see Cindy's gun hand slowly lower to the seat cushion. She waited until Cindy's eyes fluttered in an effort to keep them open. Ellen sprang from her chair, grabbed the gun and delivered a blinding series of judo moves that drove Cindy so deeply into unconsciousness that she didn't wake up until she was in cuffs. In jail.

When the cops arrived, lying on Cindy's chest was a card which read *Compliments of the Domino Lady.*

It took Mrs. Morse the better part of two hours, working with a magnifying lens and a pair of tweezers, to remove the last of the tiny glass shards from Ellen's back. She wiped the whole of it with hydrogen peroxide and pronounced it a job well done.

They went to have their coffee and sweet rolls on the patio of the Studio City house. The weather had taken a change for the better. There were a few stubborn clouds holding to the horizon, but for the most part, the sky was a broad welcoming blue.

"They're early," Mrs. Morse said, commenting on the arrival of the bull frogs among the rolling song of the chorus frogs from the pond just beyond the tree line.

"They found Joe, you know," Mrs. Morse said.

"Where?" Ellen asked.

"About a hundred yards from his apartment," Mrs. Morse said. "He made it out the window, down the fire escape, but collapsed in a neighbor's yard. She thought he was just passed out drunk. It wouldn't have been the first time. But when he was still there in the morning, and she saw the blood, she called the cops."

"What a mess," Ellen said, shaking her head.

"Any news on Anne Susan?" Mrs. Morse asked.

"She's in protective custody for now," Ellen said. "The poor kid. No child should have to go through what she's been through. It breaks my heart. She actually thought Lance was going to marry her."

"Quite a popular fellow," Mrs. Morse commented.

"He had his charms, I suppose," Ellen said. "But he was a cad, plain and simple. The best news is," her tone lightening, "Connie will be on her way home soon."

"That *is* good news."

"They say it will take a few days for her to be clear of all the narcotics they'd been pumping into her. But with some therapy and the support of family and friends, she should be okay."

Ellen and Mrs. Morse clicked coffee cups in a toast to Connie.

"There'll be a lawsuit?" Mrs. Morse conjectured.

"Of course," Ellen said. "It's what people like the Lundgrens do. But I do see their point. Connie told them right from the beginning who she was. But it seems Cindy had laid the groundwork some months in advance, so when Connie was switched out for Cindy, they'd heard it all before."

"How was the switch made?"

"Cindy had the help of an orderly," Ellen said. "She can be very persuasive."

The two women sat in companionable silence, listening to the frogs and the birds, enjoying a gentle breeze that came in through the rustling trees.

"Your mask?" Mrs. Morse asked.

"I left it in Iris' apartment. I was in such a hurry to be gone from that place," Ellen said. "I called the cops and left. The way things had been going, I wasn't sure they weren't already on their way. And the Domino Lady could not be found in an apartment with a dead woman and her murderer."

"Well, I can tell you, I'm glad it's over," Mrs. Morse said. "This will be one for the book."

"You know we've talked about this, Mrs. M.," Ellen said. "The Domino Lady will need to be well retired before you can even think about writing that book of yours."

"Understood, my dear," Mrs. Morse said with a smile. "But when the time comes, you must agree, this one, what shall we call it? The Case of the Model, Madness and Murder? It will make for a compelling read."

"No one will believe it, Mrs. M." Ellen said.

"Oh, I think they will," Mrs. Morse said. "Its no more unbelievable than the Case of the Dead Assassin."

"True," Ellen agreed. "I scarcely believe it myself, and I was there!"

The two women laughed, sipping the last of their coffee, fingers pressing the crumbs of their sweet rolls onto their tongues.

Danny made reservations at Chez Rendezvous. He requested the back table, far from the main room. He'd already ordered a bottle of Ellen's favorite white wine which was chilling in an ice bucket next to their table. He was uncharacteristically nervous. At exactly 7:00, the doors to the restaurant opened and she walked in. It was as if time held its breath, as did everyone in the place. People stopped mid-bite to watch her saunter through the room.

She was dressed in a green silk dress that caressed her shapeliness like a lover's touch. Her décolletage was low and daring. She wore a short waisted, velvet jacket that framed her breasts, offsetting the perfect paleness of her skin. Light seemed to be drawn into her long golden hair which shimmered with each sway of her hips. But that face. That face. Not perfect. Her eyes a little too large and a little too blue. Her nose, small, with the slightest bump just before the upturned tip. And lips a little too full, her lower lip in a perpetual pout. But it was the combination of those anomalies that made her stunning and unforgettable.

"Hey, gorgeous," Danny said, offering to take her jacket, but she said she'd prefer to keep it on.

"To protect against the effect of a chill," she said coyly. Danny felt himself blush as he imagined what she meant.

Ellen had known the Chef at Chez Rendezvous for several years and trusted him completely. Whatever he served them would be perfect. They started with candied walnuts, blue cheese, pears and bell peppers served on a bed of romaine and baby mixed greens tossed with champagne vinaigrette. This was followed by roast chicken stuffed with rosemary, fennel and olives served with potatoes. They ate in silence, savoring each bite. Every once in a while, their eyes met in shared appreciation of their feast.

With the plates cleared and finishing the last of their wine before the dessert, Danny said, "So, I heard from Delores yesterday."

"What does your crazy wife want now?" Ellen asked. "Has she discovered a new way to make your life miserable? Maybe she's taken up pyrotechnics as a hobby for when she gets out?"

"No, not exactly," Danny said. "Turns out she wants a divorce."

The wise crack on Ellen's tongue evaporated. "What?" was all she could manage.

"Turns out, she's fallen in love with a fellow patient," Danny explained. "A former radio actor by the name of Roy Hardgrove. They want to get married when they both get out, and she wants a divorce. She said, now, for the first time, she knows what love is."

"Well, that's great news," Ellen said, cautiously.

"I hoped you'd think so," he said, smiling.

The waiter brought them each an exceptionally rare cognac before dessert. Danny asked if she'd heard the latest on the Connie Lundgren case.

"Not really," Ellen said. "I've been trying to get a hold of her, but they keep telling me she's incommunicado under doctor's orders and that she's under sedation. I guess she's just a wreck and rightly so, with all she's been through."

"It's a pretty crazy story," Danny said. "There's a crazy twin sister, an illegitimate teen age daughter, a two bit hustler and an artist's model. And your friend, the Domino Lady is neck deep in it."

"Really?"

"Yep," Danny said. "In fact, she's the one who put it all together. The crazy sister is in jail because of her. In fact, she's the one who called it in. And when our boys showed up, the dame was out cold, with the Lady's calling card on her chest."

"Well, I'll be," Ellen said. "I guess she's not so bad after all, uh?"

"Nope," Danny said, "In fact, I think she's pretty darn swell."

He removed a small flat box wrapped in shiny white paper tied together with a black satin bow.

"What's this," she said warily.

"Just a little something to show my appreciation," he said, and pushed the box closer to her.

She brought the box to her, untied the ribbon and gently removed the paper. Carefully, she lifted the lid and folded back a square of tissue paper. A black domino mask lay coiled in the center of the box. She picked it up, looking at him, a curious expression on her face. Beneath the mask was a card. She held it to the light and read, *Compliments of Detective Danny O'Boylan.*

"I won't ask you to try it on," he said smiling. "I already know how beautiful you look in it."

She replaced the card and looped the mask back into the box and returned the lid. She gave him a smile so full of meaning, they skipped dessert.

The End

Notes on the Case

I have to admit, I hadn't heard of the Domino Lady before talking with Ron. I'd just finished a piece and was still in that writing zone and I asked if there was something I might try my hand at. He sent me the Domino Lady Bible and a story he'd written about her and I was inspired.

The opening scene of *The Case of the Model, Madness and Murder* gave me insight into how I was going to handle her character. That she's being photographed for *Harper's Bazaar* tells us she's a damn fine looking dame. Magazine model pretty. Her interaction with Nita, the photographer's assistant, about Ellen's décolletage, I hope shows her sense of humor and her willingness to have fun with her obvious charms.

I don't know how other writers write. My guess is no two of us work the same way. I don't do any plot mapping. I let the story unfold as it will, and create situations to which the characters react. Until Ellen answered the phone call in the dressing room, I had no idea what she'd be up against. When Connie said, "Oh, Ellen, I've been arrested," it set the wheels in motion.

I just want to say a little something about pacing. I like the story to unfold at a clean, even pace. Although I enjoy reading authors who can really paint a detailed picture and put you deep into it, that ain't me. I like to think I tell you just what you need to know in a cadence that flows quickly, but not rushed. I'm spare with physical descriptions. I try to get you to see who these people are through what they do and what they say. It's important that we have a pretty clear picture of what Ellen looks like. But it's left up to us to create the physiognomy for the rest of the cast. I think there's such a thing as character transference. As we read about a character, they sometimes will remind us of people we know or know about, and we transfer that to the characters in the book. If that happens, then it seems like the story becomes more personal to us. That's the goal, anyway.

The story needed a romance. Enter Detective Danny O'Boylan. They have a history. If circumstances had been different, they'd be together. But we learn why they can't. But we still sense that emotional and physical tug between them. How it plays out, we can't be sure.

As the story unfolds Ellen hears differing versions of the crime of which her dear friend has been implicated. She doesn't want to believe Connie could have committed cold blooded murder, and she fights against it. But as the stories build, one on top of another, with just enough twists, she starts to doubt her friend's innocence. And as she does, we do as well.

I tried to base each version on the agendas of the person telling it. Even the mystery man skews his version to promote an outcome. We never know who he is, but it is not difficult to imagine him working with or for the real killer.

It didn't seem feasible for Ellen to be a credible crime fighter and not have behind-the-scenes support. There'd be no way she could always be at the right place, at the right time, so not unlike Holmes' Baker Street Irregulars, she has a network of willing collaborators feeding her information she'll use to solve crime. Once I had that, I knew she needed someone to coordinate and manage the network. Enter Mrs. Morse. They've been through hell and back together, and we get a sense of the closeness of their relationship by the way they interact. Having the Mrs. Morse character let me explore the possibility that the Domino Lady was just one of many personas Ellen employed to solve crime. She's a master of disguise. Just as the Domino Lady is designed to serve a purpose, so is Lola Louise. A look into Ellen's closet reveals dozens of character costumes. It might be interesting to explore that aspect of her where she might be able to play the character of the Domino Lady against another of her personas.

As soon as the mystery man tells Ellen that Connie has a sister, things start to make sense—kind of. It explains the daughter. It could explain a lot of things. The most important thing about writing his scene was to stay out of his way. I just let him talk. He already knew what Ellen knew, so he had a good foundation on which to build his version. As his thugs take her back to her car, this version clears Connie, and as screwed up as the rest of it is, she's back to believing in her friend, but not without a twinge of guilt for having doubted her.

I sincerely hope you'll have enjoyed my take on the Domino Lady character and hope I'll get a chance to explore with her again.

TIM BRUCKNER I suppose I'm best known as a sculptor. Over the past forty-five years I've produced hundreds of action figures and collectible statues for companies like DC Direct (now DC Entertainment), Side Show, Gentle Giant, Dark Horse and many more. Early in my career I created art for several album covers. Most notably the art for Ringo's *Ringo* cover. Around that same time I worked as an illustrator and designer. In my late twenties I wrote, performed and produced three children's albums for Casablanca Records. Sandwiched in there were a couple of special effects projects, sculpting and art directing work on the alligator suit for the movie *Alligator*. These days I've semi-retired from commercial work, exploring my own creative projects and writing. I've been writing short stories since I was a kid. A couple of years ago I co-wrote *Pop Sculpture: How to Create Action Figures and Collectible Statues*, published by Watson-Guptill. Last year I published by first book of fiction, *Sensible Redhorn*, a collection of four pulp-driven stories centered around a hardnosed crime reporter. Most recently, I've had the great fortune of being able to work with Ron Fortier and Airship 27. Hold onto your seats, it's going to be a pulpy ride! Visit my site at www.timbruckner.com and visit me at Facebook for the latest news.

THE DOMINO LADY FINDS A FEW GOOD MEN

by Kevin Findley

*A*s Ellen Patrick drove down the Pacific Coast, a myriad of thoughts and emotions played through her mind. Though barely over two decades in this life, she had already known the despair of not just losing her parents, but also the rage of having her beloved father taken away by violence. Among those responsible were some of the very men he called friend and believed were on the same side of justice.

Owen Patrick's death forged her rage into a drive with no time for anything except revenge on those who believe themselves beyond the law. The sense of justice her father tried to instill in her was now a very cold and small thing. In order to achieve her revenge, Ellen quickly learned to use every tool available to her: Chief among them a mind well-trained and honed by some of the finest schools and her father's own desire to see her excel, a sound knowledge of Judo and, of course, her exceptional athletic ability and physical assets.

This is why Colonel Henry Benjamin Mayfair, USMC, confused Ellen. The decorated veteran of the Great War was one of the few men who appeared to be immune to those rather considerable assets. Other friends of her father, many of whom had known her since childhood like the Colonel, could not or would not take their eyes off of her shapely legs or ample chest. They treated her like a brainless toy at best or an object ripe for the taking at worst.

Admittedly, she did encourage the toy-like treatment as part of her disguise. Two of the men who were part of the conspiracy that murdered her father now resided in jail from their own illegal activities. They had no idea their downfall and arrest began with words from their own lips into her delicately shaped ears; the ears of the Domino Lady.

The Colonel however, looked her directly in the eyes whenever he spoke to her. He was perhaps a bit gruffer with her as an adult than when she was a child, but he neither spoke down to her nor was he ever impolite. He was also the best chance she had now to gain further information about the criminals and politicians who conspired to kill her father.

Under the pretense of catching up, Ellen had called Mayfair for a lunch date. He suggested a restaurant on the coast halfway between San Clemente and the main gate at Camp Pendleton. A favorite of the Marine, he promised Ellen excellent food for their late lunch and a chance to catch up. She smiled with anticipation and then lowered the roadster's accelerator to shrink the distance.

"Colonel Benji! It's so good to see you again! Come here and give me a kiss…and not one of those on the cheek like when I was ten, either!" With that, she leans up on her toes and gives the 46 year old Marine a big buss on the mouth. Mayfair looks displeased, but gestures her to sit down at his table. Ellen intended to continue with her spoiled, rich girl persona, but Mayfair waved his hand at her when she begins to speak again.

"I don't believe for a moment that one year traveling in Europe and the Far East reduced the bright and inquisitive young lady I watched grow up to a socialite with no common sense or redeeming qualities. Please don't insult me further, Ellen or I'll leave now."

It was rare for someone to tell Ellen Patrick to speak more intelligently, so Colonel Mayfair's words surprise her enough that she actually blushes from an embarrassment she never felt even when dressed as the Domino Lady. Once she can feel the color begin to leave her face, she starts to speak again.

"You're quite right, Sir. Since my father's funeral, I've found it much easier to play the silly socialite. Well-meaning people with nothing to say or who just want to pry into my affairs generally leave me alone much sooner."

A smile appears across Mayfair's face. "Very good, Ellen; I hoped that was the case. Now, I apologize for not getting back to you since Owen's funeral. It's very nice to see you, and while I'm sure we'll have a pleasant lunch, I doubt that you drove all the way down here just to say hello. What do you want to know about your father?"

"A few days ago, I found a second appointment book he kept in a hidden compartment of his armoire. The entries coincided with gaps in his public calendar and when he was supposedly vacationing north in Monterey or elsewhere. The subjects are all coded, as were the people he met with. I couldn't make any progress until I found the name 'H.B. Trump'. It didn't mean anything at first, but then I remembered a visit you had with my father when I was a little girl; I believe that was your first tour at Camp Pendleton. After the end of a particularly good tale, he jokingly called you

Lejeune's Trump, referring to General Lejeune, whom you served with in the Great War and Panama."

Mayfair barks a short laugh. "Now that's the young woman I remember! Excellent work, Ellen." He leans forward slightly. "One slight correction, that was actually my second tour, and you would have been eight years old. You were a little precocious even then."

Leaning back once more, "You would of course like me to tell you what we talked about and if I recognize any more of those names, yes?"

"That's correct, Sir. Anything that might help me find out what he was working on in the last few weeks before his death. I'll turn it over to the police, of course." she hurriedly adds at the end.

"Perhaps you should turn the book over to the police now, Ellen. I'll be happy to go with you and describe my conversations with Owen in depth."

"I would, Colonel, but the detective in charge of the case was just recently arrested for corruption, and a new one hasn't been assigned yet." *If one ever is* Ellen darkly thought.

"Very well, then. Do you have the appointment book with you?"

"Yes, Sir, it's in my purse."

"Don't bring it out here. Let's take our lunch on the restaurant's deck so we have a clear view of who's around us."

Half an hour later, the pair have finished their lunch and begun decoding over coffee and dessert. Mayfair taps at one page in particular. "There are three other names with the same subject next to my name, 'boxing match'. I don't recognize the other two, but I'm fairly certain that S.P. Horse refers to Frederick Scheinhorst. He's a councilman just north of here in San Pedro. I was leaving my meeting with Owen when he arrived very early, if the time next to his name is accurate." Mayfair snorts, "Of course, he blamed your father and then tried to turn on me. He behaved much better after I dressed him down."

"I wish I had been there to see that."

"Perhaps, Ellen, but if you had been there for the meeting, then you might have been there as well when Owen was murdered. Keep that in mind for those moments when you feel guilty you weren't with him."

For the second time that day, Ellen blushes. "I will, Colonel; thank you. Now what exactly did you discuss with my father? You said something about equipment thefts?"

"Yes, it was about supplies and equipment disappearing from the Marine long term storage warehouses at San Pedro. Near as the Camp Quartermaster could tell, everything made it off ship and into the warehouses, but began disappearing within several days after each delivery. The facility is guarded by civilian contractors, so the local city government is supposedly running the investigation. If it weren't for the inventory that was accomplished because of a change of command in April, it wouldn't have been caught until the end of year inventory this month."

"That's not till December, though."

"Military inventory is done end of fiscal year. That's next week, September 30th."

"Do you think Councilman Scheinhorst is part of this?"

"Probably, but he certainly won't be in charge. The man has all the intelligence of a bowl of chow hall oatmeal. According to Owen, the only reason he was elected a councilman is his own father thought him too useless to be a part of the family real estate business. Now he spends his days working to approve all zoning and other issues needed to increase his family's wealth."

"Then why would he speak to my father?"

"There's no reason…" Mayfair hesitates "…unless he was the first one to betray him. You see, Ellen, I didn't bring this to your father. He already knew it was going on, but he only had a few details."

Ellen's face hardens. "San Pedro is only about an hour from here."

"Fifty-eight miles along the coastal highway." Mayfair frowns. "You're not planning to go confront him in his offices, are you?"

Ellen shakes her head. "I don't know where the San Pedro city hall is, and I wouldn't get there in time today anyway. However, there is a friend of mine who might like to talk to him tomorrow." She looks teasingly at Mayfair. "I don't suppose you'd care to put up a lonely, young girl for the night, Colonel Benji?"

Mayfair scowls at her while Ellen happily laughs.

The Colonel, of course, found Ellen a clean bed and breakfast nearby run by a Marine widow. While the room accommodations were rather simple, the breakfast was quite good and the coffee even better. Rested and fortified, Ellen felt ready to take on the world; let alone a simple councilman.

After a leisurely drive up the coast, the vivacious young woman stops at a filling station just outside San Pedro for directions. In five minutes, she's parked in front of city hall, checked her hair and lipstick, then strolls up the stairs. Her plan was to charm a clerk into giving her Councilman Scheinhorst's home address after a little flirting and then be on her way. Fortunately for Ellen, Kermit Devereaux was on duty that morning. By Ellen's standards he was rather cute, if a little bookish and easily distracted by a nicely turned ankle. In other words, he was perfect for what she needed.

At the sound of her knock on the entryway, he begins speaking before even looking up. "Yes, may I help...ahhh...you?"

Ellen jumps in before he can recover his senses, "I certainly hope so. You see, I work at a legal office in Long Beach, and my boss wants me to get an address for a client here and how long he's lived here, only I lost the name and it's one of those funny German names and, oh, I'm in such trouble if I can't find it!" Her voice rising with every word, she also was pushing herself over the counter toward the clerk. Poor Kermit never had a chance.

"Please, Miss, calm down. I'm certain we can find out everything you need today."

"Thank you, ummmm, what would you like from me?"

Blushing at the question, Kermit stammers that all he needs are the first and last names of the person she's looking for. "If I can identify him in the city register, then we'll know his address and I can look him up in the tax records. That should tell us how long he's lived here. It shouldn't take long at all."

"Oh, well, that should be easy. Like I said, it's a German name, starts with an S."

"Let me get the right book, wait just a moment." Devereaux gets the R through T book and brings it to the counter. "Okay, what's the next letter?"

"Could we sit at the table over here? It's rather hot and that side of the office is in the shade."

"Absolutely." Moving to the table meant having Ellen sitting right next to him, and Kermit couldn't think of a better way to spend his morning.

Once seated, Ellen gives his right arm a little squeeze and tells him, "It starts with Sch, but that's where I can't remember too well."

"No problem, let's find the right page." Turning quickly, he finds the one starting with Sanders and ending with Scranton. "Okay, what's next?"

"The next letter was an e or an i."

"Let's see, there's no name with starting with schi-, the first two with schei- are Scheinhorst. They're a local family, in fact Frederick is a councilman here."

"Oh, it's the name below that one! I remember now." She points to an Ernestine Schell, squeezing a little closer to Kermit and memorizing Scheinhorst's address while doing so.

"Oh that's great!" The young clerk shakes himself out of his reverie. "Just let me get the tax records, and we'll look up how long Miss Schell has been here."

"Before you do, could I bother you to get me a soda? It's so hot and I saw that café across the street. I have a stipend for lunch, so I can pay for one for you too."

"I'm not really supposed to leave unless I get someone to watch the counter."

"Oh, I can do that!" Ellen replies with a grin. "Please?" she wheedles.

Charmed and defeated, Kermit takes a quarter from Ellen and goes to the café. In just a minute, she's copied the address from the directory and finds it in the city map books behind the counter. By the time the young clerk returns with the sodas and change, Ellen has directions to the councilman's house in her purse and is fanning herself with her driving gloves.

Five minutes later, the sodas have been finished, the information for Miss Schell has been written down, and Ellen departs. It takes Kermit another minute to realize the beautiful blonde never told him her name or even what law office she worked for.

Driving away, Ellen promised herself that she would go back sometime and have a proper lunch with Kermit as a reward for helping her. Her noon meal today, though, was a solitary affair followed by window shopping the young woman really didn't even notice. Her mind was already beginning to feel the anticipation and thrill that only her alter ego provided.

She waits out the remaining hours to sunset at a lovely restaurant on the beach, fending off men of various ages and marital status, then drives to a small motel nearby. After checking in dressed as and behaving like a woman meeting a married lover, she goes directly to her room and locks the door behind her. Ellen then strips down to her undergarments, sets the alarm on a travel clock and lays down to sleep. At 2 a.m. she awakes refreshed and ready for breaking and entering; perhaps even assault and battery if rifling Scheinhorst's papers proves less than fruitful.

The lithe, young woman lays out a now familiar white evening gown and black cloak on the bed. She quickly slips the dress over her head and down past her hips. Then Ellen adds a syringe of sedative to her garters and checks the .22 automatic and extra magazine in her purse; finally pulling on the cloak to cover her bare shoulders and hide the gown. Stepping outside, she quickly replaces her license plate with one she acquired from an abandoned car in a previous adventure. The mask will have to wait until she arrives at the councilman's home.

A short time later, the Domino Lady is in the side door of Scheinhorst's small, two-story house. It takes her only a minute to realize there's nothing useful she can find skulking in the dark, even with a flashlight; time for another tactic. She makes certain the curtains are closed to outside viewers, opens the study door into the hallway, turns on the desk lamp and begins picking things up and putting them back down; making as much noise as possible. It doesn't take long to get a response.

"Who's down there?!" The stairs creak and then a still sleepy looking Frederick Scheinhorst appears in the doorway holding a long, wooden shoe horn like a baseball bat.

"Well, well; the search for money and jewels may have been a bust, but at least there's one interesting thing to play with in this dreary, little house."

"Huh?" *Mayfair was right* she thought; *a bowl of oatmeal has more sense. At least that makes this easy.*

"All of you rich families like to stash valuables in plain, quiet hideaways like this." She puts on her best pout. "Since there's nothing here, big boy, that must mean you're the prize. Why don't you come over here and let's find out what makes you so valuable?"

"Sure thing, doll! Freddy's got a big surprise for you!"

Such a ruse never failed the Domino Lady. Men so inclined to behave in the lowest manner readily expect it of everyone around them. Once Freddy buries his face in her neck and tries to pull the gown off her shoulder, it takes but a moment to use the syringe in her left hand to inject him behind the ear. The fast acting sedative leaves the councilman unconscious before he lands on the floor.

With no need now for stealth, the blonde avenger turns on the ceiling light and begins a more thorough inspection of the desk. Finding nothing, she turns to the councilman's two bookcases. The first one reveals nothing, but on the second she finds behind an ornate bookend a locked panel that extends into the wall. Having found no keys in the desk, the Domino Lady searches an already snoring Freddy and then goes upstairs to his bedroom. It takes only a moment to find his key ring and then return downstairs.

The contents of the hidden compartment were in stark contrast to the plain little house. Inside were stacks of $20 and $100 bills along with a bag of exquisitely crafted women's jewelry and a couple of men's Heuer watches. At the back of the compartment were folders with what looked like real estate transactions, wills and other legal papers. A quick review meant nothing to her, but she takes them anyway along with the cash and jewelry.

In order to send Freddy and whoever might be in charge down the wrong rabbit hole, she pulls a stack of unused paper from the desk and replaces the documents in the folders. Then she drops them into the metal waste can and lights the contents on fire, making sure parts of the folders survive the flames. Her last act before departing is to place one of her calling cards on the desk with the taunting phrase...*Compliments of the Domino Lady!*

Ellen returned home that evening; went to bed once the excitement wore off and then awoke later that morning to examine the papers and take stock of her haul from Scheinhorst. Her adventure netted over $6,000, with the jewelry worth at least three times that. "Hiding money makes sense if you're taking bribes, but where did the jewelry come from? He certainly didn't get it from an admirer, unless they're all old enough to be his mother!" After considering her options, she decides to pay a visit to the police. The house of a friend of hers was broken into a few weeks ago, and that just might help her pick up some new information.

"So anyway, Detective Taylor...oh, may I call you Steven? Good! Anna is still soooo scared after seeing that broken window, I just had to come down and see if you've caught the bandits yet."

"I appreciate that, Miss Patrick, but the jewelry and everything else that was taken from her house was very new and easily fenced; that means sold to a crooked shop owner. It also makes it very hard to track down her property or the bandits if we don't find them within the first week after they've broken in."

"Are you trying to tell me she would have been better off if the bandits had stolen her grandmother's brooch? Well, that's just silly!"

"Older settings are harder to sell since they're not as popular as they once were." Taylor patiently tries to explain.

"I understand that no one wants to wear last year's earrings, but surely they're worth something."

"Of course they are. In fact, Ellen, an older item is sometimes worth more because of its history, but that means the thief will have to find a different kind of buyer. There are always private collectors who don't care where a new addition might come from."

"You mean there are thieves that only steal from the elderly? How awful!"

"Not exactly, Ellen, but there have been a number of older citizens along the coast this spring who have had their property disappear. All the jewelry taken was several decades old, with the most recent piece from just after the turn of the century. The owners either died and it disappeared from their estate, or they moved to a retirement home and it vanished from there after their death."

"This is all so fascinating, Stevie. Oh! Do you have any pictures of what's missing? Perhaps the next time when I'm dropping off last year's fashions at a second hand charity store, I might see them in a display case. That would be helpful, wouldn't it?" Ellen gives the detective her most dazzling smile.

The bemused look on the detective's face clearly says no, but he is more than willing to do anything short of actually beating a suspect in front of her to keep the attractive young woman in his office for as long as possible. "You wait right here, Ellen and I'll bring them over. The police need more citizens like you assisting us."

Every piece now in her wall safe was in the photos or descriptions given to the police by the insurance companies. The owners were the same names on some of the documents she took from Freddy Scheinhorst. Nothing Ellen found so far, though, connected to either Colonel Mayfair or her father. That was still a mystery. *Oh well, at least Detective Taylor was attractive enough to wile away the afternoon with; perhaps even an evening or two when this was over.*

The crime boss Freddy Scheinhorst reported to was a local figure named Carl Hayden. He was a second generation crook whose family had carved out a big enough piece of Long Beach and San Pedro that the Sicilian mobs had left him to his own devices when they moved into Los Angeles and then began spreading out.

Carl was smart enough, though, to know it wouldn't last forever. He had seen what happened to the other gangs in L.A. and realized the wolf was at his door, patiently waiting. Hayden figured that after another year or two, he could retire with no change in his lifestyle, so his primary con-

"You wait right here, Ellen..."

cerns now were to keep the peace and make as much money as possible until he started getting squeezed out.

He made Freddy Scheinhorst's acquaintance a month after the younger man was elected to the city council. Seeing how Otto Scheinhorst treated his son publicly, Hayden was certain he could use the newly minted councilman. After a few 'accidental' meetings to sound him out, Carl began letting Freddy have a peek into his world. He took to it like a crooked duck in a pond of dirty water.

They soon came up with the scheme to steal easily resold equipment from the local warehouses. Freddy not only provided the muscle to move it and a trusted fence to resell the property but, with Carl's assistance, found himself on a committee that oversaw employing guards for the warehouses. Although Hayden didn't have complete trust in Scheinhorst yet, it had been a profitable relationship for them both up until this point.

In trying to explain how he lost his boss' money, the very nervous councilman let slip about the jewelry in the wall compartment. Carl quickly realized that although this was a small con, it was one that could go on for years with no attention from the police. It might even provide a steady income after he turned over the large operations to his mob counterpart, Ignacio Dinelli.

"It's a decent scheme Frederick, and I'm honestly surprised you were able to keep it from me this long. How did you come up with it?"

"It's the same way my father got started in the real estate business, Mr. Hayden. First, you need to find a bunch of geezers ready to die, like in a retirement home. Once you make sure they don't have a family to interfere, all you have to do then is slip them a deed transfer or a new will right after their medication and they'll sign it. Most of them even say 'thank you' when they hand you the papers back." Freddy laughs. "What's even better is when they die, I say their jewelry was stolen and file an insurance claim. Since I have a fence in my back pocket, I don't even have to wait to resell it."

"So, of course, no one would have known anything if this Domino Lady hadn't broken into your home and stolen your jewelry and my money. Tell me, Frederick, have you financed this scheme with my money from the warehouse thefts?"

"Well, yes, Mr. Hayden. I did start it with your money. After the first two, it's all been strictly on my dime, though." Freddy actually digs the toe of his shoe into the carpet like a naughty child and keeps an eye on Hayden's right hand, standing behind the crime boss. "I'd appreciate it if we could keep this from my father. He only put me on the city council in order to help expand the family business, not start my own. That's why I went after old folks with property outside of San Pedro."

"Of course, Frederick! No reason at all to bring Otto into this; I admire a man who can think on his feet. To buy my silence from now on though, you'll have to bring me in as a partner. I won't take half, just a third."

Freddy's eyes go wide, but he wisely for once keeps his mouth shut.

"You'll also need to show one of my people the details of how you do this. I think with a little planning, we can expand your scheme up and down the coast. Between this and the military 'surplus' you've helped me with, I see us both continuing to make an obscene amount of money and keep your father completely out of it."

Now imagining money falling from the sky, the greedy councilman quickly agrees to everything and exits Carl Hayden's home even faster to start counting his chickens.

The crime boss motions for his right hand, "Tubarão."

"Yes, Mr. Hayden?"

"Keep an eye on Frederick. We'll keep him around if this confidence scheme pays off; it's a fairly simple cheat and should return a healthy profit for a long time. However, if the police begin poking around—or if he has any more late night visits—we'll need to know immediately."

"Yes, Sir. I'll have someone watch his house for the next couple of weeks."

"That should be sufficient. Find out what you can about this Domino Lady. If she's employed by the Dinelli family, we can work something out in terms of restitution. If she's not, there's no room for independent operators in our business. Just look at how much trouble one simple theft has caused us. Go see Sam Tweedle and take care of it."

"I'll go now. Sam's usually at Dinelli's dinner club this time of day."

The front man at the Dinelli Restaurant and Italian-American Social Club was Marco "Polo" Pagliotti. He was a concierge with no customers unless they were approved by the boss, Ignacio Dinelli, or his chief enforcer, Sam Tweedle. At five foot three, Polo hated anyone more than a half inch taller than himself; women in particular. For reasons he never shared with anyone, he apparently hated Carl Hayden's right-hand man, Tubarão more than anyone else.

"Hey, boys, look who's here! How ya doing there, Fernando?"

"I'm fine Polo, just let Sam know I'm here."

"Sure thing, Fernando." The little man strolls into the back of the restaurant and returns in less than a minute. "Mr. Tweedle is busy right now. Come back later."

"I'll wait; Mr. Hayden sent me over."

Five minutes later, Tubarão starts to get impatient but simply gets up and pours himself a cup of coffee. After another five, Polo begins needling the Portuguese thug again. "Hey, Fernando, you hungry? I'll send Eddie to get a couple of tacos off the lunch truck if you're hungry. Ha, ha, ha!"

"I'm Portuguese, not Spanish, you little runt. Get it right." Tubarão could feel his temper starting to fray and wanted to see Tweedle as quickly as possible. "Mr. Hayden sent me to speak to Sam. Now do your job and actually tell him I'm here this time."

Polo walks over and gets in the big man's face, "Tell me what to do again, you fat 'Spaniard,' and I'll teach you some manners." Then he chucks Tubarão under the chin like a sullen child needing a lesson. At that, the little Italian goes flying over the bar, breaking off tap handles and smashing bottles and glassware.

"What the hell is going on out here?!" Everyone stops cold and looks over at the source of the voice. Sam Tweedle could best be described as average looking until you saw him working over a man who owed his boss a debt. Then the description is 'deadly' followed by a string of epithets. A non-Italian high up in the 'Family,' Tweedle makes up for his lack of Sicilian blood with unswerving loyalty and a ruthlessness that impresses even the boys in Chicago and New York.

"It was my fault, Sam. I overreacted to an insult from Pagliotti there."

"Why are you here, Tubarão?"

"Mr. Hayden sent me. He wants to know if this new player in the papers, the Domino Lady, works for you."

"No, she's not one of ours. Why?"

"She lifted some merchandise from us last night from Freddy Scheinhorst. Since she's independent, we'll take care of her. Mr. Hayden just wanted to ask you out of respect to Mr. Dinelli."

"How long have you been out here waiting?"

"About ten minutes."

One of the hoods helping the fallen Pagliotti calls out, "We need to get Polo to the hospital. His face is cut up and it looks like he's busted a couple of ribs at least."

Tweedle looks at Polo and then back to Tubarão. "Okay Eddie, get him out of here." Pointing with his chin at the Portuguese, "You'll pay for the damages here out of your own pocket. You'll do this out of your respect for Mr. Dinelli and so it doesn't affect his business relationship with Mr. Hayden." Tubarão nods his assent and Tweedle turns to Pagliotti. "Polo, you're covering your own doctor bills. The next time you keep someone waiting to see me that long, I'll toss you over the bar myself."

After Eddie and Polo leave, he looks back at Tubarão. "Polo's a pain in my neck, but if you ever put your hands on any of my people again without cause, I promise you I'll personally deliver your corpse to your family in Mirandela. If Polo here is too badly busted up to do his job, I may still do it. Understand?"

"I got it, Sam."

"Get out."

"That's the story, Mr. Hayden. My temper got the better of me, and I tossed him like a sack of trash. If it helps with Mr. Dinelli, I'll pay for the runt's medical myself."

"That won't be necessary. Sam Tweedle made it clear what needed to happen, and I'll leave it at that. I've always found Pagliotti to be a nasty little piece of work, and it doesn't bother me at all if he spends a few nights in the hospital. That said, this is the last time you lose your temper while in my employ. One more incident and I'll cut you loose faster than your last ship's Captain."

"I understand, Mr. Hayden. About the Domino Lady; since she isn't working for Dinelli, I have an idea."

"Spit it out."

"She's a jewel thief, right? We'll set up one of Freddy's scams here in San Pedro and put the word out to reel her in. Once we have her, I'll find out how she caught on to him and then get rid of her."

Hayden begins to laugh, "If Otto finds out about this, he'll have a fit!"

Tubarão just shrugs. "Yes Sir, but since Freddy is his only son, it won't really affect our operations. I know the guy the boys in Los Angeles use for making accidents happen. They can arrange the same solution for Otto if we need it."

"Very good then! Oh, one more thing about Scheinhorst. His people are supposed to pull more property from the Marine warehouses tomorrow. I think due to the unwanted attention Freddy just received, this should be the last time for a few months. Make sure we have someone there as an extra lookout this time."

"I've already made plans to be there myself."

"Excellent! That's all for tonight, then. Good evening, Tubarão."

"Good night, Mr. Hayden."

The next day, Ellen calls Colonel Mayfair to update him on what she found at Scheinhorst's home and the time spent with Detective Taylor. Unfortunately, he doesn't recognize any of the names from the folders.

"I went through my father's coded appointment book, but I couldn't find any match to the names or subjects."

"My code-breaking skills were never that good, Ellen, but if you bring both next time we meet, I'll see if I can find anything."

"Thank you. Do you have the address for the Marine warehouse in San Pedro? My friend who paid Councilman Scheinhorst a visit thinks it should be the next place to examine."

"Exactly who is this friend of yours? Detective Taylor or some kind of private operator?"

"She's neither one Colonel. The press has named her the Domino Lady."

"That jewel thief I've read about?" Ellen can picture Mayfair shaking his head at the other end of the phone. "You're keeping strange company, Ellen."

"She's more than that. The Domino Lady has…suffered like I have. I guess you could say I'm sponsoring her efforts."

"Fine then, have her meet me at the warehouse tonight, and I'll escort her through the gates."

Ellen hesitates. "She really prefers to be a lone operator, sir; I don't think she would show up if she had to meet someone. Getting her checked in would be difficult anyway. After all, Colonel, she does wear a mask."

"All right; I'll give you the address. If she finds out anything useful, I want to know tomorrow. If she's caught, though, your friend will have to face the authorities by herself. This is a military warehouse, breaking in will be a federal offense and not just simple trespassing."

"Thank you, Colonel. I'll make sure she understands."

At Dinelli's Social Club, Tweedle is preparing for the dinner rush when Eddie comes running out of the back.

"Mr. Tweedle! I got a call from our guy at Little Company of Mary Hospital. Polo just died, and our guy says the police are coming here to ask questions. I guess that Portagee did him more damage than we thought."

Sam looks at the seafood clerk, "Scram!" and turns back to Eddie. "Clear everyone out, lock up before the cops get here and keep the boys out of sight for a few days. Once you get home, call in a new cashier and a couple of waiters for tomorrow morning to answer their questions. Make sure none of them have worked here before. They can answer truthfully they don't know anything so the cops won't get anything out of them."

"Can do. You keepin' low, too, Sam?"

"No, Mr. Dinelli needs to be informed, and then I've got a promise to keep." Tweedle picks up the phone behind the bar, stops and then tells Eddie to wait. "Do you know the warehouse where Hayden lifts all that gear and other stuff from the Marines?"

"Naw, but I can find out in a few minutes. My brother works for a guy…"

"Just do it, Eddie. Robbing those warehouses is Hayden's favorite scam right now. If Tubarão doesn't know about Polo yet, maybe I can find him over there and fix this tonight."

Tubarão and Scheinhorst's movers are already loading the truck when the Domino Lady arrives. The blonde avenger quickly realizes the two security guards are part of the theft and decides to deal with them immediately. Switching the .22 for the syringe on her garter, she simply walks softly up to the guard in the shack and injects him behind the ear. After laying him out to make it look like a heart attack, and with a devilish grin, she puts her lips together and blows a low whistle.

At the sound, the other guard starts moving backward toward the shack, "What is it Stan?" After no response, he turns around and walks into the shack. "Stan!" he screams and bends down to help the other guard. The last thing he feels is a hand grab his neck and then the rest of the knockout drug takes care of him. With both guards down, the Domino Lady places a call to the police, telling them about dead guards, brutal thugs and that if they move quickly, they'll catch them all.

Checking the truck cab, she looks through the glove compartment and then uses the pocket knife she took from one of the guards to slice through the valve stems on the passenger side tires. Once done, she moves around to the side of the warehouse and slips in.

Edward "Shifty" Green and his crew specialize in stealing large items from rich homes and warehouse storage using the Greenback Moving Company as a cover. Between their knowledge of every alley and forgotten backstreet in San Pedro to Shifty's brother-in-law reselling the stolen goods in his fence/pawn shop, they can make anything smaller than an elephant disappear. A skill put to bad use by Otto Scheinhorst, his son Freddy, and eventually Carl Hayden; he also spots the Domino Lady spying on them just as they put the last crate on the truck.

"Everything loaded?"

"Yeah, Tubarão. We got everything on your shopping list. We've also got a little bird watching us from the warehouse. A blonde one with a mask."

"Let's get you out of here. I think this is the little bird I've been trying to meet, and now is as good a time as any to make her sing."

They move to get in the truck, and Shifty's partner notices the flat tire. "We got a problem, Boss. Check the back tire. This one, too."

Tubarão goes to chew out the guards only to find them unconscious. He starts rubbing his hand over his face, trying to keep calm and decide what to do next.

"Shifty! Can you get the tires aired and drive out of here?"

"No can do; the valve stems have been cut. I can't patch those."

"*Damn!*" He takes his keys out of his pocket, removes the mail key and hands Shifty the rest. "Take my car and get out of here; that blonde *bruxa* probably called the cops, too. You know where I live, right?"

"Yeah sure. You had us over to listen to the play-offs last month."

"Get everyone where they need to go and then park it out front. Drop the keys in the mail slot. Once I find out how she knew to be here, I'm going to take tonight's loss out of her skin."

Tubarão re-enters the warehouse and calls out, "Domino Lady! I know you're here. Come out and tell me what you want!"

Confident that she can beat him, the lovely crime fighter steps out of the shadows, and as she approaches, flips her cloak back over her shoulders to reveal her décolletage. "Let's make a trade, big man. Tell me what I want to know, and then I'll answer your questions." With that, she starts to back up inside the warehouse.

The big thug chuckles, "Impressive, but I've spent a lot of years visiting islands where the women wear a skirt and nothing else." He starts moving to follow her. "Now come here, little miss; I need to find out what you know about Freddy's scam and how you knew to come here tonight. If you're lucky, I'll leave you someplace where Mommy and Daddy can find enough to bury."

As he reaches for the statuesque crime fighter, she quickly sidesteps, grabs his arm using a Te-Waza technique and then uses his own momentum to force him off-balance. As he tries to regain his footing, the Domino Lady easily slams him into a support beam and then bounces him to the floor. Tubarão gets up with new respect in his eyes, but doesn't lose any confidence.

"Judo? I learned a bit of that when there was a Jap onboard my ship in the South China Sea." Smiling broadly, he motions Domino Lady to come closer. "Let me show you what he taught me."

Moving in more cautiously this time, she blocks a throat grab, a punch, slides around another and tries another arm throw only to find herself the one flying through the air. Struggling quickly to her feet, the Domino Lady just has her .22 drawn before catching a crushing blow over her left kidney and then another on the right. She goes down again in agony.

"If you're going to last any longer in this business, then you're going to have to learn how to take a punch." Tubarão strikes her twice between the shoulder blades, knocking the wind out of her. "But it's too late for that now, I suppose." He squats down beside her to grab the automatic when he hears a voice that stops him cold.

"Tubarão! This is Sam Tweedle! Pagliotti just died in the hospital. Come out now and I'll make it quick. Two in the pump so your family can have an open casket after I take you back."

Tubarão looks down at the Domino Lady again, nervous for the first time. "I guess we'll have to finish this later. I've got to leave now, so here's your chance to crawl away." With a smile at her look of anger, he gets up and then disappears into the stacks of crates. All she can do is throw a few loose nails from the ground in Tubarão's direction to put Tweedle in her attacker's direction and off of her own.

After making her way back to her car, Ellen furiously rips off her mask and throws it on the floorboards.

" 'Crawl away,' he said and that's just what I did!" Up till now in her personal crusade, she hadn't found an opponent she couldn't either outsmart or outfight. Bad enough the thug put her down with little effort, but then to taunt her the way he did made her more furious than the actual beating.

Hearing police sirens in the distance, Ellen realizes she has only moments to get away. Swallowing her anger and pride, she turns over the motor, throws the roadster in gear and carefully drives away to avoid attention from any arriving police cars.

Despite a long, hot bath and half a bottle of liniment, Ellen still awoke late the next morning stiff as an old washerwoman. The bruising on her shoulders, ribs and back was already beginning to show. There was no way she could meet Mayfair without him knowing instantly it was her behind the mask. She would have to risk meeting him as the Domino Lady and hope he didn't look at her as he would Ellen Patrick. Time to see how much the Colonel trusted her.

She approaches Mayfair with the hood of her cloak pulled low. Thankful for the poor lighting inside the dive bar, it allows her to keep her face in shadow; obscuring everything except for her mouth and chin. "Colonel Mayfair? Ellen Patrick asked me to meet you tonight. I'm the Domino Lady."

"Is Ellen all right?"

"Yes, sir. She's going over some papers that I found at Scheinhorst's home. I wanted to speak to you personally about who I found at your warehouse last night."

"Then please sit down."

"Thank you." Moving carefully, the Domino Lady slides into the booth.

"Ellen tells me you interrupted the theft long enough for the police to arrive. They didn't catch anyone, but the Corps didn't lose any property last night. Thank you for that."

"You're welcome. I'm glad I got that right, at least."

"You're obviously in pain, so I'm guessing you ran into someone you couldn't beguile with that outfit last night?"

Temper flaring, she angrily spits out, "I fight better than the average man, Colonel! This one was just a little better than the average. He won't surprise me again."

Mayfair looks past her to the thug walking up. "Here comes your chance to prove it."

"Those stems are calling me from across the room, baby. Let Arnie buy you a drink." He nods at Mayfair. "This old man can't do anything for you I can't do better."

The Domino Lady looks up and smiles sweetly. "Thanks for walking over, Arnie. This is just what I need." Then she kicks him in the knee.

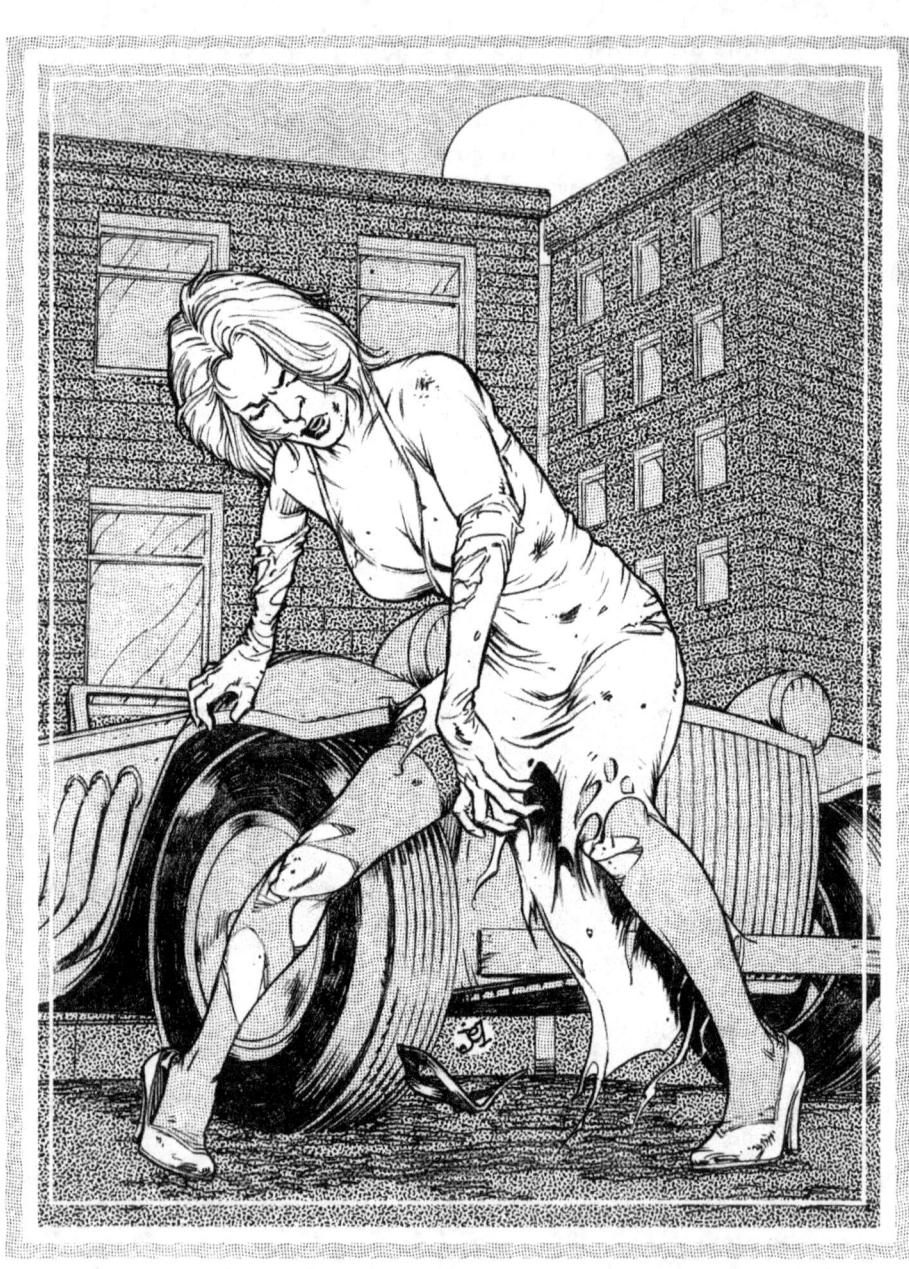

Ellen furiously rips off her mask…

The thug howls and bounces back on one leg. "You crazy broad, I'm gonna push in your face!" With that, he lets go of his knee and takes an angry swing at the blonde manhunter.

Not bothering with an arm lock or any traditional Nage-Waza, the Domino Lady simply sidesteps the blow and punches Arnie in the throat. While he's gagging, she hooks her left foot behind the same knee she kicked before in an Ashi-Waza and brings the goon down on his back so hard every glass in the dive bar shakes. Kicking hard enough to flip him over, the Domino Lady grabs an ear and pulls his head back with a high heel stuck in his spine.

"Like I said, Arnie, this was just what I needed." Pulling one of her calling cards from her evening glove, she shoves it in his open mouth. "Now get out of here before I start breaking off pieces you can't replace."

Slapping the back of his head for good measure, she sits down again without bothering to watch Arnie stumble out of the bar.

"Did I pass the test, Colonel?"

"You've earned some respect. That was quick, efficient, and you channeled your anger usefully rather than let it distract you like Arnie. Whoever taught you Judo was thorough. Every other thug and crook in this bar is too scared of you now to even look in your direction. That's only going to last for a few minutes, however, so go ahead and finish your story before someone drinks enough courage to try again."

Taking in a painful breath she relates what happened at the councilman's home and then tells Mayfair about the previous evening's adventure. "Another crook called him Tubarão. It sounded like Spanish, but I didn't recognize the name."

Mayfair looks thoughtful for a moment. "It's not a proper name; it's Portuguese for shark. Did he say anything about the sea or being on a ship? If he's from Portugal, then he may have signed on with the Merchant Marines at some point. Most Portuguese make good sailors; every job from cook to ship's captain."

"Yes, he mentioned being on a ship in the South China Sea. Does that mean you can find out who he is and where I can find him?"

"Most likely, yes. I have a contact at the San Diego office who owes me a favor or two. Describe him for me."

The lithe crime fighter unconsciously sat up straight and answered, "Six feet perhaps, but he wasn't as tall as…six foot one." The young woman almost slipped and said her father. Hoping Mayfair didn't notice, she continued. "Dark brown hair, brown eyes, medium complexion, but obviously spent many years in the sun. His accent was mild and his English was quite good. He had a large mustache and goatee." She grimaces, "along with rough hands and a pretty good knowledge of Judo."

"What about jewelry or tattoos?" Mayfair snorts, "Some of them think an earring makes them look like a pirate."

"No jewelry, and he was wearing long sleeves so I couldn't see if there were any tattoos." Then she remembered a comment. "Oh! He mentioned having a shipmate from Japan when he was in the South China Sea. That's who taught him Judo."

"That might be enough; especially if he was tossed off his last ship with a bad report from his Captain." Looking quizzically again at the Domino Lady, "You said someone else called him by name. Did you recognize him or know why he was there?"

"No, the other one said he was Sam Tweedle, but I don't know the name." She repeats to Colonel Mayfair word for word what was said in the warehouse and most of what happened afterward.

"I don't know Tweedle or Pagliotti. Anything else about the crooks loading the crates or the truck itself?"

"I heard Tubarão call one of them 'Shifty,' but no real names. There was no name on the truck, but there was an invoice in the glove box with the name Greenback Moving. There's no listing with information in San Pedro, Long Beach or even Los Angeles, though."

"I'll check with the transportation company. If we use them on Pendleton, I can get an address and phone number." Mayfair smiles and leans forward. "Maybe you'll get lucky, and those two will kill each other before anyone else gets hurt. Do you have a police contact that might know who Tweedle or Pagliotti are?"

"No,, and I don't think Ellen should approach Detective Taylor again so soon. I do know a private investigator who owes me a favor however." She moves, slowly, to get up. "Thank you for your time."

"As far as your evening plans go—and from the bruises I saw—I'd suggest a full tub, hot as you can get it, with a large cup of Epsom salts. They don't have to be completely dissolved before you get in, but pour them over the closed drain so you don't accidentally sit on them. Stay in the tub until the water becomes just warm. Get out, dry off quickly and then wrap your ribcage to lessen movement. Not too tight or you'll be too uncomfortable to sleep."

"I appreciate that Colonel. If I find anything useful, I'll let you know through Ellen."

One very hot bath, a wrap and a soft robe later, Ellen calls Roger McKane from her bedroom. An old friend, former paramour and current private eye, his service didn't know where he was yesterday but said now he was in San Diego tracking down an errant wife. Knowing which hotel he preferred, she dialed it and asked for him.

"Hello, Roge! How's my favorite private dick in California?"

"Ellen, baby! How are you? Still breaking hearts? I know mine never recovered."

"You're a dear, Roge. Now hush a moment and listen. I'm trying to discover a few things for the Domino Lady."

"I'm almost all ears, baby."

"Yes, and I'd bet I can guess what the rest of you is."

"You know me too well, Ellen."

"Down, boy. Our mutual friend recently ran into a man named Sam Tweedle. He was after another criminal named Tubarão for killing someone named Pagliotti, and she got squeezed in the middle. She has a line on the Portuguese bad man, but nothing on the other two names."

"I don't know who Tubarão or Pagliotti are, but Sam Tweedle is familiar. The Domino Lady is lucky she was able to walk away after running into him. Sam works for the Dinelli family operating out of Long Beach and San Pedro. They run nearly all the docks around there."

"So he's rather important."

"That's an understatement. As Ignacio Dinelli's right hand man, he's as high up as a non-Sicilian can get with these people, and he earned it by being tougher than every dago between him and that job. His personal loyalty to the old man is so tight that a Fed who spoke to Sam once about turning on him disappeared. Rumor has it that Tweedle killed the guy in front of Ignacio to prove himself."

"That explains why a thug as tough as Tubarão got nervous when Tweedle showed up."

"Seriously, Ellen, if the Domino Lady has to deal with him again, she better call in the Marines for back-up."

"She just might do that, Roge. Now be a good little private eye and tell me all about this naughty wife you're chasing down there in San Diego."

After running from the warehouse encounter with Sam Tweedle, it takes Tubarão several hours before he feels safe enough to stop and telephone Carl Hayden, waking him up with what happened. The crime boss rips into him for a full minute before calming himself.

"Wait until dark and then get over to the office we keep on Highland. I don't think Dinelli's people know about it, so make sure you're not followed. I'll call Ignacio in a few hours to see what can be salvaged out of this mess."

That night, while Ellen continues making nice with Roge, Tubarão continues to try to calm down a still angry Carl Hayden. "I swear to you, sir, I wasn't trying to kill the runt. When I left Dinelli's social club, he was cut up yes but he was fine otherwise. He even walked out on his own feet."

Hayden slams both hands on his desk. "Apparently, the doctor who signed the death certificate felt differently! This is a disaster, Tubarão. The warehouses are now off-limits to us for the near future. If Camp Pendleton decides to replace the guards with their Marines or just have all property delivered the next day, we'll never make another dime off of them."

"Since the Domino Lady knocked out the guards, sir, the cops aren't looking at them."

"Cold comfort, Tubarão, especially since you couldn't even get rid of that one broad!"

"Yes, sir. I did beat her pretty bad before Sam showed up. I don't think she's going to turn up again anytime soon."

"Let's hope not." Dropping into his chair, Hayden continues, "Also, because Freddy is somehow tied into this, we can't use him to monitor city hall or expand his real-estate confidence game right now."

Hesitating to bring it up but knowing he has to, "If you need to cut me loose, Mr. Hayden I understand. I can get out of here right now and be in Mexico in two hours. From there I can catch a berth to almost anywhere in less than a day."

"Not just yet. You'll have to leave, but you're going to clean up this mess first. I promised Dinelli entirely too much to keep the peace, so find out how much of the military surplus Shifty's fence still has in his possession. If there's enough, we can hand it over to Ignacio and keep Sam Tweedle from killing you here at least. You can leave town without having to look over your shoulder, and I can keep Dinelli from deciding I'm no longer worth keeping alive."

"Thank you, Mr. Hayden."

"Don't thank me yet. Part of the deal is you hand over everything you have except the clothes on your back. It's supposed to go to Pagliotti's family as restitution. I'll get you to Mexico, and then you're on your own. Tweedle is supposed to hang back for a day, but that doesn't mean he won't have people following you. Understand?"

"Yes, Sir."

"One other thing, did we start using Shifty Green on Freddy's recommendation?"

"Yes, we did…Oh, I got it now. Freddy recommended him because Shifty's moving company works with his family's real estate business."

"Do we have to get rid of both of them?"

"No, Sir. Shifty has no respect for Freddy or his father. He's even said flat out to me that he'd rather work for us."

"He may get his wish. Call Freddy and get him over to our regular office; we'll see if he's still trustworthy. If you see anyone following you, ignore it. Ignacio gave me his word you won't be touched until after the meeting, and he's always lived up to that before."

"Yes, Sir."

Waiting long enough to make sure the Portuguese has left the outer office, Hayden flips an intercom button. "Zelda, get me Ignacio Dinelli on the phone. We have some details to work out."

The next morning, Ellen wakes to a cold rain outside. She calls Mayfair to let him know about Roge's information on Sam Tweedle. The Colonel has a little info to give in exchange.

"Greenback Moving is used to pack up and transport household goods from Camp Pendleton to the docks when we transfer Marines overseas. It's got a decent reputation, but Transportation doesn't like to use them."

"Why not?"

"The owner, Edward Green, has been handing out business cards for—and encouraging Marines to use—his brother-in-law's pawn shop if they need extra cash. There's nothing illegal about that, but when one of our young men starts living past his means, it's only a short time before things start disappearing. We can't outright ban him, so Green gets just enough business to keep him from complaining."

"So Freddy sets up the thefts, Green actually steals the property and then uses his brother-in-law's business to resell it."

"That's my guess and it may explain the cash you found in that wall panel."

Feeling the thrill of the hunt starting, Ellen quickly asks, "Did you get an address for Green?"

"Yes, but the Major running Transportation says it's just an office. I also have one of the cards for his brother-in-law's pawn shop. Got a pencil handy, Ellen?"

Wearing a very expensive brown wig, Ellen has her head covered with a cheap kerchief and a raincoat over an equally cheap, low-cut dress she picked up at a department store. Parking her roadster a half dozen blocks from her destination, she boards the next bus and arrives at The Lucky Pawn just before noon.

The layout was pretty typical, eye-catchers in the front window, easy resell items on the front shelves, with the cheap bins in the back of the store and the best quality items behind the counter. The young man sitting there looked at her clothes and went back to reading his dime novel.

Ellen starts to ask him a question when another man walks out. "Marty, looks like we got a little function to take care of tomorrow night."

"Are you talking about a party? You boys need any entertainment?" At that she removes her raincoat, leans over the counter and pulls her sunglasses down just enough to flash her brown eyes at them. "I've got a couple of friends that love parties almost as much as I do."

"Ah, umm, naw. This is strictly a business meeting, but maybe we can talk about a little party on Friday."

"Sounds good to me." Ellen purrs, "How about I just wait over there while you two finish talking about all that boring business then?" With that, she walks away, swaying like an unlatched gate in the wind. Marty puts down his magazine and pays careful attention.

"Where was I, Marty? Hey, look at me!"

"Sorry, Ronnie."

"Barney called. He says we got two big players coming tomorrow night, each with a crew. Shifty's boss at city hall is with one of them. We're going to play host and move the rest of that..." glances over at Ellen who pretends to look at a display case, "surplus we got on hand. They'll be here around eleven. Shifty said he'll fill us in on the rest later."

Turning to Ellen, "Hey, doll! Come over here."

Sashaying back, Ellen spends the next five minutes describing her friends and working out the party details. While Ronnie just leers at her with a growing grin, Marty actually helps her on with her raincoat, walks her out and waits with her for the bus, trying to arrange a private date.

Once she arrives back at her roadster, Ellen sheds her kerchief and wig. She pulls out a driving cap and gloves from the trunk along with a demure sweater to wear over the dress and a set of flats to replace her high heels. After applying a better shade of lipstick, she drives to a familiar café in Long Beach to think and plan. Their excellent blueberry pie has proved to be a great source of inspiration in the past.

If the big players Ronnie mentioned are Tubarão, Tweedle and their bosses, then she certainly can't take them alone. Getting Scheinhorst locked up where he belongs for a very long time means she has to try, though. Recalling Roge's words, the blonde beauty knows she needs help, but at what cost?

Her reputation as the Domino Lady is one of a jewel thief, yes, but she's also spoken of with no little respect by some in the underworld. Enough people have seen her beat down men twice her size that the fences in L.A. know better than to try to cheat her when she sells off stolen jewelry or launders money taken from criminals.

Even with that, she's still seen more as a nuisance than a rival. If she starts walking into situations with her own gang, then bullets are going to fly every time she shows her face. Even worse, the police will have to start taking her seriously as well. Right now, men like Detective Taylor get a good laugh out of her tweaking the noses of criminals and taking their ill gotten gain from them. Until she finishes her revenge on the men who killed her father, that can't change.

After another twenty minutes and a second piece of pie, Ellen finally decides to call Colonel Mayfair. The Domino Lady is going to need someone for whom a handful of criminals are just another walk on the beach.

"Go on in, Councilman. Mr. Hayden isn't mad at you; just think of this as a promotion interview." *One you better ace,* Tubarão thinks to himself.

Hayden is waiting in his office for Freddy, a drink in each hand and a big smile on his face. "Come in, Frederick! Please have a seat. Here, I believe scotch and soda is your choice of poison isn't it?" He sits down at the small table with the nervous young man.

"Yes, Mr. Hayden. It is." Freddy takes the glass with two shaking hands and downs half the contents in one swallow.

"Why are you nervous. Frederick? Has the Domino Lady come by for another visit?"

"Oh no, sir! I haven't seen her at all!"

"Good. Now, as Tubarão said, you're not in trouble. In fact, I'd like to bring you into the fold a little closer, if that sounds good to you."

"I'd like that very much, Mr. Hayden. What do you want me to do?"

"Nothing really. I'm meeting personally with Ignacio Dinelli tomorrow evening, and I'd like you to be there with me. It'll show Dinelli that I have trust in you and he should feel the same." *Otto should have kept the boy closer to hand*, Carl thinks, *he's too eager to please anyone in authority who shows him any interest.*

"Mr. Dinelli? Even my father tries to stay clear of him if he can."

"Ignacio is a perfectly reasonable man. Despite some of the more lurid accusations in the press, he isn't some criminal mastermind trying to steal San Pedro from the local Protestants." He leans toward the younger man with a concerned look. "You'll be there with me, won't you, Frederick? I'd like to show Dinelli that not everyone believes that nonsense."

Freddy can barely contain himself, "Absolutely, Mr. Hayden, you can count on me!"

For the next fifteen minutes, Hayden continues to bring Scheinhorst to his side; alternately complimenting and then pretending to confide in him. By the end of it, he signals to Tubarão that they will keep the councilman around after all.

"Have Zelda get Ignacio on the phone, please. It looks like we'll be adding one more to the guest list tomorrow."

This time, the two meet at a bar just outside San Pedro. The Domino Lady is waiting for Mayfair this time and waves him over to her corner booth. She quickly lays out everything she knows about tomorrow's meeting and what she hopes to do.

"So there we are, Colonel. The whole cast of characters will be there; along with their bosses."

"Why don't you just call in the police like you did previously?"

"With the heads of two organizations at the same location, I'm certain there will be no chance the police can show up without one or both men being tipped off. Also, I don't just want the thieves caught; Scheinhorst has to be arrested as well."

"I understand Ellen's desire for revenge because of her father. My question is: why are you here? She said she's sponsoring your activities and that you suffered like her, but I'm not convinced." He raps a knuckle on the table. "Convince me right now, or I go back to Pendleton, call the police myself on the location of the Corps' property and forget I ever met you."

Hesitating, but knowing she needs his help, the young woman tells Mayfair as much truth as she possibly can, adding details from one of the folders she stole from Scheinhorst. "I lost my parents within six months of each other when I was ten. They were good people, but there was no extended family for me to go to. What little they had disappeared in the court system, and I went into foster care. I was lucky; a good family took me in and, while they weren't my parents, it was a decent life.

"After I reached majority and left the system, it still took me two years to get the rest of my records. Somehow, Freddy Scheinhorst's father Otto got himself appointed as the executor of my parents' estate. I never met him before or after their deaths. All he did was file delays, rack up attorney's fees and incur other costs. By the time everything was done, he owned everything that should have been mine and it was all nice and legal."

"His son was probably still in school himself when this happened." Mayfair points out.

"You're right, but he's engaging in the same dirty tricks as his father did. I can't get back what was taken from me, and I haven't found a crack big enough in Otto's business to exploit yet, but I can stop Freddy from doing it to someone else. Just like I can help Ellen." She looks expectantly at Mayfair.

"I'm still not convinced you're telling me the whole truth, but I do believe you want to stop these people for the right reasons. Here's something else to consider: my contact at the Merchant Marines got back with me after Ellen called. This Tubarão is most likely Bernardo Cerqueira. He's been a sailor since he was fifteen and in trouble since his first Merchant vessel. He was tossed from his last ship eight months ago for fighting and insubordination."

"Not a good man then."

"Hair trigger temper and the fists to back up the anger. In my opinion, he's just one step up from a mad dog that needs to be put down. One last thing: Ellen does not participate. If I even think I see that little red flivver of hers, I'll call this off. It's you, me and whoever I bring in."

"You, me and your Marines, Colonel; I can promise you no one else will show up."

"Good. Let's get over to that warehouse and see what I can set up for you. If they're all going to be in one area, then perhaps we can get them to thin the herd for us."

"Thin the herd, Colonel? This isn't a cattle drive."

"No, but the same principle applies. We make it look like they're shooting at each other in order to get them to actually do it. By the time they stop, you may be down to a manageable few."

"Then what? Calling the police would still be useless."

"If you take down enough of them, you can deliver the rest—with the stolen property—to the nearest police station. Call far enough ahead and the Camp Quartermaster at Pendleton can meet you there to identify the property and force an arrest."

"My intimidation skills don't usually apply to forcing men to load crates and then drive themselves to jail."

Mayfair snorted, "Not with that little .22 you keep at hand; or should I say at thigh."

The Domino Lady laughs, "Why Colonel! How kind of you to notice!"

"Very amusing, Domino Lady." He scratches his chin, "Come to think of it, it might actually be useful if the cops *are* bought off. Tell me, have you ever handled a Thompson submachine gun?"

"No, I haven't, but I'm starting to like where this conversation is going."

The next evening, Ellen is surprisingly nervous. After scouting the warehouse and working out the details with Mayfair, she knows that she'll be in little physical danger. If something goes wrong, it will be her criminal persona that suffers. She has to be seen doing this on her own.

Reaching into her closet, Ellen removes Domino Lady's silk evening dress, cloak and mask. She lays them on the bed and then pulls the pins from her hair, shaking loose her natural curls to fall to her shoulders. She then slides her dressing gown off her silken shoulders, letting it slide past her shapely legs and onto the floor. She looks at herself in the mirror, alabaster skin still marred by the bruises left from the beating Tubarão gave her three nights ago.

After a moment, she slips the white evening gown over her head and gives a quick shake to make it fall into place over her trim waist and full hips. Arming herself with the .22 and syringe, she silently promises herself that the Portuguese thug will pay for what he did, and soon.

Mayfair had carefully examined the pawn shop storage yard and surrounding neighborhood last night. Picking a spot a block away, Mayfair requested she meet them there and then they'll make their way to the warehouse. Once she parks her car borrowed from the family groundskeeper (who was happy to drive the roadster for a few days), the Domino Lady climbs into Mayfair's Packard. The Colonel is behind the wheel and his three men are in the back. He quickly makes introductions.

"All of these Marines are California boys. They also have a lot in common with your friend and patron, Ellen Patrick. Each of them have lost family members to organized crime, crooked politicians, or both."

"This is First Lieutenant Edward Mills. He's from Sacramento."

"Good evening."

"Next to him is Staff Sergeant Francis Kilpatrick. He grew up right outside the gate in San Clemente."

"Hello, Miss."

"This is Lance Corporal Daniel Armenta, he's a Chumash Indian from the Santa Ynez Reservation north of here."

"Good evening, Ma'am."

"Ma'am? How old are you?"

"Nineteen. My parents signed the papers to let me join the Corps at sixteen."

"Even so, don't call me Ma'am. Domino Lady will do just fine."

"Yes, Ma'am."

The Domino Lady couldn't help but feel a thrill to see these men, dedicated to their country, now ready to fight at her side. Her heart swelled with pride as apparently did her chest. The three younger Marines suddenly found it almost impossible to continue looking her in the eyes and even Mayfair found something interesting on the roof of the car to study.

"Thank you, gentlemen for helping me tonight. The criminals we're going after have not just stolen from you, but have used the money from those thefts to intimidate people into selling their land or pay men to kill them outright. They're the worst our beloved California has to offer, and tonight we'll put an end to at least some of them. This is only a one-time

Arming herself with the .22 and syringe…

request for assistance, and if the men I'm after aren't here tonight, we'll shake hands and depart company."

She hesitates for a moment then presses on. "I realize that you'll want to try and do more than I ask, but I need you all to stay back as much as possible. I know Colonel Mayfair told you about my previous encounter with one of these men, but that's why I need to be the only person they see. I have to rebuild my reputation, small as it is right now."

A short time later, they've all entered the storage yard through the hole Mayfair carefully cut in the fence the previous evening. After making certain that Ronnie and Marty were still in the Lucky Pawn and unaware of them, they quickly settle into their positions and wait.

Ignacio Dinelli looked nothing like a gangster. His appearance was much like his father, a talented baker in Sicily and then later in New York. Out of respect, he keeps a bakery named after his father open in Long Beach run by his numerous cousins. It also serves as a good front for running various numbers games. Everybody loves pastries.

"Good evening, Carl. I wish this meeting was under better circumstances." He brushes dust off of his coat. "Not to mention a better location." Satisfied, he looks up. "We never just meet to talk, do we?"

"Newman's perhaps, Ignacio? Sunday brunch at 10:00?"

"Lunch at 12:00 would be better. My wife prefers the late morning Mass."

"Done. I'll make the reservations." Looking around, "Shall we get down to this evening's business then?" Dinelli nods.

Tubarão clears his throat. "I would like to formally apologize for what happened. I overreacted to Pagliotti's remarks, and I regret the difficulty this has caused you, Mr. Dinelli. To make up for this and to relieve everyone of any difficulty with the police, I will accept the responsibility for Polo's death, provide restitution to his family and leave town tomorrow." Looking at Tweedle, "I also accept that this does not stop anyone from coming after me, just that it gives me 24 hours to clear my personal issues and depart."

"You should just let me kill you now, Tubarão. It'll be much quicker."

"I'll take my chances, Sam. Come see me in Portugal, and we'll see if you still think it'll be that easy."

Taking that as a cue, the Domino Lady signals to Lt. Mills. He taps

Sergeant Fitzpatrick's foot and the Marine NCO fires one shot close by Dinelli's bodyguard to strike Tubarão in the shoulder. At the sound of the first shot, Corporal Armenta fires a round from a Springfield twin to Fitzpatrick's, striking Tweedle high in the thigh. Mayfair instructed them all to avoid fatal shots if possible, but not at the expense of their lives. Both men go down, chaos erupts and then each side unleashes hell on the other.

"Kill that double-crosser!" Hayden yells while running for cover. One of his bodyguards begins firing toward the mob boss, drawing their return fire while the other man runs next to Hayden, trying to protect him.

Dinelli quickly shows how he commands the loyalty of men like Tweedle, running to grab the man's collar and drag him out of the way; firing all six rounds from the .32 in his coat at Hayden.

"Finish them off! Whoever kills Hayden gets a third of his business!"

With both of Dinelli's men aiming for him, Hayden's first bodyguard goes down like a shredded tissue, twitching for a few moments and then stopping. Before they can capitalize on it, Tubarão draws his .45 and begins sending his own slugs in their direction. One man goes down, holding his stomach, but still firing back. The big Portuguese takes another bullet, this one to the chest, collapsing a lung. He tries to push himself on his back out of the way.

As both crews continue thinning the herd, Ronnie and Marty execute the better part of valor, running back into the Lucky Pawn and then out again, smashing through a glass case on the way to the front door. They finally get picked up a block away by a patrol car. Since the cop is on Hayden's payroll, he takes them to the nearest hospital as instructed and spends the rest of the night cursing the two for getting blood on the back seat of his prowl car.

Back in the yard, Shifty Green and Freddy Scheinhorst do their best to crawl under the flying bullets. Shifty makes his way to the fence and crawls under to escape. It takes him another five minutes to realize he's ripped his pants and himself in a very delicate place. One round finally finds its way into Freddy, grazing his left arm. The councilman screams as if he's been mortally wounded.

"Lousy shooting," mutters Lt. Mills from the shadows, and then puts one squarely into Freddy's right knee to keep him down. Colonel Mayfair, realizing that it's almost over, motions to the Domino Lady for her .22. She hands it over with a curious look and then watches in amazement as Mayfair waits for a lull in the shooting and then drills Dinelli's second bodyguard through the eye. The Marine hands it back with a harsh look of satisfaction and whispers one word, "Reputation."

Hayden and Dinelli both finally realize that someone else is in the shooting match and start yelling to each other.

"Carl, we've got a third player!"

"I figured that out! Let's get out of…." Then the yard erupts in .45 staccato and everyone puts their heads down again. Raising them up after a few seconds, they hear a voice only Tubarão and Freddy have heard previously.

"Gentlemen! Toss your guns and step out where I can see you! If you can't walk, drag yourself."

Hayden's bodyguard sneers, "Toss yourself doll!"

Rat-a-tat-tat! "Got another opinion now, 'doll?!' Get moving, Freddy ,and drag Tubarão with you."

Hayden calls out, "Let's do it Ignacio. The lawyers can clean this up."

Dinelli looks down at Tweedle. He's already pale from blood loss. "Do what you have to, Sir."

The mob boss tosses out both of their weapons. "We're coming out!"

Both groups walk or stumble out to see the Domino Lady standing with a canvas bag over one shoulder and the Thompson ready. She waves the Tommy gun at them. "Face that way, across the street." Once they do, she calls out to Scheinhorst, "I told you to drag Tubarão out with you, Freddy."

Blubbering like a baby burned on a hot stove, Freddy angrily cries out, "He's already dead!"

Looking back, Mayfair is signaling the Domino Lady's attention, letting her know that the Portuguese sailor is indeed dead. She nods and then takes the bag off of her shoulder and throws it. It lands next to Hayden's remaining bodyguard with a rattle. "Here's some jewelry for you boys. Put it on. There are also bandages once you're chained."

"But I'm hurt!" howls Freddy.

"Keep crying, you little daisy, and I'll finish you off myself," Hayden growls at him.

"Next time, boys, don't associate yourselves with men who steal from old people. Even jewel thieves have standards." Taking a deep breath, she launches into the speech she worked out with Mayfair while walking around to face them.

"I don't care about your numbers, protection rackets or who you have bought off on the police force. All I want to do is to grab a few pretties, the odd automobile for a little fun and maybe some cash now and then. If I take too much, just put the word out and we can always work out a deal. I'm not greedy, just high maintenance."

Looking harder and pointing the Thompson directly at Hayden, she continues, "Sending someone to kill me is another matter. The next time it happens, I won't be nice and leave you for the police. Everyone chained together now? Good. Into the truck then."

Once they're loaded up and the end of the chain is locked to a ring on the tailgate, the Domino Lady walks over to where Tubarão lies still. She leans over the still warm body and softly whispers, "I guess I'm going to learn how to take a punch after all." She looks up to see Mayfair nod and then he and the other Marines leave to wait for her with the Colonel's Packard.

Making sure the remaining crooks are secure, she places an anonymous call to the San Pedro *News-Pilot* crime desk. In less than five minutes, The Lucky Pawn is swarming with reporters and photographers. By the time the cops and lawyers arrive, each man has been photographed in their chains, ready for fame on the front page. Tucked in the driver's window is a black and white card that reads *Compliments of the Domino Lady!*

The day after Tubarão fought the Domino Lady, agent Gerald Fagan carefully supervised the transfer of his new source and eventual witness into an ambulance. "We appreciate your help and cooperation Mr. Pagliotti. We have the best plastic surgeon on the West Coast waiting in San Francisco to take care of the injuries to your face." Despite his position as lowest rung on the Dinelli ladder, Polo had kept his ears open and was proving very useful to the FBI. "For your recovery, you'll be in the wing of a private hospital that only the Bureau has access to."

"Thanks, Jerry. For a G-Man you're okay."

"You're quite welcome, Marco. Just so you know, we arranged for a 'distant cousin' to come and claim your body right about now. That way none of your family can reveal anything to Dinelli or any of his people."

"Ha! That idiot Tweedle left me to hang, and now he and Dinelli are going to pay for it." A rueful smile splits the bandages on his face. "You know, Jerry, I was a lousy crook. Heh! I'm probably better off selling tuna on Fisherman's Wharf."

"If that's what you'd like when this is over Marco, we can arrange to set you up with a stand."

Polo Pagliotti would live a long life and eventually die in his bed talking about his best buddy, "Jerry the Fed," the only five foot three agent in the FBI.

This time, Ellen made sure her meeting with Mayfair took place in a public diner frequented by the younger Marines. It amused her to know that the Colonel's stodgy reputation would soon be ruined all over Camp Pendleton by having lunch with a much younger woman. The cooler day allowed Ellen to wear an outfit that covered her now fading bruises.

"The San Pedro Police have been busy since we left, Colonel. According to the *News-Pilot*, Freddy Scheinhorst is in the prison medical ward along with Tweedle. After his father publicly cut him out of the family, he hasn't stopped singing to the police about every dirty deal the old man put together over the last twenty years." Pointing at the newspaper in front of her, "According to this, the San Diego Sheriff's Department caught Otto Scheinhorst and Shifty Green in a moving van heading for Mexico."

"That's good news for everyone in San Pedro. I hope they pay more attention to who they elect to their city council this time."

"I guess we'll have to wait and see, Colonel. I'm surprised Hayden and Dinelli are still in jail; happy, but surprised."

"With the Federal charges due to our stolen property, it's going to be tough to beat. Has Scheinhorst said anything about meeting with your father?"

Ellen shrugs, "I don't know. No one from either the San Pedro or the Los Angeles Police Departments have come to ask me any questions."

"What about the other two names we saw next to the subject 'boxing match' in Owen's appointment book?"

"They don't appear to match any of the other people we've come across in this. I'm not sure if this means it's another series of warehouse thefts or if Dad had other sources we just don't know about."

"Are you worried that if Scheinhorst does say something, it will just be swept under the rug?"

"Yes, I am because the police have produced nothing on their own!" Ellen looks at Mayfair with heat in her voice but not a tear in her eyes, "The only people involved in my father's death that have been prosecuted are the ones the Domino Lady brought down. Even then, they're in jail for other crimes and not for murdering him. It galls me that I had to settle for that with Scheinhorst as well."

Sensing Ellen's mood, Mayfair tries to steer the subject, "When do you believe your friend will hang up her mask and cloak, then? She got her revenge on Otto Scheinhorst after all. Will she help you check off every name in Owen's appointment book, or will she try to bring down every single criminal in California?"

"Of course not, Colonel. She's only pursuing the smaller set of villains."

"Which all happen to have some connection to your father." Ellen looks up at that, but Mayfair just shakes his head, "Ellen, my dear, anyone with a passing familiarity with Owen and his work is going to soon realize that everyone the Domino Lady has brought down has some sort of connection to him. From there, it's just a good guess that you're…supporting her activities."

"So she should stop out of fear? Should I?"

"Of course, but realizing that neither of you will, perhaps you should pursue a few gangsters not connected to Owen or the people he was investigating. Stopping some smugglers, sinking a gambling boat or even just harassing a few of the more public faces of organized crime might be useful. It's called picking the low-hanging fruit."

Ellen couldn't help but laugh. "Sinking a boat, Colonel? Isn't that a job for the Navy or even the Coast Guard?"

Now it was Mayfair's turn to chuckle. "You'd be surprised what an enterprising young woman can accomplish below decks in just a few minutes when no one knows she's there."

"So this is an offer of training then?"

"Yes, for both of you. She was right about being seen as a lone operator. Staying in the shadows will keep the police away, but that's no reason for her to rely only on luck. She's going to have to find something else to wear, though. I won't teach her how to scuttle a ship or hit a target with her little popgun if she's wearing that silly evening gown." They both laugh at the thought of it. "It's only going to be over the next three months or so. This tour at Pendleton will be up after the New Year and then I'll be off again; back to Panama, most likely."

"The Canal?! Oh, that sounds positively romantic!"

"As long as I can avoid getting malaria, of course. Who knows, I might just stay there too. A number of my fellow Marines have retired there to help manage Canal operations or open businesses supporting it. Many of them even find the time to finally start a family." It was the first time Ellen ever saw the man look wistful.

"So you're not coming back?"

"I'll no doubt be back at some point, just not assigned to Pendleton." Smiling at Ellen, "No witty remark or further flirting?"

She laughs, "I think I've already learned that doesn't work with you, Colonel but I do insist you join me for Christmas Dinner. You'll be missed."

"Thank you, and I accept the invitation. Now, give your friend, the Domino Lady, my offer and some advice when you see her next. This fight of hers, regardless of the motivation, has a thrill that few people know or can even begin to understand. If she's not careful, it will consume her life, and she'll get up one morning to find her youth has fled and the next generation is impatiently waiting for her to leave the parade ground."

With a puzzled look, Ellen has to ask, "Then why are you offering to help?"

Mayfair smiles, "Because I remember those days in my own life. No one could have stopped me as a young Captain, but a wise, old Sergeant Major preparing to retire after the War and over 30 years of service once told me the very thing I just said to you."

"Don't worry, Colonel, I'll make sure she gets the message."

The End

WRITING DOMINO LADY

Whattaya mean how did I write this? I sat down and kept my butt in the chair until I had at least 500 words every day, Monday through Friday; 200 words on Saturday and Sunday; that's how. Some days I wrote more (my best day was 1,134) and some days it showed as less in the total. If that doesn't make sense, that was after I figured out that Ellen could not have met with Mayfair face to face with bruises all over. I must have deleted at least two pages and then started that meeting and subsequent beat down over again. Once that was done, I realized it made a scene later in the tale unnecessary and there went another page. Frelling internal continuity!

On days like that, I had to go back and fix what I could before my eye started twitching. If I couldn't get a good handle on it, I blocked it off with hash marks and then went on to the next scene. It was then I figured out that when I want to bang the laptop on the desk until something breaks is the best time to write an action scene. The Domino Lady stomped Arnie really well after one of those incidents. Besides, it's always fun to write about a beautiful woman kicking some guy's tail as long as it's not mine getting the kicking.

The best part of writing a pulp story, though, is adding to the history of the character and hopefully building on it. The Domino Lady had only six stories from the Age of Pulps compared to Doc Savage or the Shadow. There is just something about her that is much greater than a slinky dress and a syringe full of sedative. As far as I'm concerned, she is the archetype of the "tough broad" brought to life by actresses like Barbara Stanwyck and Bette Davis. I'm very happy to join the list of caretakers who have added to her legend and hope to do more in the future.

For the Camp Pendleton references and the local area, I had some help from a gentleman who was stationed in that area during WWII. He was in the Navy back then, so of course I use the term 'gentleman' loosely. No one get offended by that, please. I ran the joke by him before submitting this, and he nearly fell out of his chair laughing. The exact stories he told didn't make it in, but I did lift a few details with his approval. He also gave me a good feel for the era and what San Pedro and Long Beach were like back then.

In case anyone is wondering, there really is a café in Long Beach with blueberry and peach pie that good. You'll just have to find it for yourself.

KEVIN FINDLEY was raised by a kindly couple in a small town in Kansas. Unfortunately, he misplaced his blue suit and red cape as a child, so he has been a freelance writer for the last two years. This is his first published work in the wonderful, macabre world that is Pulp. For three years before that, he edited websites for a number of commercial businesses.

Prior to that, he served 20 years in the U.S. Air Force. He retired as a Logistics Specialist with the rank of Major back in 2009. During that time, he was able to travel and live in various places to include Austria, Japan, Egypt and many more. Surprisingly, he is still allowed in all of those countries. He is married with two kids still at home and more scattered throughout the U.S.

His wife is very happy he finally listened to her and took up writing as something other than a hobby. It keeps him home, makes a few bucks and keeps him out of trouble for the most part. If you want to tell him how much you loved his tale of the Domino Lady, or even if you didn't, you can contact him at www.linkedin.com/pub/kevin-findley/35/208/36a/. Expect more from him at Airship 27 and other Pulp-related corners of the internet.

DOMINO LADY & ME

*S*hortly after entering the world of New Pulp, I discovered the Domino Lady via a reprint collection of all six of her six called "Compliments of the Domino Lady," published by Rich Harvey's Bold Venture Press. It featured a cover by the legendary Jim Steranko. Sadly it was, in my humble opinion, the worst Steranko cover ever done. When you purposely hide the face of a beautiful woman...well, your gimmicky concept fails immediately. Still the stories themselves were a hoot.

The Domino Lady was a masked heroine who first appeared in the May 1936 issue of *Saucy Romantic Adventures*. All her stories were published under the house name of "Lars Anderson" owned by the publisher, Fiction House. To this day the author's real identity is unknown.

The Domino Lady is really University of California, Berkeley graduate, socialite Ellen Patrick. When her father, District Attorney Owen Patrick, is murdered while she is away on a post-grad tour of Europe, she is devastated. Upon her return home she learns the corrupt authorities have no intention of finding her father's killers. Thus she puts on a domino mask and a backless white dress to avenge him. She would arm herself with a small .22 silver-plated automatic and a syringe full of knockout serum, but her best weapon was her beauty, which often distracted and entranced opponents, or at the very least led them to underestimate her, allowing her to outwit them.

She steals from her targets, donating most of the profits to charity after deducting her cut, and leaves a calling card with the words "Compliments of the Domino Lady". In order of their appearances, these were her six original adventures.:

"The Domino Lady Collects" *(Saucy Romantic Adventures, May 1936)*

"The Domino Lady Doubles Back" *(Saucy Romantic Adventures, June 1936)*

"The Domino Lady's Handicap" *(Saucy Romantic Adventures, July 1936)*

"Emeralds Aboard" *(Saucy Romantic Adventures, August 1936)*

"Black Legion" *(Saucy Romantic Adventures, October 1936)*

"The Domino Lady's Double" *(Mystery Adventure Magazine, November 1936)*

With the birth of Airship 27 Prodcutions, it was a simple jump to want to publish a brand new anthology of stories featuring this sexy crime fighter, and so I set out to put one together. I managed to solicit four stories, one of them penned by yours truly, and was set to go to press when our then publisher backed out of the project leaving us high and dry. A few months later, while at the Windy City Pulp & Paper Convention in Chicago, I reported all this to my good friend, and Moonstone Book Publisher, Joe Gentile. Gentile offered to take on the project, add more writers and get the damn thing out.

True to his word, Joe doubled the stories and in 2009 Moonstone Books released *Domino Lady – Sex As A Weapon,* edited by his sister, Lori Gentile. I recommend it highly and I will always be grateful for Joe for his help when I most needed it. Of course, Airship 27 Productions would eventually bounce back when we became an independent publisher beholding to no one but ourselves and our dreams. Still you have to know, there was always that nagging itch to get an original Domino Lady book out with our imprint on it. What you hold in your hand is the result of that five year itch...finally scratched to perfection. Ha.

I have to tip my pulp fedora to the amazing team that made this book a reality. Uppermost are the four new writers who signed immediately when I first put out the word for submissions. Greg Hatcher, Gene Moyers, Tim Holter Bruckner and Kevin Findley have all turned in wonderful tales true to the character in so many ways.

As for our artists, I knew at the offset we would need people who could draw beautiful women and we lucked out in recruiting two of the best in the business. James Lyle, who provided the 12 amazingly gorgeous interior illustrations, is a good pal and his work speaks for itself. As for the cover, months ago I tripped over Ted Hammond when he began posting his stunning pin-up work on Facebook. What can I say that his cover does not? If a picture is worth a thousand words, Ted's is worth a million. That is the Domino Lady in all her beauty and deadliness.

And finally, a huge applause to my partner in crime, our very own Art Director, Rob Davis who pulled it all together. He never fails to surprise me with just how great a designer he truly is.

So there you have it, my long, long journey with the Domino Lady. And least you think it ends here, but nothing could be further from the truth. Even as I write these words, I am currently writing two new comic book series for Joe and Moonstone Comics, both of which feature our dazzling vigilante, so keep your eyes out for *Black Bat – Domino Lady: Danger Coast to Coast* and *Guns of the Black Bat.* And finally, our own Airship 27 Productions Volume Two is already in the works.

Ron Fortier
3/26/2015
Fort Collin, CO

The Queen of Escapes

CURTIS FERNLUND

HATS OFF TO THE SERIAL CLIFFHANGERS

The time is 1935. After a decade of fame as the Queen of the Serials, Hollywood actress Gloria Swann is dismayed to see her box-office numbers dwindling with each new production. Desperate to reclaim her popularity, she bankrolls her own film project; an over the top jungle adventure to be shot on location in the wilds of the Amazon rainforests of Brazil.

After the crew and cast arrive at their isolated destination, a series of accidents occur threatening the lives of several of the players. The main target of these unexplained mishaps is Swann's younger stunt double, Angela Morgan. She suspects there are evil forces lurking in the jungle that threaten their safety. Her only ally in this belief is veteran stunt coordinator Karl Braun. When Gloria Swann mysteriously disappears, Angela may be the only hope the Queen of Escapes has to survive.

Writer Curtis Fernlund's homage to the classic film serials of yesterday is a rousing, fast paced adventure that speeds from one danger-filled cliffhanger to the next. James Lyle provides marvelous interior illustrations and Andy Fish captures all the fun in his gorgeous cover painting, packaged and designed by Rob Davis.

AN AIRSHIP 27 PRODUCTION

Airship 27 Productions

New PULP

PULP FICTION FOR A NEW GENERATION!
FOR AVAILABLITY CHECK AIRSHIP27HANGAR.COM